Second Bloom

Sally Handley

A Holly and Ivy Mystery

Printed in the United States of America

Cover Design: www.carolmonahandesign.com

First Printing, 2017

DEDICATION

To

Mary Ellen Handley

and

Nina Augello

ACKNOWLEDGEMENTS

First, I'd like to thank my sister, Mary Ellen Handley, who has been my faithful gardening companion through the years and who was with me the day I got the inspiration for this book.

Secondly, I'd like to thank Nina Augello, my dear friend and life coach, who cheered me on through self-doubts and moments of despair and without whom I would have abandoned this book long ago.

Thirdly, special thanks to Carol Monahan, graphic artist extraordinaire, who designed my new logo, book cover and book marks. Carol has been a great friend and seen me through many transitions, not just graphically, but personally as well. (www.carolmonhandesigns.com)

I must, of course, thank my beta readers--Virginia Handley, my mother, Gretchen Bank, Julia Crislip, Laura D'Aprix, Jay Johnson, Joanne Manse, and Lois Tylutki, who read rough drafts and still encouraged me to keep on going.

Next on my list to thank, Lauren B. Davis (laurenbdavis.com), author and writing instructor extraordinaire, as well as all the participants in her

Sharpening the Quill classes who provided the very first critiques of this book when I just began writing. Lauren's edits, encouragement, insights and inspiration have been invaluable to me.

Special thanks to my Cozy Mystery critique partners, Judy Buch (www.judybuch.com/), Cindy Blackburn (cueballmysteries.com) and Diana Manley whose genuinely constructive critiques and suggestions have helped me in ways that be cannot measured.

Finally, thanks to Sisters in Crime (Sistersincrime.org), both the national and my Upstate South Carolina Chapter (sincupstatesc.blogspot.com) and Malice Domestic (malicedomestic.org). I appreciate the many kindred souls these organizations have linked me with, both published and unpublished writers, who constantly amaze me with their generosity of spirit and willingness to share their knowledge and experience.

1 A CHANGE IN PLANS

Holly Donnelly sped up the ramp to the parking deck connected to Newark Airport's Terminal C. She pulled into the first empty spot she found, jumped out of the car, and ran down the escalator, out of breath by the time she reached the flight arrivals board. Scanning the flight information, she exhaled, stretched her neck, rolled her shoulders and smiled. Her younger sister Ivy's flight just arrived at the gate. In spite of having lingered too long in the garden that morning, trying to get everything perfect for Ivy's visit, she wasn't late. Now she only had to wait at the baggage claim for her sister, grab her luggage and head home for the start of a delicious, carefree two-week visit of gardening, grilling and sight-seeing.

Holly glanced up at the board again. The number five began flashing in the baggage carousel column. She headed over to the baggage area and stopped, facing the escalator nearest carousel five. As she focused her eyes on the top of the escalator, she felt an ache in her stomach remembering how forlorn Ivy looked when they said good-bye at the airport in South Carolina just three months ago after Dave's funeral. Holly had wanted Ivy to come back with her to New Jersey then, but Ivy said she needed some time to sort through things and deal with the will, life insurance and other business matters. Holly so wanted to stay and help, but with only a few weeks left until the end of the semester, she had to return to New Jersey to deal with exams and final grades.

Before long, Holly spotted Ivy on the escalator. She smiled, shaking her head as two men, probably in their thirties, did a double-take. Wearing black skinny jeans and a fitted red denim jacket, the petite, blue-eyed, blonde Ivy still turned heads at 52.

When Ivy caught sight of Holly, she gave a wave and a big

smile. At the bottom of the escalator, the two sisters embraced and tears welled up in Holly's eyes as she hugged Ivy tightly.

"I'm so glad you're here," she said.

"Me, too," said Ivy, equally teary-eyed. "Were you waiting long?"

"No, actually I was afraid you were the one who was going to be stuck waiting. I lost track of time in the garden, and when I checked the flight status and saw your flight was due fifteen minutes early, I nearly panicked. Fortunately, traffic was light. Hey, isn't that your bag with the blue ribbon on the handle?"

"Yeah, that's it."

Together the sisters grabbed the suitcase and pulled it off the carousel. A woman standing beside them touched Ivy on the arm and said, "I would have known that was your sister, even if you hadn't told me she was meeting you. You two look like twins."

"We get that a lot," Ivy replied laughing. The woman, she told Holly, had sat next to her on the plane.

"I never get tired of hearing that we look like twins," Holly chimed in. "I'm the older one."

"Let's go," said Ivy, rolling her eyes and giving Holly a good-natured shove.

Holly smiled as she pulled on the luggage handle, leading the way to the parking garage. In the car, she asked, "So, the flight was okay?"

"Yeah, no problems at all."

"The weather's supposed to be great the next three days. Isn't that perfect? I made chicken cacciatore in the crockpot today, but we can grill tomorrow and Sunday."

"Chicken cacciatore! Mmm, my favorite."

"Hungry?"

"Starved!"

On the drive home Ivy updated Holly on her dealings with the lawyer, the bank and the insurance company.

"Thank heaven I'm done with that." She started to cry. "It's been so hard for me. I hated having to talk to those people. They were just so … I don't know. They just made it so hard to understand everything. I don't know what I would've done if I didn't have you to call and talk me through it. What a nightmare."

Holly reached over and patted her sister on the knee. "I know, but it's over. You're here now. Let's just enjoy every minute together. We can do whatever you want. I thought maybe tomorrow we'd just go to the garden center and buy plants. If you like, on Saturday, we could go to New York and see a matinee."

Ivy nodded, drying her eyes, and the sisters lapsed into a comfortable silence.

This is going to be great. Holly relaxed as she drove homeward. She so wanted Ivy to sell her place in South Carolina and move in with her. When she was younger, she'd never minded living alone, but now she often felt lonely. Ivy balked when she suggested the move last month. Holly realized she'd brought up the subject too soon after Dave's death. If all went as planned this week, she was sure Ivy would come around. She just had to be patient.

As Holly turned the corner and her Tudor house came into view, Ivy exclaimed, "Wow! The yard looks beautiful. I've never seen those roses along the fence look better."

Holly beamed. When they opened the front door, Lucky, Holly's border collie, practically did backflips at the sight of Ivy. She couldn't stop wagging her tail.

"I told you your favorite aunt was coming to visit," Holly joked. Ivy made her usual fuss over Lucky and the dog lay at her feet under the table all through dinner.

After dinner Holly grabbed the leash and the pack of three headed to the park at the end of the block. They rounded the duck pond and came out the other side of the park on Crescent Drive.

"Let's cross here," Holly said." Did I ever introduce you to Edna Hagel?"

"I don't think so, but I remember your talking about her. She's in your garden club, isn't she?" Ivy asked as they crossed the street, arriving directly in front of a one-story brick colonial.

"Yep. This is her house. Come with me." Holly headed up the driveway. "I want to stop and thank her for hiring Juan. You know him -- my landscaper. Edna asked me if I knew anyone who could do some work for her and I recommended him. His wife just had a baby and he was really happy for the extra work."

Holly rang the doorbell. When no one answered, she leaned over the banister and peered in the front window.

"Guess she's not home," Ivy said.

"I don't know." Holly shook her head, turned and started back down the steps of the front stoop. "Let's go around back. She might be in the kitchen and can't hear the bell."

As they came around the side of the house, Lucky put her nose to the ground and picked up her pace, straining the leash. When they reached the back patio, she spotted a squirrel and took off after it pulling the leash from Holly's hand.

"Oh, no," said Holly taking off after the dog, Ivy right behind her. At the left far edge of the patio, Lucky leaped up two stone steps and bounded down the pea stone footpath that ran through the yard.

"Lucky, you come back here right now!" Holly shouted as she watched the dog leap past some overgrown shrubbery that blocked the path, disappearing from view.

"Uh-oh," said Ivy as both of them stopped in front of the shrub barrier. "What should we do?"

Holly sighed. "I guess we better just wait here. The property is completely fenced on three sides, so she can't get out. I just hope the leash doesn't get caught on something. I'd hate to have to make our way through this jungle to get her. Some days I wish I could return that dog to the shelter."

"Yeah, yeah ..." Ivy smiled, turning to look around the yard. "What a beautiful piece of property. With some work, I imagine this would be paradise."

Holly turned and nodded. "It really is something, isn't it? You'd never believe you were in a city in New Jersey."

Arborvitae formed a lush green wall completely screening the house to the left. About forty feet from where they were standing, a white picket fence marked the end of the property. A row of trees along the back fence almost completely blocked the view of the neighboring house that faced the next street over. On the right, various shrubs and trellised vines stood in front of a six-foot, white, vinyl, privacy fence separating the Hagel yard from the neighboring property on that side.

"You're right. I'd never believe I was in northern New Jersey. That pine over there really makes me feel like I'm in a forest."

Holly followed Ivy's gaze upward to the top of the 35-foot tree towering above the privacy fence.

"Remember going out to the lake when we were kids and playing blind man's bluff around the pine trees there?"

"Yeah, you were really good at that."

"That's because I always tried to stay near those trees. I could feel the softness of the needles through my sneakers. If I stood still, somebody always came close just as a teaser. It didn't matter how quiet they were. As soon as they stepped on the needles, I could smell the pine. That's when I'd pounce."

"You're kidding? That was your secret? Here I thought my big sister had x-ray vision."

The two laughed and gazed dreamily upwards, admiring the pine tree, when suddenly Lucky appeared with a grin stretching from ear to ear, the leash dragging behind her.

"Oh, you!" Holly glared at the dog and bent down to retrieve the leash. "Bad dog."

Ivy chuckled. "By the looks of her wagging tail, 'bad dog' doesn't mean the same thing to her that it does to you."

"C'mon," Holly said, turning and heading back down the path to the house.

"Look at this shed!" Ivy exclaimed, as they descended the stone steps to the patio. "I completely missed it on the way in."

To the right stood a shed custom-built in the style of a cedar-shingled Cape Cod half-house. A blue door and two shuttered windows with flower boxes beneath graced the front façade. Dead plants filled the flower boxes and the shutters needed paint.

Holly shook her head and sighed. "It's so painful to see all this in such a run-down condition. You should have seen this place in its heyday. I remember coming here for the Hagel's 50th anniversary party, probably twenty years ago. There was a moonflower vine in the center of the side fence over there. That vinyl fence wasn't here then and the pine tree wasn't so tall. The vine was so loaded with white flowers that it almost looked like a constellation, like a mini Milky Way. And the scent! Positively intoxicating. The whole night was magical."

"Look at this rose bush." Ivy stopped to admire a bright red shrub rose bush planted on the far side of the shed in front of the arborvitae. "This woman really knows her yard. There's an awful lot of shade back here, but this spot seems to get just the right amount of sun for a rose bush."

"Yep, she's been a master gardener as long as I know her," Holly said.

As they continued toward the house, Ivy pointed to a cleared section extending from the shed to the house. "It looks like this area's been weeded."

"You're right. Juan must have started."

Holly crossed the patio, tied Lucky's leash to a patio table leg and headed to the back door. "You can see why she needed help. Last month I saw her walking in front of the house with a nurse. That's when she asked me if I knew anyone who could give her a hand with the yard work. She used to do most of it herself, but she's probably in her nineties now."

This time Ivy sighed. "Is this what we have to look forward to? I just hate getting old."

Holly stopped and grabbed Ivy's arm. "Hey! Stop that. We're not there yet. C'mon."

Ivy followed Holly up the steps to the back door. Holly rang the bell. When no one answered, she leaned over the banister and peered through the kitchen window.

"We've been back here quite a while," Ivy said. "Wouldn't she have noticed us by now if she was home?"

Holly pushed back from the banister and pulled her cell phone from her pocket. "I guess so. I just can't imagine her being out this time of day. It's nearly seven."

Holly put the phone back in her pocket and knocked on the door. "Maybe the bell isn't working." She cupped her eyes with her hands and looked through the glass panels of the door. "Wait a minute."

"What is it?" Ivy asked.

"I can't be sure." Holly moved her head trying to find a better angle to see inside. When that didn't work, she leaned over the banister again. "Hold on to me," she directed Ivy as she leaned far enough to grip the window sill and raise herself to see deeper into the kitchen.

"Oh, no!" She jumped back. "Edna's lying on the floor."

"Quick. Call 911."

Holly got her phone out and tapped 911 as she descended the steps to the patio looking out on the back yard.

"Hello? This is Holly Donnelly. I just found -- uh -- I'm at 12 Crescent Drive. Yeah, in Pineland Park. I'm in the backyard with my sister. We see Mrs. Hagel inside. She's on the kitchen floor. Can you send..."

Holly turned back to face the house, but Ivy was nowhere in sight.

"No, no. I'm still here. Wait a minute. The backdoor is open. It looks like my sister got into the house."

Holly walked to the foot of the steps and stopped, "No, I don't know anything about her medical condition. Can you send someone quickly? Great."

Holly turned off the phone and hurried up the steps. As she opened the screen door about to enter the house, Ivy appeared.

"No, Holly," she said, blocking her path. "We're too late."

2 A SURPRISE VISIT

As they stood at the foot of Edna Hagel's driveway waiting for the EMTs to arrive, Holly looked down at her cellphone clock, then over at Ivy. "They should be here soon. I'm so sorry about this," she said.

"It's not your fault," Ivy replied, bending to pet Lucky. The dog had lain down on the pavement, mirroring the subdued mood of her two human companions.

"It's just that this is not exactly how I wanted to start your visit here." Holly sighed.

"Relax. It's okay. In thirty years of nursing I've had to learn to deal with death. It's never easy. I'm actually glad I'm here with you and you didn't discover Mrs. Hagel by yourself."

Ivy stood back up and squeezed Holly's arm. "I'm sorry about your friend."

"Thanks." Holly frowned, looking at her cellphone again.

"Here they come," Ivy said, pointing at the Rescue Squad ambulance coming down the street.

The vehicle pulled into the driveway. A man was driving and a woman sat in the passenger seat. The two, wearing matching white tee-shirts and baseball caps with the letters EMT emblazoned on the front, parked and emerged simultaneously. The female EMT opened the back door of the rescue vehicle, while the man approached Holly.

"I'm Holly Donnelly. I made the call. This is my sister, Ivy."

"Hello. I'm Jamal Benson. That's Sue Wardell. Where's our

patient?" Benson turned to help Wardell remove a stretcher from the back of the ambulance.

"You'll have to go around the side of the house and in the back door. She's in the kitchen," Holly answered.

"She has no pulse and her body's cold," Ivy added. Benson stopped and stared at Ivy.

"I'm a registered nurse," Ivy volunteered in answer to the unspoken question. "While Holly was on the phone, I tried the door and found it open. I only felt for a pulse."

"Are you related to the patient?" Benson turned and resumed helping his partner with the stretcher.

"No, I'm a friend of Mrs. Hagel's," Holly replied. "We just dropped by ..."

"Can you call a family member?"

"I don't have any numbers."

"Okay, ladies," Benson said. "We'll take it from here. Give us your contact information, and if we need to talk to you, we'll give you a call."

Holly gave the EMTs her phone number and address. She and Ivy stood watching as the two responders moved quickly up the driveway and disappeared from view around the side of the house.

"I guess that's it," Holly said, turning to Ivy.

Ivy nodded. "C'mon. Let's go and let them do their job."

Holly hesitated and looked back up the driveway.

"Holly, let's go. There's nothing else you can do here. Let's finish our walk around the park and go home."

"Okay." Holly tugged on the leash, and Lucky rose, leading the way down the street.

****

Back in her kitchen, Holly detached the leash from Lucky's collar and hung it on the hook near the back door. "What do you want to do?" she asked walking over to the sink, looking out the back window.

Ivy smiled, sitting down at the kitchen table. "We don't have to do anything. You want to talk?"

Holly turned, bit her lip and stood just looking at Ivy for a moment. "I know," she said, snapping her fingers. She crossed the kitchen, entered the dining room and went over to the liquor cabinet. Bending down, she opened the cherry wood doors and pulled out two, Waterford Crystal, old-fashioned, rocks glasses and a bottle of Jameson whiskey. Returning to the kitchen she placed the glasses and bottle in front of Ivy.

"We'll have a mini-wake for Mrs. Hagel. I feel like I need to do something to honor her."

Ivy nodded as Holly got a water glass out of the cupboard and filled it with ice. Ivy rose and located a small water pitcher from another cupboard, filling it with tap water. Both returned to the table and remained standing across from each other. The ice clinked as Ivy dropped the cubes into each glass. Holly opened the Jameson and poured. Ivy added the water. They each lifted their glasses.

Holly began the toast. "Edna Hagel was a wonderful person. She was a good neighbor and a fantastic gardener. She will be missed." She raised her glass just a bit higher. "To Edna."

"To Edna," Ivy echoed, also raising her glass.

Each took a swallow, lowered her glass, and sat down. After a few more sips, Holly smiled and said, "I do feel better now."

Ivy laughed. "That's just the whiskey."

Holly reached for the bottle. "If that's the case, then let's have just a bit more."

As she started to pour, Lucky stood up and began to bark, heading to the front door. "Somebody must be walking up the street with a dog," Holly said.

When the barking got louder, Ivy got up, walked into the dining room and looked through the front windows.

"Holly, there's a really good-looking man, dressed in a suit and tie, standing at the front gate. Do you have something to tell me?"

"Right," Holly replied, rolling her eyes. "He's probably somebody with the wrong address," she said as she came up alongside Ivy and peered through the blinds. "Yeah, he's nobody I know. Definitely at the wrong house."

Outside, the muscular stranger pulled a cellphone out of his pocket and put it to his ear, placing his free hand on the gate. Ivy looked at Holly. "Go comb your hair and put on some lipstick."

"Seriously?"

"Seriously."

"Get out of here. That man is not here to see me. If he's not lost, he's probably an insurance salesman or a Jehovah's Witness." Holly turned, walking through the arched doorway into the hall. "Quiet, Lucky. It's okay."

Ivy turned back to the window, parting the blind slats to get a better look. "I never saw a Jehovah's witness with dark, wavy hair like his. And if he's an insurance salesman, I'd consider upping my coverage."

"Get out of the window," Holly said, kneeling to calm Lucky.

"Uh-oh," Ivy said.

"What?"

"A police car just pulled up."

Holly stood up and looked through the glass panes of the front door. A patrol car, lights flashing, parked in front of the house. A uniformed female police officer got out, walked over and said something to the man at the front gate.

"He must be a policeman," Ivy said. "He just opened the gate, and they're coming up the walk."

Holly started to feel an adrenaline rush through her body, the one she sometimes felt right before she stepped in front of a microphone at a public speaking engagement. She shook herself. What did she have to be nervous about?

Lucky resumed barking. Holly reached down and grabbed her collar as the man in the suit reached the front stoop. She opened the door.

"It's okay, Lucky," she said. The dog got quiet and sniffed in the direction of the two visitors.

"Are you okay with dogs? She's friendly," Holly said.

The man bent forward and offered Lucky his downturned hand. Lucky sniffed and walked past him to the uniformed officer who did the same.

"I'm Detective Manelli with the Pineland Park Police." The suited stranger held up his identification.

Just like in the movies. Holly looked at the ID pretending she could actually read it without her glasses.

"This is Officer Rivera. Are you Holly Donnelly?"

"Yes."

"We'd like to talk to you, Ms. Donnelly."

Holly stood looking from the detective to the policewoman to Lucky.

"Can we come in?" he asked.

"Of course. I'm sorry. Come in." Holly opened the door wide, knocking into Ivy who had been standing right behind it. "Sorry."

She sighed and walked past Ivy through the arched doorway opposite the dining room into the living room. Ivy remained by the door.

"Hello. I'm Ivy Donnelly, Holly's sister. I just arrived today from South Carolina."

Detective Manelli nodded and followed Holly into the living room.

"Are you twins?" Officer Rivera asked as she entered the hallway.

"No, no. Just sisters." Ivy giggled and shut the door once Lucky was inside.

"Have a seat." Holly said, pointing to the two wing chairs on either side of the fireplace. She sat on the couch facing the fireplace and Ivy sat beside her.

"We just came from the Hagel residence," Manelli began. "You placed the 911 call, Ms. Donnelly. Is that right?"

"Oh, that's why you're here," Holly said, feeling her tensed shoulder muscles relax. "Yes, I placed the call."

"Why were you there?"

"My sister and I were walking the dog, and I told her I wanted to stop by and thank Mrs. Hagel for hiring a landscaper I recommended. He ..."

"How well did you know Mrs. Hagel?"

"Pretty well. We've been neighbors for more than twenty years. We belonged to the garden club together."

"Why did you go to the back door?"

"We tried the front first. I knew Edna was hard of hearing, so when she didn't answer the front doorbell, I thought we should try the back."

"When she didn't answer there, you just let yourselves in?"

"No..."

"Holly didn't go in," Ivy volunteered. "I did."

"Why?"

"When Holly looked through the window and spotted Mrs. Hagel on the floor, I told her to call 911. While she was on the phone, I tried the door and it was open." Ivy shrugged.

"So you just walked in and decided to examine the body?"

"Yes. I wanted to help if I could. I'm a registered nurse."

"What exactly did you do?"

"I went in, walked over to Mrs. Hagel and felt for a pulse. Her body was cold. No pulse."

"Then what did you do?"

"I stood up and went over to the kitchen counter to look out the window and see where Holly was. I didn't want her to come in and see her friend's body."

"Did you touch anything?"

"No. Wait a minute. Yes. I knocked a pill bottle on the floor, so I picked it up and..."

"Wait a minute!" Holly interrupted. "What's going on here?"

Detective Manelli didn't answer, but merely stared at Holly. After a lifetime of working for male bosses, Holly recognized the look. Condescending and meant to intimidate, the look that always made her spine turn to steel. She lifted her chin, returning the stare, determined not to blink.

Manelli turned back to Ivy. “What did you do next?”

Holly leaned forward, about to stand up. Ivy put her hand on Holly’s arm. “It’s okay.”

Holly sat back as Ivy continued.

“I stood up and went back to the door. Holly was on the stoop. I stopped her and said we were too late.”

“Then what?”

“We searched the house for valuables, stuffed our pockets and went out front to wait for the EMTs.” Holly’s words dripped with sarcasm as she glared at Manelli.

“Holly!” Ivy sighed. “You’ll have to excuse my sister, Detective. She’s quite upset over Mrs. Hagel’s passing.”

“Did you try to move the body?” Manelli asked.

“What? I don’t believe this,” Holly said, looking at the policewoman, sitting quietly across from her.

Ivy shook her head. “No. There was no reason once I knew she was gone.”

“So you didn’t see the knife in her chest?”

Ivy’s eyes widened and she stared at Manelli, speechless for the first time. Holly snapped her head back in Manelli’s direction.

“What did you say?”

“Mrs. Hagel had a knife in her chest.”

“Oh, no!” Holly covered her mouth with her hand. Ivy reached over and squeezed her other hand. Holly began to shake. “I can’t … I … who would do such a thing?”

“That’s what we’re trying to find out,” Manelli said.

Ivy looked from Holly to Manelli. “Mrs. Hagel was on the floor face down. I only felt for a pulse, Detective. As soon as I realized Mrs. Hagel was dead, I stood right up and went to the window to look for Holly. I understand why you need to question us, but surely you don’t think we had anything to do with murder. My sister was Mrs. Hagel’s friend and I didn’t even know her. What motive could we possibly have?"

Manelli looked down at the notepad in his hand and continued. "Did you see anyone else around the house before you went in? Anything seem unusual to you?"

Holly shook her head. Ivy said, "I can't think of anything."

"The landscaper you recommended. What's his name?"

"Juan. Juan Alvarez, Holly replied.

"Do you have his address and phone number?" Manelli asked.

"Yes, but Juan wouldn't ..."

"What's the address?"

Holly just blinked, not moving or answering.

"We need the contact information," Manelli said looking at Ivy.

Ivy turned to Holly. "Where do you have Juan's address and phone number? Can I get it for you?"

"It's on the side of the refrigerator," Holly answered, barely whispering. She sat still just looking down at her hands.

Ivy went to the kitchen, returned with a slip of paper and handed it to Manelli. He thanked her, stood up and handed it to Officer Rivera who copied down the information.

"Juan Alvarez is incapable of murder," Holly said, still focused on her hands in her lap.

Manelli glanced at Holly, then looked at Ivy. "Because you had access to the crime scene, we'll need you both to come down to Police Headquarters tomorrow for fingerprinting."

Holly bit her lip and brushed away a tear starting down her cheek. Ivy put her hand on Holly's shoulder and said, "Of course."

"Here's my card, and Officer Rivera will give you hers. Call her tomorrow morning. If you think of anything that might help us, call me."

Ivy took the card from the detective as Officer Rivera rose, returned the slip of paper with Juan's contact information and added her business card. Holly remained seated on the couch, rubbing her forehead with her hands, her eyes closed. Ivy escorted the pair to the front door. After closing and locking the door, she returned to the living room. Holly looked up. “I think I need another Jameson.”

3 POLICE HEADQUARTERS

At 12:52 PM the next day Holly eased into an open parking space marked visitor behind Pineland Park Police Headquarters and turned off the ignition. Their appointment was scheduled for 1:00 PM. As she reached to unfasten her seatbelt, Ivy placed a hand on Holly's forearm.

"Now, remember, you promised me you would stay calm today."

"And I will," Holly reassured her. "I promise."

Ivy let go of Holly's arm and reached to unclasp her own seatbelt. "Why am I not convinced?"

"Look, I don't know what got into me yesterday. When I realized that detective was questioning you like a suspect, I got a little crazy. And when he said Edna was murdered, I lost it, I admit. I was caught off guard. Today's different. Today I'm prepared."

"Okay, then let's go."

Inside the front entrance the two sisters were instructed by a policewoman to put their handbags on a conveyor belt and step through a metal detector. "I feel like I'm back at the airport," Ivy said.

I wish we were. If only we could start this visit all over again. Holly hoped that after this ordeal, they would be able to go to the garden center, buy some bedding plants and put this all behind them. When it was her turn, she held her breath as she walked through the metal detector. *Thank heaven--no buzzers.*

After clearing the initial security checkpoint, they had to stand in line to speak with a police officer seated at a desk located in front of another set of doors. Holly looked around at the drab green walls and spotted some water stains on the ceiling. “You know, I’ve never been here before and I’ve lived in this town more than twenty years.”

“I can’t say I’ve ever been to a police station either. I guess we’ve been pretty lucky.”

“Until now.” Holly frowned.

“Relax. This is just because I touched the pill bottle and we both touched the railing. Our fingerprints won’t be on the murder weapon and that will be the end of it.”

“Next,” snapped the chubby, balding police officer behind the desk. Holly and Ivy approached.

“Names,” he said without looking up.

“Holly and Ivy Donnelly.” Holly answered.

“Who are you here to see?”

“Officer Yolanda Rivera,” Holly read off the business card they’d received the night before.

The officer picked up a phone. “Holly and Ivy Donnelly to see you.” The policeman looked up at them for the first time and grinned. “Yeah. Okay.” He hung up the phone and asked, “Are you really twins?”

“Wrong,” Holly said, rolling her eyes and shaking her head. “Ouch!” Holly glared at Ivy who’d just pinched her. Ivy smiled at the policeman and fluttered her eyelashes. “Don’t mind her, Officer,” Ivy gushed. “She’s just annoyed because she’s younger than me.”

The policeman laughed and said, “Go through the doors and wait there for Officer Rivera. She’s on her way.”

“Thank you so much,” Ivy said, as she looped her arm through Holly’s and led the way.

As soon as they got through the doors, Holly asked, “Why did you say that I was younger?”

Still holding onto Holly’s arm, Ivy whispered, “To defuse the situation. In spite of your promise to stay calm, you were already getting testy with a man who was just making conversation."

Holly swallowed hard and raised her chin. "You're right. I'm not normally rude."

"No, you're not. You're just nervous. Now snap out of it."

"Okay, okay."

Officer Rivera appeared. "Good morning, ladies. Thank you for coming in."

Holly wanted to ask if they had a choice. Instead she just said, "You're welcome." After all, this young woman was being polite, just doing her job. This morning she looked much younger than she had sitting in Holly's living room the night before.

"Follow me," the policewoman said. "I'll escort you to the lab."

As they walked down the corridor, they passed Room 101. On the door was the name "Detective Nicholas Manelli." Holly felt that same tingling rush of nerves she felt the night before when Manelli and Rivera had walked up to her front door. She exhaled through her lips when they walked past and saw Room 101 was empty.

"You understand why we need to do this, don't you? We need to be able to identify your prints and distinguish them from any other prints we find at the scene," Rivera said.

"Yes," Ivy replied. "That's what I told Holly. My fingerprints will be on the pill bottle and not on the murder weapon."

"That's right." Officer Rivera looked from Ivy to Holly and back. "It really is amazing how much you two look alike. It's just your eyes are different."

Ivy grabbed Holly's arm before she could respond. "Yes, mine are blue and Holly's are green. Holly's actually three years older than me, but who can tell?"

"Not me," Rivera said as they reached their destination. "Here we are. Inside Officer Brennan will fingerprint you. He'll contact me when you're finished and I'll be back to escort you out."

Twenty minutes later Officer Rivera again was holding the door as Holly and Ivy exited the finger printing lab.

"That wasn't so bad, was it?" she asked smiling.

"No, it wasn't," Holly replied. As they retraced their steps back down the long corridor, Holly looked over at Rivera. "Officer, have you spoken with Juan Alvarez yet?"

The smile left Rivera's face as she nodded. "Yes."

Holly waited for the policewoman to say more. When she didn't, Holly probed. "He's not a suspect, is he?"

"I can't discuss the case with you, Ms. Donnelly."

"You can't tell me anything? Not even if he's been brought in for fingerprinting?"

"No, Ma'am. I'm sorry."

"Officer, Juan has worked for me for over ten years. He's an honest, hardworking, gentle man. He's incapable of hurting anyone."

Officer Rivera raised her left eyebrow and nodded as if in agreement, but said no more. As they reached the middle of the entry lobby, a middle-aged woman wearing a no-nonsense, navy blue business suit and crisp white blouse came up to Officer Rivera and handed her a manila folder. "Manelli said to tell you to call him with the results as soon as I gave them to you," the woman said.

Officer Rivera took the folder. "Thanks." She turned to Holly and Ivy and said, "Sorry, I have to run. The exit door is right over there," she pointed and turned back in the direction of the corridor they'd just come through. "Thanks again for coming in," she said over her shoulder as she hurried off.

Just as Holly and Ivy started walking to the exit, swinging doors burst open from a corridor to their left. Two uniformed policemen entered the lobby escorting a man in handcuffs.

"Oh, no!" groaned Holly.

"What?" Ivy asked.

"That's, Juan." Holly turned and headed in the direction of the three men.

"Holly, wait."

Holly didn't look back. As she got closer, the policeman on the left realized she was approaching them, and held up his arm, his palm facing out.

"Ma'am, stop," he shouted. "You don't belong here."

Holly stood still. "I know the man you've got in handcuffs. I just want to talk to him."

The policeman, who could have played fullback for the NY Giants, shook his head and positioned himself directly in front of Juan. "No. You can't. You need to leave."

Suddenly, the swinging doors opened again, and Detective Manelli came striding through.

"Great," he said when he saw Holly. He walked over and got between her and the policeman. "Ms. Donnelly, what are you doing here?"

Before she could answer, over his shoulder he yelled at the police officers still standing behind him, "What are you waiting for? Move it!"

As the police officers turned and resumed their walk across the lobby, Holly caught a glimpse of Juan in grass-stained jeans and a faded tee-shirt. Looking pale and frightened, he called out to her as he was led away. "Ms. Donnelly, I no do this. *Ayudame, por favor.* Please, please help me."

"What are you doing here, Ms. Donnelly?" Manelli repeated.

Holly stood watching as Juan and the two police officers disappeared through the corridor arch. She turned and frowned at Manelli.

"We're here at your request, Detective. Remember?"

Ivy came up alongside her, latching on to her arm. "We were on our way out when the policemen came in with Juan."

"Why were you alone?" he demanded.

"Because someone handed Officer Rivera a folder and said you wanted her to call you as soon as she got it. She, too, was following your orders." Holly nearly spit out the words.

Ivy sighed loudly. "Holly, really. Detective, we're sorry ..."

"Sorry? Sorry for what?" Holly asked, scowling at Ivy. Turning to Manelli, she asked, "Why was Juan Alvarez in handcuffs?"

Manelli stood, returning her glare, his arms folded across his chest.

"Let's go." Ivy tugged Holly's arm.

"No, I want to know why Juan's in handcuffs. We were questioned and fingerprinted and we weren't handcuffed. Is it because he's Mexican, Detective?"

Except for a visible tightening along the line of his jaw, Manelli didn't move or change expression.

"She didn't mean that," Ivy said looking from Manelli back to Holly. Raising her voice, she said, "We're leaving right now!"

Ivy pulled so hard on Holly's arm that she spun her slightly around. With momentum on her side, Ivy pushed Holly to the door. Manelli remained standing in the center of the lobby shaking his head as he watched them exit.

4 WHAT TO DO?

The sisters didn't speak a word on the way home. In the kitchen Holly dropped her handbag on the table, went over to the refrigerator and pulled out a pitcher of iced tea.

"Want some?" she asked, making eye contact with Ivy for the first time since they left police headquarters.

"Yes," Ivy answered going over to the cupboard to get glasses. "Can we sit on the patio?"

"Sure. Bring the glasses." Holly held the door open. Lucky ran out first.

The sisters stepped under the green canvas canopy that shaded the patio and walked over to the round cast-iron table nestled in the far corner of the 10-ft. x 10-ft. space. Ivy placed the glasses on the table and Holly poured. Ivy took her glass and dropped onto the cushioned chaise in the corner opposite the table.

"Your houseplants certainly look happy out here," Ivy said looking at the two baker's racks spilling over with lush, green foliage at the patio's edge. When Holly didn't respond, she continued. "Do you feel like going to the garden center to get plants for those?" She pointed to empty clay pots that lined the shelves of a two-tiered plant stand that matched the patio furniture.

Holly bit her lip and sank down on the loveseat angled to the right of Ivy's chaise. "Listen. There's no way that Juan could have murdered Edna."

Ivy sighed. “How can you be so sure?”

“Because I know him. He’s one of the most honest men I know. You have no idea how many times I run out to do errands leaving the house unlocked when he’s working in the yard. He’s never even stolen so much as a garden tool, and he certainly had ample opportunity. Besides, what reason could he have for killing Edna? It’s just not possible.” Holly shook her head and looked out to the raised vegetable beds at the back of the yard.

“All right. He does work for you. But how well do you really know him?”

“Are you kidding me? I know everything about him. Whenever he works on daylong projects, I make lunch, and we eat in the kitchen or on the patio. I speak about as much Spanish as he does English, so we manage to communicate pretty well. He’s told me all about his life in Mexico and his two sons who are still living there with his parents. Even though he misses them, he doesn’t want to bring them to America until they‘re finished with high school. He’s worried they might get involved with gangs if he brings them here too young.”

“And he’s not worried about gangs in Mexico? I read they’re a real problem there.”

“That’s in the cities--not in the country where his parents live. You should hear him talk about the garden he had there and his fruit trees. Does that sound like a murderer to you?”

“No, I admit he doesn’t sound like a murderer. But you ...” Ivy looked down at the glass of tea in her hand.

“What?”

Ivy looked up and frowned. “I’m sorry, but you are a bleeding-heart. Always the champion of the underdog.”

“Is that so wrong?”

“It’s not wrong, but the guy works for you occasionally. I’m just saying you may not know him as well as you think.”

“He more than works for me.” Holly stood up, walked over to the table and put her glass down. With her back to Ivy, she said, “We’re *compadres*.”

Ivy sat up straight. “What does that mean? You’re friends? Lovers? What?”

"No. Being a *compadre* is a special relationship." She turned and faced Ivy. "I'm his daughter's Godmother."

"What! How old is she?"

"Five."

"Why didn't you ever tell me?"

"Because I felt that you and Dave wouldn't approve. Am I wrong?"

"It's not that we wouldn't have approved. Dave just always worried that as a single woman by yourself, you're what he called an 'easy touch.'"

"Really?"

"Not just him. I worry the same thing. You're too open sometimes."

"Look, I'm an old maid with no children. If I want to spend a little on this child, why shouldn't I?"

Ivy stopped, shrugged and took a sip of tea. "First of all, you're hardly an old maid, but you are right. You worked for what you have and should be able to do whatever you want with it. But right now, I'm concerned about your getting involved trying to help someone who could be a murderer."

"I know." Holly sank into a chair near the table. "I'm so sorry. Why did this have to happen now, when you're here?"

"I don't know. Maybe I'm here to stop you from doing anything crazy."

"Crazy or not, I know I have to do something."

"Why? I know you want to help, but realistically, what can you do?"

"But I feel partly responsible."

"What are you talking about? How are you responsible?"

"If I hadn't introduced Juan to Edna, this never would have happened to him."

"Please. I can't believe you're even thinking that. Aren't you the one always stopping me dead in my tracks when I start blaming myself for things? You're the first one to say that you can't control what other people do. Besides, you did a good thing. You said Juan was happy for the extra work."

"I know. I know." Holly sighed and moved to the edge of her chair. "What's killing me is Juan doesn't have anybody to turn to. You saw how the police reacted when I tried to say anything positive about him. If I had evidence against him, I'm sure they'd sit me right down and take notes. Juan's Mexican. Therefore, he must be guilty. They don't want to hear anything that might contradict their take on things."

"So let's just say I agree with you. My question still is what can you realistically do to help him?"

"I'm not sure. At least I can speak up for him. Be like a character reference, right?"

It was Ivy's turn to sigh. "I suppose so."

"Maybe I should I go back down to Police Headquarters and see if they'll let me talk to him." Holly stood up again, pacing this time. "He probably needs to make bail. Maybe I could help with that. I know he doesn't have any money. And he's going to need a lawyer, too. The court will appoint a lawyer, but you know those guys aren't the best." She shook her head and shrugged. "The police seem so sure it's Juan that they may not even look any further, and a mediocre lawyer isn't likely to investigate other suspects." She stopped pacing and turned to Ivy. "What do you think I should do?"

Ivy sat up straight, smiled a weak smile and took a deep breath before she began her reply. "First of all, slow down. Even if I agree that Juan doesn't sound like a killer, I'm not convinced that you can help him. You can't put up his bail or pay for a lawyer. He could never pay you back. And, if the police and his lawyer won't investigate other suspects, honestly, how can you?"

"I don't know." Holly dropped heavily back into her chair.

Ivy shook her head. "You know I've always admired your ability to speak up when everyone else was afraid, but this is different somehow. Talking to that detective last night made me uncomfortable. Maybe it's just getting older. I only know I feel more vulnerable now. I know you're worried about Juan, but I'm worried about you."

"I get that," Holly replied leaning back in her chair, looking upward. After a moment she sat forward and clenched her fists.

"I, too, hate getting old. I didn't want to admit it before when you said it. I used to be brave, but now I feel afraid. Sometimes, if I'm someplace where people are talking politics, I don't even want to express an opinion. Can you imagine that?" She clutched her hand to her chest. "Me? Worried that someone might do something to me because I disagree with them on a political issue. I won't even let anyone put campaign signs in the yard, because I'm afraid the opposition will trash the place or hurt the dog. Isn't that just pathetic?" Her eyes glistened.

"No. It's normal to feel that way. That's what everybody feels mostly all the time. And if the way you spoke to the police yesterday and today was your idea of being afraid, then I'm really worried about you. Can't you just for once let someone else battle the bad guys? Someone younger?" Ivy's shoulders sagged and she sank back into the cushioned chaise.

"That just breaks my heart," Holly lamented. Getting up from the table and walking over to the loveseat, she propped a pillow on the arm and lay down. "I feel exhausted," she said closing her eyes.

With only the sound of a light breeze ruffling the leaves of the trees, before long the sisters each drifted off to sleep.

****

Around 5:30, Lucky's bark woke them. Holly grilled steaks while Ivy made the salad. After dinner, they walked around the park, avoiding Crescent Drive. Neither mentioned Juan or Edna.

Back home, the sisters agreed on a full line-up of sitcoms on CBS. At ten o'clock, Ivy stood up and stretched her arms over her head. "In spite of that nap earlier, I'm tired."

"Me, too. Maybe I'll read in bed awhile." Holly said, sitting up.

"Not a murder mystery, I hope."

"No," Holly laughed. "I'm reading Anna Quindlin's *Still Life with Breadcrumbs*. It's actually a bit of a romance."

"Speaking of romance," Ivy said bending to pick up her shoes, "what do you think of that detective? In spite of the fact that talking to him scared me a little, he was kind of a hunk, no? And no wedding ring either."

"First of all, I think he's a racist, sexist creep, and secondly, how do you notice things like wedding rings when you're being questioned about a murder?"

"How do you not notice?" Ivy shook her head. "No wonder you never got married."

"Don't let's get started on that topic." Holly aimed the remote at the TV, shutting it off. As she went to check that the front door was locked, she said, "I wonder how Juan is doing right now."

Ivy heaved a weary sigh, shaking her head. "Do me one favor. Just get some sleep. Who knows? Maybe by morning the police will realize that Juan is not the murderer, and we can go to the garden center, pick flowers and play in the dirt to our hearts' content tomorrow."

"Wouldn't that be great?" Holly said, starting up the stairs. "Did you notice I put a TV in your bedroom?" she asked over her shoulder.

"*My* bedroom? Don't you mean the guestroom?"

Holly reached the upstairs hallway and turned to face Ivy. "I've come to think of it as your room. It could be yours, permanently," she said.

"Now it's my turn to say 'don't let's get started on that topic.' I told you before. I'm not ready to even think about moving, and if you're going to spend the rest of my visit trying to get me to ..."

"Okay, okay," Holly held her hands up in a gesture of surrender. "Not another word. I promise."

"Like you promised to stay calm this morning?" Ivy asked as she stepped into the guest room.

Holly grimaced as she stood in her bedroom doorway facing Ivy. "I ..."

"Good night," Ivy said as she closed the bedroom door.

5 KATE FARMER

"Mirror, Mirror on the wall, will I be able to sleep at all?" Holly stared at her reflection in the bathroom mirror and shook her head. Returning to her room, she closed the door, careful not to make any noise. She grabbed the accent pillows from the bed and tossed them in the corner beside the nightstand. Pulling back the fluffy comforter she sat down at the edge of the bed.

Was there any point in lying down? She thought of Juan trying to sleep in a jail cell. Shaking herself, she stood up and walked over to her glider/recliner. Sinking down into the chair, she put her head back and closed her eyes. Just as she started to relax, she again pictured Juan's face as he walked across the police lobby in handcuffs.

She turned on the reading lamp beside the chair, bending down and flipping through the magazines in the basket on the floor: *Martha Stewart Living*, *InStyle*, *Redboo*k. She sat back up and instead reached for *Still Life with Bread Crumbs*, resting on the table beside the chair. Standing up, she shut off the table lamp, got in bed, and after just a few pages, she started feeling drowsy. Shutting off the light, she sank into the pillows, hopeful this time she would fall asleep.

The image of Juan, scared and pale, popped back up, and Holly began clicking through her mental checklist of what she would do in the morning. After an hour of tossing and turning, she once again sat up. Turning on the nightstand light, she got out of bed and listened at the door. The TV was still on in Ivy's room, but she knew that didn't mean Ivy was awake. She smiled thinking about how Ivy always set the sleep timer for the maximum amount of time, and then fell asleep after about five minutes into a program.

Holly went over to her nightstand, sat down on the bed, picked up the phone and speed dialed number 2.

"Hello."

"Kate, it's Holly. Did I wake you?"

"Are you kidding? Of course, not. But what are you doing up this late?"

"I couldn't sleep. I just had to talk to someone."

"Hey, wasn't yesterday the day Ivy was supposed to arrive? Is something wrong with Ivy? Is she okay?"

"No, no. Everything is okay. Ivy arrived on time and she's fine."

"Then what's up?"

"I don't want to tell you right out. I want you to do a reading. I know it's late and this is an imposition ..."

"Don't be silly. Hang on while I go get the Tarot Cards."

Holly propped up three of the four pillows against the headboard, lay back and pulled the top sheet up to cover herself. She smiled picturing her friend rummaging through her "Tarot Bag" at the bottom of her bedroom closet in upstate New York.

"Okay, I'm back," Kate said. "I'll shuffle as you focus on your question. By the way, do you want me to do a full reading?"

"No, just the three cards."

"Okay. I'm going to hold the cards up to the phone. Blow into the speaker."

Holly laughed out loud. "Are we crazy, or what?"

"Probably, but then, who isn't? Now shut up and blow."

Holly did as she was told and waited. At the other end of the line, she heard an audible gasp.

"What is it?" she asked sitting up in bed.

"Holly, what's going on down there?"

"You, first. What are the cards?"

Kate sighed heavily. “Okay. You drew Death, the Tower and, amazingly, the Ten of Cups.”

“That’s bad, right?”

“I don’t know. The death card doesn’t necessarily mean death. It can just be the end of something or a warning not to waste time, or ...”

“It means death, Kate. A neighbor of mine was murdered yesterday.”

“Oh, no! I’m so sorry. Who was it?”

“Edna Hagel. I don’t know if I ever told you about her. She lived across the park from me.”

“Is she the master gardener who gave you the Gertrude Jekyll rosebush?”

“Yes.”

“Isn’t she, I mean, wasn’t she old? Who would want to murder her?”

“Before we discuss that, please finish the reading.” Holly nestled back into the pillows.

“The tower card shows a bolt of lightning hitting it. Like the death card, it usually means the end of something or it could be about a sudden change that we’re resistant to.”

“And the Ten of Cups?”

“Now that’s the odd thing. The Ten of Cups is about love, romantic love. It doesn’t seem to go with these other cards at all. Unless ...”

“Unless what?”

“Unless you’ve met someone. Are you holding out on me? Have you met a man?”

“No! Of course, not.” Detective Manelli’s face popped into Holly’s head.

“The problem with you is that Prince Charming could knock on your door, and before he could say anything, you’d tell him he must be at the wrong house.”

Holly grimaced remembering that was exactly what she said

when Ivy told her there was a good-looking man at the gate the night before.

When Holly didn't reply, Kate continued, "Think. You must have encountered a man somewhere for that card to ..."

"Look, I didn't call you in the middle of the night to give me another lecture on how I need to make an effort to meet men. That's your fantasy, not mine. Let's get back to Edna Hagel." Holly recounted the events of the last two days.

"Wow!" said Kate. "No wonder you can't sleep. What are you going to do?"

"That's just it. I don't know what to do, but I can't not do anything." Holly sat up again. "Why did this have to happen while Ivy is here? I planned to woo her with a perfect two weeks--all her favorite things, all her favorite foods, and then try to convince her to sell her house and move here with me."

Kate didn't comment.

"What do you think I should do?" Holly prompted.

"To borrow a phrase, Ivy's moving here may be your fantasy, not hers."

"I'm talking about Juan, Kate. If you saw his face... I have to try to help, don't I? My question to the cards was what should I do?"

"Let's think. I've heard you talk about Juan so much over the years that I feel like I know him myself. And I've known you over 25 years. I know you'd never be able to live with yourself if Juan went to prison and you hadn't tried to help him."

"That's right. You get it. I'm having a hard time getting Ivy to understand that."

"I'm sure she's just worried about you. The big question is 'What can you do'? Maybe you can't do anything, but maybe you know someone who can."

"That's good. That's really good. Let me think. Who do I know who can help?" Holly looked up at the ceiling as if the answer might be printed there.

"You were on that zoning commission in town for a while. You think anybody there could help?"

"Wow! You are amazing. I don't think the zoning commissioners can, but those people, they know people. Okay. This is great. You always have the answer."

"No, you always have the answer. Remember, like the Tarot cards, I only help you see what you already know."

"You always say that, but you know you've got a sixth sense about things."

"I'm not sure what I've got, but I was watching a re-run of *Ghost* the other night and it hit me that I'm a little like the medium in that movie, the Whoopi Goldberg character, Oda Mae. Sometimes an idea pops into my head, or a feeling that I have to do something, but it's never completely clear why. It's always just a piece of something that I can't connect to anything with any certainty. So who's the guy?"

"I already told you there is no guy."

"I don't believe you."

"Listen, I don't want Ivy to know about the Tarot thing. She still goes to church on Sunday. She'll never move here if she thinks I've gone over to the dark side."

"Nice dodge, Holly, but don't think you're fooling me. And don't worry about me telling Ivy anything. From up here in the Catskills, I'm unlikely to have an opportunity to talk to her."

"By the way, how's your garden growing?" Holly asked.

"Looks like a bumper crop of garlic again this year. Too early up here for anything other than lettuce and spinach. You're probably ready to harvest."

"Yeah, we'll have zucchini by the end of the week."

"Show off."

"Hey, thanks for the reading. I better try to get some sleep."

"Pleasant dreams. Keep me posted on any men you meet."

"Good night, Oda Mae!"

6 WHERE'S HOLLY?

"Dave! But you're … you're …"

"Dead, Ivy?" Dave smiled, his head framed by glowing white light.

"Yes. How can this be? What are you doing here?"

"I just needed to let you know I'm okay and that you need to help Holly."

"Help Holly? Of course. I always help her with the gardening."

"She needs your help with more than just gardening, Ivy."

"No, Dave. Holly's the one who always helps me. Remember? She never needs my help."

"Only you can help Holly." Dave began to fade.

"What do you mean?"

"You know what I mean, Ivy."

"No, I don't. Wait. Come back, Dave." But he was gone.

Ivy opened her eyes, sat up and looked around. It took a few seconds to realize she was not in her own bed, but in the guest room at Holly's house in New Jersey. She looked at the clock. 7:12 AM. That's funny. *Holly never sleeps this late, and she always checks to see if I want to walk with her and Lucky.*

Ivy got out of bed and picked up the bathrobe she'd laid across the rocker in the corner. Something wasn't right. *Been awhile since I haven't slept in my own bed. That's all.* She shook her head as she tied the belt around her waist. Wait a minute. I was dreaming. What was I dreaming? She couldn't remember.

Ivy crossed the room and opened the bedroom door. Up popped Lucky, tail wagging. "Good morning, Lucky. Were you guarding my door?" She patted the dog, and together they headed to the steps, the aroma of coffee beckoning from the kitchen.

Downstairs Ivy saw a full pot of coffee nesting in the coffee maker, but no Holly. She walked over to the stove and lifted the lid on the frying pan sitting on the front burner. Four breakfast sausages, nicely browned, sat in the pan. Ivy sniffed and smiled, putting the lid back in place. She turned and nearly tripped over Lucky, the dog's nose pointing upward in the direction of the aromatic sausages.

"No, no. Those aren't for you. Those are for your mother and me, wherever she is. Do you know where she is, girl?"

If Lucky knew, she wasn't telling.

Ivy looked out the window to the garden, but Holly wasn't there either. She went back upstairs to the bedroom and put on the jeans and tee-shirt she'd worn the night before. She scurried downstairs and out the front door and round to the side patio, but again, no Holly. *Where could she be?*

"What am I thinking? She wouldn't go outside and leave you inside, would she, Lucky?" Ivy turned around and went back inside. "I know," she said snapping her fingers. She opened the basement door and went down the steps straight to the garage door. Pearl, Holly's beige-colored Cadillac CTS sat parked safely inside. *Well, at least she can't have gone too far on foot.* Ivy returned to the kitchen, poured herself a cup of coffee and sat down at the kitchen table. Lucky sat down beside her. Ivy petted Lucky's head, rubbing behind her ears.

"Lucky, your mother makes me crazy sometimes." Ivy surveyed the countertops. "She didn't even leave us a note. Where could she be?" Ivy leaned back in the chair. "I bet she walked to the bakery to get those bagels I love. She'll be right back, won't she, Lucky?" The dog wagged her tail in reply. "That's it. She'll be right back."

Ivy sighed as she continued to pet Lucky. This vacation was not starting out quite the way she'd imagined. She wondered if they would get to do any of the things they'd planned. She hadn't seen Holly this upset about anything in a long time. Shaking her head, she smiled remembering how Holly had always been on some crusade or other when they were younger. From stopping the bombing in Cambodia to changing the grammar book at the school where she taught, to passing the Equal Rights Amendment, Holly was quite the activist. And she always had a plan, always seemed to know the right thing to do.

Ivy looked at the clock again. 7:45 AM. *Where could she be?* Ivy began to pace, circling the dining room table. She stopped at the window and parted the curtains looking up and down the street.

"I know, Lucky," she said, sprinting back upstairs. "I'll call her cell phone." Ivy ran to the bedroom, grabbed her pocketbook and dug past the Kleenex and her wallet to locate her phone buried at the bottom. *Why hadn't I thought of this sooner?* She searched for Holly's name and hit "send." She rolled her eyes as she heard the theme song from *Rocky* playing across the hallway. Entering Holly's bedroom, she saw Holly's I-Phone on the dresser. *So much for that idea.*

Ivy turned and there was Lucky in the doorway watching her. "Don't worry. I'm not going to steal anything." She walked over and knelt beside the dog, putting both hands on either side of her furry neck.

"I'm just being silly to worry. Right?"

Ivy jumped to her feet. *A woman was murdered in this neighborhood. If Juan didn't do it, then the murderer is still out there. What if Holly went back to Mrs. Hagel's house? What if the murderer returned to the scene of the crime?*

"Holly, Holly, Holly, where are you?" Ivy walked back downstairs and over to the front living room window. On a table in front of the window were several family pictures, including one of her and Dave on their tenth anniversary.

"That's it! That's what I dreamt. I dreamt about Dave," she said aloud. Just flashes of his face came back to her. *What had he said?* She couldn't remember. *Wait. Dave told me to help Holly. Why would I dream that?* Suddenly she remembered what she saw in Mrs. Hagel's kitchen. *But I could be wrong.* As she looked up, through the window she spotted Holly opening the front gate.

7 A PLAN

Ivy flew to the front door. “Where have you been?” she demanded, arms crossed tightly across her chest, eyes blazing.

“Just down the street at the Flynn’s.” Holly bent to pick up the newspaper on the stoop, brushed past Ivy, and headed to the kitchen.

Ivy slammed the door. “How could you go out without letting me know?” she shouted. Holly stopped in the kitchen doorway and looked at Ivy in surprise.

"I was worried sick,” Ivy said. “A woman was murdered in this neighborhood yesterday, and I wake up and find you’re gone, without your cellphone, without the dog, without a note!”

Holly put her hand on Ivy’s arm. “I’m sorry, Ivy. I guess when you’ve lived alone as long as I have, you just don’t think about letting someone know where you are. I didn’t realize you might be worried. I really am sorry.”

“Okay, but don’t leave this house again without telling me or without letting me know where you’re going.”

“Okay. I promise.”

“Another promise,” Ivy said under her breath, shaking her head. She followed as Holly turned and went straight to the kitchen counter, plugged in the waffle iron and dropped the newspaper on the table.

“Waffles and sausages?” Ivy asked.

“Waffles and sausages,” Holly replied, getting a mixing bowl of waffle batter out of the refrigerator.

Ivy got two dishes out of the dish cupboard. "So why were you at the Flynn's?"

Holly's expression changed from penitent to gleeful as she gave the waffle batter a stir. "I don't know why I didn't think of it last night. Frank Flynn is a retired policeman. He's an early riser and I caught him as he was going out to the gym this morning. He told me he'd find out if Juan had been transferred to Pineland County Jail, and let me know. He said if the charge is first degree murder there most likely would be no bail. He also said I could visit Juan, and probably the best thing I could do would be to talk to Juan's court appointed lawyer. Isn't that great?"

Ivy let out a big sigh and sat down at the table. "So much for sleeping on it."

"I did sleep on it. Not very well, I have to admit." Holly frowned at the light on the waffle iron, then turned to Ivy. "But this is good. I feel better now that I talked to Frank. I have to say I didn't like the idea of talking to the Pineland Park police again, but I'm not afraid to talk to Juan's lawyer. At least I can offer to be a character witness and maybe that will help."

"There go our gardening plans for today." Ivy frowned, looking past Holly out the kitchen window.

"No, no, we're going to go to the Garden Center right after breakfast, and we can buy all the plants, just like we planned. I'll call Frank when we get back to see what he finds out. Ah, the light finally went out." Holly poured batter onto the waffle iron, closed the lid, and started cleaning up the counter.

Ivy picked up the newspaper and scanned the first section of national news. When she got to the local news section, she grimaced at the headline. "Local Stationer Found Dead."

Holly walked over to the table with the milk pitcher. When Ivy didn't look up, she glanced down at the headline. "Does it say anything about Juan?"

"Yes."

"Go ahead. Read it to me."

Ivy hesitated, then looked down at the paper and read, "Pineland Police have in custody Juan Alvarez, a local landscaper. Detective Nicholas Manelli would not comment on the evidence against Alvarez, stating that forensics tests are incomplete at this time."

Holly walked back over to the counter. "It's okay. I'll go see Juan and talk to his lawyer."

"And you're sure that's what you want to do? Have you really thought this out?" Ivy asked.

"Yes. I mean, what could go wrong?" Then she burst out laughing. Even Ivy had to laugh as her sister handed her a steaming plate of waffles and sausages.

8 THE GARDEN CENTER

At the Garden Center Ivy found a cart and headed to the back of the building, Holly close behind. “Where should we start?”

Ivy stopped to survey the seemingly endless rows of shelves lined with flats. Scarlet, white, pink, purple, orange yellow, coral and lavender blooms spilled out of their containers. Begonias, petunias, geraniums and fuchsias dangled gracefully from the roof edge of the Garden Center’s back porch.

“Isn’t this just a feast for the eyes?” Ivy sighed.

“It really is,” Holly agreed. They stood listening to the gentle sound of trickling water from the newly installed water pond on their left, inhaling the mixed scent of basil and rosemary wafting over from the herb section on their right.

“Excuse me,” said a voice from behind. A man pushing a cart wanted to get past them.

“Sorry,” Ivy laughed, moving her cart to make way for him. “We got carried away by the view.”

Holly found some empty flats and positioned them on the cart’s top rack. Ivy aimed the cart at the impatiens aisle and they immediately began filling the flats.

“I’m just so glad we’re finally doing this,” Holly said as she guided the cart from the front.

“Me, too.” Ivy grinned. “Remember when you first moved in? It was a lot easier back then.”

"Why? Because there were fewer flower beds or because we were younger?"

"Ha! A little of both I think."

"All I know is I used to be able to do this all myself," Holly said, shaking her head. "Fifty may be the new forty if you're a movie star, but not if you're a gardener."

"What do you think?" Ivy asked as she held up a gorgeous fuschia/purple/ lilac petunia combination.

"Ooh, I love those colors. Absolutely get those." Holly reviewed the cart contents. "I think after this we need to check out. We can't fit any more on the cart."

After checking out at the outdoor register, the sisters headed to the car, passing three young men standing talking near a pickup truck loaded with top soil.

"Yeah, that's what can happen when you hire wetbacks," said a tall, young man wearing a red baseball cap bearing a pine tree logo.

A shorter fellow in an Allwood Landscaping tee-shirt smiled and said, "You got that right, Richie. What the hell was he thinking? How *estupido* could he be?" All three laughed loudly.

Holly stopped, looking over at the braying trio. Ivy maneuvered the cart between Holly and the men. The third man leaning against the truck smiled and ran his hand along his unshaven cheek. "Yeah, well, it looks like they caught the dumb bean eater."

Ivy darted a look at the men, turned to Holly and asked, "Do you think we can plant all these flowers this afternoon?" Ignoring her, Holly crossed in front of the cart and turned towards the men.

"Holly, wait! Don't ..."

"Excuse me," Holly said. The three men turned and looked at her. "I couldn't help overhearing your conversation. I assume you're talking about the murder in Pineland Park. Just in case you skipped school that day, let me tell you that in the United States you're innocent until proven guilty."

"We weren't talking to you." The unshaven fellow stood up straight and pulled his unbuttoned flannel shirt over his bulging middle.

"Really? You were talking loud enough for everyone to hear. What if I called you red-neck trailer-trash?"

The fellow in the Allwood tee-shirt stared open-mouthed while the bristly-bearded one stuck out his chest and hitched his fingers in his belt. Before either could reply, Holly continued. "What's the matter? Don't you like being addressed that way?"

The man called Richie started to move toward Holly, when two garden center employees came out of the store, walking in their direction. Richie stopped, pushed up the brim of his baseball cap and said, "Look, we were just talkin'."

"In the future, don't assume everyone is as bigoted as you are, *la boca grande*," Holly snapped, and turned back to the car. Looking over her shoulder, she added, "Just in case your Spanish doesn't extend beyond '*estupido,*' that means big mouth."

When Holly got to the car, she found Ivy arranging the flats in the trunk. She looked over at Holly and asked, "Feel better?"

"Yes. Yes, I do," said Holly, as she got in the car and turned on the ignition.

9 PINELAND PARK COUNTY JAIL

Back home, Holly and Ivy unloaded the flats and potting soil. Ivy went straight to the shed to get the gardening tools, and Holly headed into the house to call Frank Flynn.

"Okay," she said when she came back out to the patio. "Juan is in Pineland County Jail and visiting hours are one to four." She hesitated, then asked, "You'll come with me, won't you?"

"I guess so," Ivy replied, rummaging through the tool bucket. "But only if you promise not to get …"

"Not to get what?" Holly arched her back and placed her hands on her hips.

"That!" Ivy punctuated the air with her garden trowel. "You see how you answered me? You're just itching for a fight. You're a 55-year-old woman who just confronted a group of young men in a garden center parking lot. If we go to a county jail, and you do the same thing, the outcome could be a trip to the emergency room. That isn't exactly how I want to spend my vacation."

Holly dropped her hands to her side and lowered her head. "You're right. I guess it was a stupid thing to do, but I just got so mad when I realized those ignoramuses were talking about Juan."

"You can't help Juan if you get hurt."

"Those guys wouldn't have hurt me. The ring leader was just a big bully."

Ivy shook her head. "I don't agree. I saw him looking at your license plate as we pulled out of the garden center lot. That scared me. You embarrassed a man in front of his friends. Men don't like that, Holly. You don't know what they might do."

"All right. Look, I promise I won't talk to anyone but Juan, okay?"

Ivy pointed her trowel at Holly. "You'll have to excuse me if I don't feel reassured. You've broken just about every promise you've made since I got here and I haven't even been here 48 hours." She turned and went over to the baker's racks and started to tear open a bag of potting soil. Holly stood silently watching her. *Get a grip, Holly.*

****

On the drive to the county jail, Holly kept going over Ivy's admonitions in her head. How could she ever convince Ivy to move in with her if she kept making these horrendous blunders? Besides, Ivy was right about everything. She shouldn't have left the house without leaving a note, and what in the world was she thinking when she approached those young men in the garden center parking lot?

Holly parked the car in a surface lot across from the county jail. "Ready?" she asked.

"As ready as I'll ever be."

Together they crossed the street and walked to the end of the line behind twenty or more people waiting for the doors to open. Men, women and a few children populated the queue, mostly young, mostly subdued, speaking quietly in a variety of languages--Spanish, Polish, Arabic. More than a few curious stares followed them as they walked past. When they reached their place at the end of the line, Holly turned to Ivy.

"Look, I'm really sorry to have dragged you into this, but I want you to know how grateful I am that you're with me. I don't feel quite as brave here as I did back at the garden center."

"Glad to hear it." Ivy looked around, lowered her head and whispered, "You know, I don't see this much diversity in a year in South Carolina." They were definitely the minority here.

Inside the sisters sat on a wooden bench and waited for their names to be called. After just a few minutes they were summoned to follow an officer down a hall to a room with seating areas separated by wooden partitions. Some visitors were already seated talking on phone receivers to inmates on the other side of a glass wall. Holly and Ivy sat down. Juan was brought in wearing an orange jumpsuit. His hair needed combing and he looked as if he hadn't slept. .When he saw Holly, his face brightened just a bit. He picked up the phone receiver.

"Ms. Donnelly, thank you so much for coming here."

"Hi, Juan. This is my sister, Ivy."

"*Sí, Sí.* I can tell," he smiled, but the smile faded quickly. "I so sorry you have to come here. You know I did not kill Señora Hagel. I use the garden knife, but no to kill."

"Juan, I know. Were you at the house on Wednesday? Can you tell me what happened?"

Juan recounted his arrival at Mrs. Hagel's on Wednesday around 8:00 a.m. He explained that he went straight to the backyard to continue work on the weeding he'd begun the day before. At noon, he rang the back doorbell and told Mrs. Hagel's nurse that he was leaving and explained he wouldn't be back until Friday because he had another job.

"Did you see Mrs. Hagel?" Holly asked.

"No, I no see her." Juan continued partially in English, partially in Spanish. He said the police came to his house late Wednesday night, brought him downtown for questioning and held him overnight in an interview room. In the morning they fingerprinted him. Then they questioned him again about jewelry. After that they arrested him for attempted robbery and the murder of Mrs. Hagel. His fingerprints matched the prints on the garden knife and two gold bracelets were found in the garden tool bucket in the shed. He told them he didn't do it, but they just read him his rights, put him in cuffs and took him to a holding cell. That's where he was headed when Holly and Ivy saw him in the lobby.

"Juan, do you have any idea how the bracelets got into the tool bucket?" Holly asked.

He shook his head no. "Ms. Donnelly, you know I no steal. I no do this."

"I know, Juan. I believe you," Holly said. "Did the court appoint a lawyer yet? *Abogado*?"

"*Sí.* The lawyer came to see me. We talk five, ten *minutos* only. She say she come again on Monday."

"She?" Holly looked over at Ivy. "A woman lawyer. Maybe that's a good thing. Juan, what's her name?"

"Sheryl Robinson."

"I'm going to try to talk to her. If there's anything I can do, I will do it. I am so sorry this is happening to you. *Lo siento mucho*."

"Gracias, Ms. Donnelly. *Gracias."*

****

Holly didn't say a word as she and Ivy walked to the car. When they got in, she turned and said, "I've never in my life felt less sure about what to do. After coming here, I feel exhausted and hopeless and really like a fish out of water."

Ivy sat silently as Holly put her head down on the steering wheel. "I just want to go home and forget the whole thing, but I can't." Sitting back up, she turned to face Ivy. "I know I have no right to drag you into this mess with me, but I don't think I can do this without your help."

Ivy sat forward. "Now I remember! I had a dream the other night. Dave told me to help you."

"Really?"

"Really." Ivy turned and faced Holly. "All my life I've felt like I could never repay you for all you've done for me. I guess now's my chance."

Holly raised one eyebrow and smiled, "Payback's a bitch, huh?"

"Yeah," Ivy said. "But after this one, I think we're even."

10 SHERYL ROBINSON, ESQ.

The two-story brick building that housed Sheryl Robinson's office had no lobby or elevator. The outer door opened into a small vestibule with one unmarked door to the right and a flight of stairs with worn carpet treads leading to the second floor.

The door at the top of the stairs read "Sheryl Robinson, Esq." Holly knocked. An African-American woman in a white, man-tailored shirt and gray pant suit opened the door.

"Ms. Robinson, I'm Holly Donnelly and this is my sister, Ivy. I'm a friend of Juan Alvarez."

Unsmiling, the lawyer shook hands with Holly and Ivy. "Have a seat." She pointed to the two chairs in front of her desk, and sat down herself. Rifling through the papers on her cluttered desk, she found a dog-eared file folder that looked as if it had been re-cycled more than once. Not looking up, Ms. Robinson said, "At the moment, it doesn't look good for Mr. Alvarez. His fingerprints were all over the murder weapon, a *hori hori* knife I believe it's called."

"Of course, Juan's fingerprints would be on that. He was doing gardening work for Mrs. Hagel. Isn't that just circumstantial evidence?" Holly asked.

"That's not all the police have against Mr. Alvarez. Stolen jewelry was found hidden in the tool bucket he was using. The police are looking at this as an attempted robbery gone wrong, Ms. Donnelly. I think the best Mr. Alvarez can do is plead guilty to felony robbery and voluntary manslaughter and hope for a six, maybe three-year sentence."

Holly's cheeks burned and tears stung her eyes. She stared at the lawyer, started to speak and stopped. Sheryl Robinson dropped the folder on her desk, leaned back in her chair and waited. Finally, Holly spoke.

"Ms. Robinson, Juan has worked for me for over ten years. I've left him at my house with the doors unlocked numerous times." Holly stopped and leaned forward bracing her hands on the lawyer's desk. "He's never stolen anything."

The lawyer just frowned and shrugged.

"Were Juan's fingerprints on the jewelry?" Holly asked.

Ms. Robinson paused, picked up the file and perused it again. "The report doesn't say."

"See." Holly moved to the edge of her seat. "Maybe somebody else put that jewelry there to frame him. I know Juan is incapable of murder."

The lawyer looked at Holly, heaved a sigh and replied, "Ms. Donnelly, I appreciate your genuine interest in Mr. Alvarez, but the report may just have omitted the fingerprints on the jewelry. I can check, but under the circumstances, based on the evidence, a plea bargain is the best I think we can do."

Holly sat back silently, gripping the arms of her chair. She and Sheryl Robinson just stared at each other. Ivy's voice broke the uncomfortable silence.

"Has there been an autopsy, Ms. Robinson? What did the coroner list as the cause of death?" she asked.

"The autopsy isn't complete yet. I think it's obvious that stabbing was the cause of death."

"Maybe not," Ivy conjectured.

Holly and the lawyer both stared at Ivy.

"She was stabbed. There's no doubt about that." The lawyer pursed her lips.

"Yes, I know that, but--I can't be absolutely sure--but when I looked at the pill bottles on the counter the day we found Mrs. Hagel on the floor, I saw there were two prescriptions. One was for Digoxin and the other was for Ativan. Both of those pills are white, so they could easily be mixed up."

“So what are you saying?” asked the lawyer, looking at her watch.

“Digoxin is used to treat heart conditions, like atrial fibrillation, atrial flutter and sometimes heart failure. Ativan is a sedative.”

“How do you know that?” the lawyer asked, looking over her reading glasses at Ivy.

“I'm a registered nurse.”

Ms. Robinson leaned back in her chair and folded her arms across her chest. ”Okay. So what if those pills were mixed up?”

“Well, Ativan is a sedative. Too much could be fatal to an elderly person, especially someone taking numerous medications.”

“Fatal?” the lawyer said unfolding her arms and sitting forward.

“Yes. When I was in the kitchen after I discovered the body, I saw there were several paper pill cups lined up on the counter that could easily have gotten mixed up. The wrong doses in the wrong combination could result in cardiac arrest.” Ivy bit her lower lip.

“What?” Holly gasped. “And you didn't tell me?”

Ivy looked over at Holly and took a deep breath. “I could be wrong. I only got a glance at the pills in the paper cups, but I think there may have been Ativans in each of the cups, and that drug should only be given once a day. I'm just suggesting the autopsy results and toxicology report may just show something no one is looking for because of the stabbing.”

“Ivy, how could you…”

Sheryl Robinson intervened. “So what you're saying is someone drugged her, then stabbed her? Why would anybody do that?” Ms. Robinson asked.

“If the real cause of death was an overdose of Ativan, and you wanted to make it look like a stabbing and a robbery, the real murderer could have planted the jewelry in the tool bucket and stabbed Mrs. Hagel with the garden knife after she was dead knowing Juan's fingerprints would be on it.”

“So that would prove Juan was framed, just like I said,” Holly interjected.

“We’re a long way from proof, Ms. Donnelly,” Ms. Robinson replied.

Ivy sighed. “Here’s the thing. I didn’t think about it at the time, because once I knew Mrs. Hagel was dead, I stood right up and went to the door. But that night, after the police told us Mrs. Hagel had been stabbed, it bothered me that I hadn’t noticed any blood near the body. If she’d been stabbed while she was alive, I should have noticed blood.”

Ms. Robinson stared at Ivy, moving her jaw from side to side. After a few seconds, she said, “All right. I’ll call the coroner and see what I can find out. I’ll also check to see what medications were confiscated at the crime scene.” She closed Juan’s file and stood up.

“Holly, shall we go?” Ivy asked

“Uh--yes.” Holly replied. “Ms. Robinson, you’ll call us if you hear anything, or if there’s anything we can do?”

“Yes,” said the attorney as she walked them to the door and shook their hands. ”And thank you for coming in. If the medication was mixed-up, we may have something to raise reasonable doubt in the jurors’ minds. If you’re right, you may have just saved Mr. Alvarez from a prison sentence.”

****

Back in the car, Holly turned to Ivy. “Why didn’t you tell me about the pills? What were you thinking?”

“I’ll tell you what I was thinking. I was thinking that the police would certainly discover an overdose of the wrong medication. If I spotted it, wouldn’t the forensics people? Besides, I couldn’t be absolutely sure that what I saw had anything to do with Mrs. Hagel’s death. And now that I think about it, the police had to know the lack of blood meant she was stabbed after she was dead.”

“Great. So, now the police are involved in framing Juan?”

“No, I don’t think that. Remember Manelli said Edna had a knife in her chest. He didn’t say it was the cause of death.

Police sometimes keep details about the crime scene to themselves. Remember, we were suspects when he talked to us."

"Go ahead. Defend the police."

"I'm not defending anyone. Besides when the autopsy results are finished, what I saw may not even matter."

"If you didn't think it mattered, what made you tell Sheryl Robinson just now?"

Ivy took a deep breath and exhaled slowly. "When the lawyer said Juan would go to prison for three to six years, I got sick to my stomach. I don't know Juan as well as you do, but I have to agree with you. I can't believe that gentle man we met at the county jail would kill anyone. At Mrs. Hagel's house, with all those police around, I felt afraid to say something I wasn't sure about. Here, I wasn't afraid to tell the lawyer what I thought I saw."

Holly gripped the steering wheel and leaned her head back against the car seat. "Oh, Ivy, I'd be really mad at you right now, if I didn't think you maybe just saved Juan."

On the drive home, Holly burst out laughing. "I almost fell off my chair when you asked the lawyer about the autopsy. When you started talking about the pills you sounded like an expert witness on the stand. You really amaze me sometimes."

Ivy giggled. "Did I sound like I really knew what I was talking about?"

"Are you kidding? You stopped Sheryl Robinson right in her tracks. She seemed to be just going through the motions with me, but once you started, you had her full attention. Ivy, Ivy, Ivy. You always underestimate yourself."

"I just didn't want to say something and be wrong. But after you said that maybe somebody else put the jewelry in the tool bucket, it got me thinking that if someone really did want to frame Juan, they could have killed Mrs. Hagel with drugs and then stabbed her to cover up the overdose. That's when I knew I had to say something even if I was wrong."

"Thank heaven. Now let's just keep our fingers crossed that what you saw actually helps Juan."

11 A CHANCE ENCOUNTER

The next day after breakfast the two sisters decided to work in the garden a few hours in the cool of the morning and then drive out to Well-Sweep Herb Farm in Hackettstown after lunch. Ivy continued mixing and matching flower combinations for some hanging pots for the back patio, and Holly returned to the front yard to weed the border bed along the fence. She just finished clearing the weeds from two fence sections, when she heard her name.

"Holly? Is that you?"

Holly stood up and saw a young man dressed in a suit, standing on the sidewalk, facing her neighbor's house.

"Ira? Hello." Holly smiled and waved. The young man walked over, and she took off her gardening glove, reaching over the fence to shake hands.

"What brings you here?" she asked.

"Your neighbors have some work for me," he replied.

"They don't want to sue me, do they?" Holly joked.

"You know attorney/client privilege," he replied laughing. "But no, I can tell you they aren't suing you. So, how have you been?"

"Pretty well, thanks. You know, I was actually thinking of calling you," Holly said.

"Are *you* planning to sue someone?"

"No, no." Holly chuckled, shaking her head. "Are you still on the zoning board?"

"Yes. We still talk about you, you know."

"Don't tell me that. I can just imagine what's being said."

"It's all good. Really. Are you planning some work? Do you need a variance?"

"No, I didn't want to talk to you about a zoning issue. It was about Mrs. Hagel's murder."

Ira's expression shifted from a smile to a frown. "Really awful, isn't it?"

"Yeah, I can't believe it," she replied, gripping the fence rail.

"Why were you going to contact me about that?"

"The gardener who's being held for Mrs. Hagel's murder--I introduced him to Mrs. Hagel."

"You certainly have no liability there," Ira assured her.

"I'm not worried about that. I know the gardener well, Ira. He's worked for me for years. He would never kill anyone."

"I'm not a criminal lawyer," Ira demurred.

"I know that, but the reason I was going to call you was just for some guidance on whom I might talk to in town in order to help this guy. My neighbor two doors down is a retired policemen and he found out for me where Juan--that's his name--is being held. I visited him and talked to his lawyer."

"Sounds like you didn't need me at all."

"I don't know about that. I feel I need every bit of help I can get."

"Who's the lawyer?"

"Sheryl Robinson."

"Court appointed?"

"What do you think?"

"What did she tell you?"

Holly recounted what transpired at the lawyer's office, including Ivy's revelations about Mrs. Hagel's medication.

"Wow. Do you and your sister want jobs? I know a few attorneys who could use people to do paralegal work."

"Please!" Holly rolled her eyes. "Seriously, Ira. What do you think?"

"I think you'd run rings around these kids coming out of college and paralegal schools," Ira teased.

"You know that's not what I mean. I'm talking about Juan. Do you have any suggestions about what I could do for him?"

Ira got quiet and looked down at the rosebush. Holly waited. Having worked on the zoning board for nearly two years, she learned to recognize when a lawyer was internally analyzing the question asked and formulating a prudent response.

Ira looked up again, all traces of playfulness gone from his face. "If your friend, Juan, didn't murder Mrs. Hagel, someone else did, and that could be anyone. A family member, a neighbor, a random thief. You may want to think about that before you get involved any further. As a neighbor who lives just a block away from the Hagel house, quite frankly, I'm terrified thinking there is a murderer on the loose."

"Gosh," Holly said as she ran her hand through her hair. "I hadn't even thought about that. I've been so focused on helping Juan, I didn't give any thought to who might have actually killed Mrs. Hagel."

"My advice to you is leave this to the police."

"But the police seem to have already made up their minds that Juan is guilty. I don't think they're even looking for other suspects. And Juan is such a good man. I know he didn't do it."

"You asked me. I've given you my best professional advice, even though I understand your concern."

"Thanks. I appreciate what you've told me. Right now there really isn't anything more I can think to do. I just hope the autopsy clears Juan. But listen. If you think of anything that can help, just give me a call. Okay?"

"Sure. It was good to see you. And let me know if you change your mind about working for lawyers." Ira smiled.

"Get out of here before I turn the hose on you." Holly laughed as she put her gardening gloves back on.

"See, now that's the Holly we miss on the Board," said Ira, laughing as he walked away, heading back to the neighbor's front path.

Holly watched Ira disappear into the neighbor's house. She looked down the street in the direction of the park. Ira was right. If Juan didn't kill Mrs. Hagel, someone else did. Who in the world would want to kill that nice old woman? She only had one son. He would inherit everything when she died, and she always bragged about how well her son ran the family printing and stationery business. Why would he kill his mother now?

"Holly! Holly!"

Startled, Holly turned to see Ivy standing at the bottom of the front steps, holding a pot of red and white impatiens with vinca gracefully trailing down the front.

"What were you so deep in thought about? I must have called your name five times."

"Oh, nothing," Holly lied. "That pot looks gorgeous, " Holly said as she picked up her tool bucket. "I think it's quitting time. Let's get cleaned up and have some lunch."

****

After her shower Holly returned to the kitchen. Ivy was just finishing a plate of leftover chicken cacciatore.

"I made you a salad. I figured you would have leftovers, too."

"You figured right." Holly grabbed a plate.

"You think I can get a bay plant like yours at the herb farm?" Ivy asked.

"Probably."

"Do they have a gift shop?"

Holly laughed loudly. "Yes, they have a gift shop. It's in a big barn. You'll love it. Of course, I do believe you've never been to a gift shop you didn't like."

The phone rang. Holly walked over to the counter. The caller ID showed Sheryl Robinson, Esq. She quickly picked up the handset. Ivy put her fork down and waited, exhaling when she saw Holly's face break into a big smile.

"Okay," Holly said. "We'll be there."

"Juan's being released!" she beamed as she hung up the phone.

"Really? Tell me what she said," Ivy demanded.

"The coroner said the cause of death was cardiac arrest, not stabbing. Mrs. Hagel was dead before the stabbing." Holly sat down and squeezed Ivy's hand. "They're still waiting for the toxicology report to confirm the drugs in her system, but the coroner suspects an error or overdose in medication as the cause of death."

"You mean I was right after all?"

"You were right. Sheryl Robinson said the coroner and police might have reached the right conclusions eventually, but she pushed them based on what you told her, and she thinks that made a difference."

"What great news."

"And Juan's fingerprints were not found on the jewelry, any of the medication or anywhere in the house, so he's being released today!"

"Fantastic," Ivy replied. "We can celebrate at the herb farm."

"Well--I sort of agreed to drive over to Paterson and pick Juan up and bring him home."

Ivy looked crestfallen.

"Please don't be disappointed," Holly said. "We can go to the herb farm tomorrow. Once we get Juan home, we're completely free to start our vacation over. Tomorrow we do only what you want to do, and nothing you don't. I promise."

"Another promise?"

"Yes. I promise, as soon as we drop Juan off at his house, we can hit a cosmic reset button. We'll start immediately by doing a little shopping at the Promenade Shops and then have dinner at Joe's Crabshack."

"Can we order those rum drinks and ask them to dance the Macarena?" Ivy asked.

"All night long if you want!"

12 A NURSE IN NEED

Both Holly and Ivy were feeling content and mellow on the drive home after dinner at Joe's Crabshack. As Holly turned the corner of her street, she spotted two people on her front doorstep.

"Who could that be?" Ivy asked.

"It's Juan, but I don't know who the woman is."

"She's in nursing scrubs," Ivy said.

Holly parked the car in the driveway and the sisters walked around to the front of the house.

"Hola, Juan. I thought you'd be home celebrating with your wife and daughter," Holly said.

"Gracias, Ms. Donnelly. I so happy. Thank you. My wife, she say to thank you, too."

"I already told you, my sister is the one who deserves the thanks. She's the one who saved you." Holly laughed, putting her arm around Ivy.

Juan smiled at Ivy, but then looked to the young woman beside him and the smile left his face. "*Esta es* Elena Gomez, Ms. Donnelly. Her *madre,* she work for Mrs. Hagel."

Elena dabbed at the corners of her swollen eyes with a shredded, crumpled tissue. She wore a white, fleece hoody over blue nursing scrubs. *Too young to be a nurse*. Holly's eyes widened as she realized this girl's mother was the woman she'd seen walking with Mrs. Hagel in front of her house.

"Hello, Elena," Holly said.

"Hello," the tearful brunette replied, her eyes darting from Holly to Ivy, then to Juan who put his hand on her shoulder and nodded in the direction of the sisters. She hesitated, looked down at the tissue in her hands, then finally at Holly. "My mother was arrested today. They say she killed Mrs. Hagel." At that Elena burst into tears. Juan squeezed her shoulder and reached in his pocket, pulling out a clean tissue.

Holly and Ivy exchanged expressionless glances. "Let's go inside," Holly said, unlocking the door and leading the way. "Sit down. Please," Holly pointed to the couch, left the room and returned with a box of tissues she placed on the coffee table in front of Elena.

"Thank you," the girl sniffed.

"Elena, why do the police think your mother killed Mrs. Hagel?" Holly asked.

The girl took a deep breath and began, "Because her fingerprints are on the pill bottles. And the jewelry. They say she drugged Mrs. Hagel. They say she put some jewelry in the garden tool bucket and stabbed Mrs. Hagel to frame Juan. The Hagel family now say other jewelry is missing." Elena sat forward clenching and unclenching her hands. "The police came and searched our apartment, but they didn't find anything because my mother, she didn't steal anything and she didn't kill Mrs. Hagel."

"I'm so sorry, Elena. I'm certain your mother didn't do this, but I'm not sure why you're here," Holly said.

"Juan said you helped him." Elena ran the tissue across her cheeks. "Please. Please. My mother--she's working to put me through nursing school. I'm only eighteen. I don't know what to do."

Holly looked from Juan to Ivy. "Don't you have any other family?"

"No. My father died when I was ten. There's only me and my little brother and sister." Elena again leaned forward moving to the edge of her seat, lightly drumming her fisted hands in her lap. "My mother didn't do this. She couldn't do this." Elena began sobbing this time, burying her face in her hands.

"I'd like to help, but I don't know what I can do," Holly said. "I spoke to the police and the lawyer because I knew Juan personally and thought I could be a character witness, but I don't know your mother..." she trailed off as the young woman sobbed even louder.

"Holly." Ivy tipped her head in the direction of the kitchen.

"Excuse us a minute," Holly replied. Juan took Elena's hand, trying to comfort her as the sisters left the room

"Oh, boy!" Holly stood with her back against the kitchen counter. "What am I going to do?"

"You're going to tell her we'll help her," Ivy said calmly.

"What?" Holly exclaimed. "Aren't you the one who told me to let the police handle it when I said I wanted to help Juan?"

"Ssh! Keep your voice down." Ivy covered her mouth with her index finger. "I know what I said, but she's so alone and she needs help."

Holly stood silently staring at her sister. After a moment, she let out a deep breath and said, "Oh, I get it. It's because she's studying to be a nurse, isn't it?"

"Okay. Partly. But I just can't believe a home health care aide who's sending a daughter to nursing school would kill her employer and frame somebody else. She'd have to be a monster, and I don't think a monster could have raised that young woman out there."

"But what can we do? At least with Juan, I felt I could be a legitimate character witness."

"You can talk to Elena's mother, can't you? You can talk to her lawyer, too. Elena won't know what to ask. Believe me. I know what that feels like. That's what *you're* good at. Maybe you could learn something that could help Mrs. Gomez."

"*Me* or *we*?" Holly raised both eyebrows.

"Okay, *we* could talk to the lawyer, but you know you're better at talking than I am."

"I can talk all right, but remember? You were the one who helped Juan. I was actually quite useless."

"No, no. If it was up to me we would never have gone to see the lawyer, so don't say that. Look, I'm completely on board. Elena has no one to turn to. If, after we talk to her mother and the lawyer, you think there's nothing we can do, then we'll just have to tell her that."

"Are you sure? You really want to get involved in this?"

"I do. Elena and her mother are in the business of nursing people and nurses are not likely killers. Let's just do what we can."

"You realize this means those fabulous plans we made for the herb farm and a Broadway show are on hold again?"

"What's another day or two?" Ivy shrugged.

With a weary sigh, Holly nodded and the two returned to the living room.

"Elena, is your mother in the Pineland Park Jail or the County Jail?

"Pineland Park."

"Okay. Tomorrow Ivy and I will go downtown and talk to your mother."

"Thank you. Thank you so much." For the first time, Elena's face brightened.

Holly shook her head. "You must understand that we are not lawyers or investigators, and we're not even sure we can help your mother."

"I understand. I understand. If you could just talk to my mother. See if there is anything I could do to help her."

"Okay. We just don't want you to think we can do something we can't."

"No. No. I understand." She nodded her head, reminding Holly of a puppy, excited and eager to please.

"*Vamanos*," said Juan, getting up to go.

Holly and Ivy walked them to the front door. As Elena descended the front steps, Juan turned to Holly.

"*Muchas Gracias.* God bless you, Ms. Donnelly."

"Juan," Holly began quietly, "I'm not sure…"

Juan squeezed her hand. "*Rezaré a Dios. Esta en Su manos. Buenas Noches.*"

Holly closed the door and she and Ivy watched as Elena and Juan got inside a beat-up Honda that had to be more than ten years old.

"What did he say to you?" Ivy asked.

"He said he would pray to God. It's in his hands."

"Prayers can't hurt, can they?"

"No, but Juan may have just used up all his spiritual mojo cashing in his own heavenly get-out-of-jail-free card. Let's hope Mrs. Gomez has some of her own celestial credits."

13 SLEEPLESS IN PINELAND PARK

Holly crawled into bed, exhausted, hoping she would fall asleep immediately, but as soon as she closed her eyes, her mind kicked into overdrive. *Who killed Mrs. Hagel?* From the moment she'd seen Juan in handcuffs, her total focus had been on helping him. Not trying to find a murderer.

Against her better judgment, she agreed to talk to Elena's mother. For all she knew, the woman may have actually committed the murder. But Juan brought Elena to her because he clearly did not believe Mrs. Gomez was guilty. That had to count for something, especially since the charges included trying to frame him.

Holly dreaded going back down to the police station the next day. Tossing and turning for half an hour, she finally jumped up and turned on the light, muttering, "What the hell?" She reached for the phone and hit Speed Dial 2.

"Kate?"

"Hi. You know, I was just thinking about you. How's it going down there?"

"You want the good news or bad news first?"

"Good news, of course."

"Juan was released."

"That's wonderful news. How'd you manage that?"

"I had very little to do with it. Ivy saved him." Holly recounted the visit to Sheryl Robinson's office.

"Amazing!" Kate said. "Kudos to Ivy, huh?"

"Really. You know I've always felt guilty because growing up I usually got credited with being the smart one, but that's only because I was more assertive. Ivy's way smarter than me."

"You also like being the center of attention, and the few times I've been in Ivy's company, I can tell she doesn't. She seems more content to follow."

"Yeah," Holly paused. "But every now and then, she can surprise you, like when she up and joined the Army on her twentieth birthday."

"I forgot that. I still can't imagine that 95-pound blonde in the army."

"We used to call her Private Benjamin." Holly laughed. "One of these days we'll have to get together so she can tell you some of her army stories."

"So what's the bad news?"

Holly threw her head back onto the pillows. "Ugh! For a moment there I almost forgot."

She told Kate about Juan's visit with Elena Gomez and their promise to talk to Mrs. Gomez the next day.

"And this was Ivy's idea?"

"Yep."

"I'm becoming more and more impressed with your sister."

Holly sat up. "But, Kate, I think this is going to be a train wreck. I didn't know what to do to help Juan, but at least I was sure he didn't do it. I don't even know this woman."

"Do you think she could have done it?"

"Probably not. But the only solution is finding who did kill Mrs. Hagel, and I definitely don't know how to do that."

"You didn't know how to help Juan, either."

"Hey, you're supposed to tell me 'Holly, you're right. Tomorrow go to Well-Sweep Herb Farm with Ivy and forget about the whole thing.'"

"If I said that you'd hang up and continue to toss and turn all night."

Holly sighed. "You're right. What am I going to do, Kate?"

"I just happen to have the Tarot cards right next to me. Shall I shuffle?"

"Go ahead. They can't make things any worse." Holly nestled back into her pillows and pulled the comforter up to her neck.

After a moment, Kate said, "Blow."

Holly took a deep breath, blew into the phone and waited.

"Ooh. Interesting."

"Are you going to ooh and aah, or are you going to tell me what came up?"

"Okay. You've drawn the Seven of Wands, Justice and the King of Wands."

"What do they mean?" Holly sat up again, this time throwing her legs over the side of the bed and leaning forward.

"The Seven of Wands is about persistence and resilience, about hanging in there to get what you want. Hold on. Let me look at my notes." Holly could hear paper rustling.

"Here it is. Face challenges one at a time. and you will succeed."

"This doesn't sound like it's telling me to go to the herb farm tomorrow." Holly lay back across the bed.

"No. Afraid not. I think Justice is pretty self-explanatory in this instance, don't you? But here we go with the King of Wands. Again a strong, male figure. Let's see what my notes say. He's someone who dominates by strength of will. A leader of people and he sincerely wants everyone to share in the benefits of group efforts. Strong-minded. Okay. Who's the guy?"

Holly remembered Detective Manelli's tightened jawline when she asked why Juan was in handcuffs. "For heaven's sake, there is no guy," she blustered. "So this reading is telling me to go to the jail tomorrow?"

"Pretty much. Wish I was there to go with you. I think someone needs to be looking for your King of Wands, because you're simply not paying attention."

"I saw one of my Zoning Board cronies this morning. Maybe he's the King of Wands. Hate to disappoint you, though. He's married and twenty years younger than me."

"Happily married?"

"Good night, Kate."

14 LEONELLE GOMEZ

The next morning as Holly put her oatmeal in the microwave the phone rang. Elena Gomez said her mother was still at the Pineland Park jail and had not yet been transferred to the county jail. She agreed to meet Ivy and Holly downtown at 10:00 a.m.

At 9:55 Holly pulled into the parking space behind Police Headquarters. "I pray we don't run into that stupid detective again."

"Me, too, but if we do, please control yourself." Ivy unbuckled her seatbelt, turned and put her hand on Holly's arm. "Seriously. Remember what Dave always told me. Don't make enemies you don't need to."

Holly nodded. "You're right."

As they approached the front doors of the building, they spotted Elena. She smiled and ran over, giving Ivy a hug. "I'm so happy you're here," she said as she hugged Holly next. Holly looked over Elena's shoulder at Ivy, grimacing. Together the three women worked their way through the security line.

Inside the visitation room Elena began crying as soon as she saw her mother. Leonelle Gomez wore her jet black hair pulled back from her face and tightly braided. Her brown eyes were puffy, as if she hadn't slept. She stood up straighter when she saw Holly and Ivy. Sitting down she picked up the phone, blinking rapidly to keep her tears in check, her mouth turned downward in a doleful expression. After a brief exchange in Spanish, Elena stood up and handed Holly the phone. Holly sat down on half the chair and Ivy sat beside her. They put their heads together to share the phone.

Holly gave a weak smile, nodded at Leonelle and began. "Mrs. Gomez, I'm not sure if we can help, but why don't you tell us what happened the day Mrs. Hagel was… the day Mrs. Hagel died."

Leonelle Gomez explained that the day of Mrs. Hagel's death she needed to leave early to take her son to the dentist. Mrs. Hagel's son, his wife and their daughter stopped by around ten and left by ten-thirty. Leonelle prepared lunch at noon and after Mrs. Hagel ate, Leonelle cleaned up and left at one-thirty. Her eyes met Holly's. "I didn't steal any jewelry, and I didn't kill Mrs. Hagel."

Holly nodded. "So Mrs. Hagel was well enough to be left alone?"

"*Sí*. I didn't have to leave early too much. When I did, I put a frozen dinner in the microwave. Mrs. Hagel had one of those …*come se dice*?" She pointed to her chest and looked at Elena.

Elena, who was standing close behind Holly and Ivy listening, said, "A medical alert button."

"*Sí*, and I always put the phone next to her when I go."

"Her family couldn't stay with her?" Holly asked.

Leonelle looked down. "No."

"What about her medication?" Ivy asked.

Leonelle stiffened. "I don't know how the pills got mixed up. Every day before I go, I put the pills for tomorrow in the paper cups. So much to do in the morning. Get Mrs. Hagel dressed and cook breakfast. The pills, they look alike. I always open one bottle at a time and close it as soon as I take out the pills." Leonelle again made direct eye contact with Holly, leaned forward, her palms flat on the table. "I never make a mistake. That morning, I did the pills right after breakfast because I knew I had to leave early. When I left that day, the right pills were in the right cups."

Holly again nodded. "Your fingerprints were on the jewelry…"

Leonelle closed her hands into fists and sat up straight. *"Verdad,* my fingerprints are on the jewelry. Mrs. Hagel liked to wear a piece of jewelry even in the house, so every day she look in the jewelry box, and she pick a necklace or a pin to wear. I help her. My fingerprints are everywhere," she said, her whole body shuddering.

"Mrs. Gomez, someone switched those pills and then tried to frame Juan," Holly said. "You were with her every day. Can you think of anyone who might do that?"

Leonelle sighed loudly. "I don't know. That family of hers. They not nice. The son, he only comes with papers for her to sign. He never stay. His wife, she only comes with her daughter when they want money. They no care about her. It make her sad, I know. But kill? I don't know." She looked down at her hands, shaking her head.

"Was there anyone else who came to the house that day? Friends? Neighbors? Workmen?"

Again, Leonelle shook her head. "No when I was there. Only the son, his wife and the granddaughter."

Holly didn't know what to ask next. After an uncomfortable moment of silence, Ivy asked, "You locked up before you left?"

"Sí, I know I locked the doors. I always check before I go."

"Somebody had to have come in the house after you left. Was there a break in?" Ivy continued.

"*Ese es el problema*," Leonelle said, clenching her fists again and lightly pounding on the table in front of her. "The police say it was me because I have a key and nobody broke in."

"Who else has keys to the house?" Holly jumped in, her brain freeze melted by Ivy's line of questioning.

"Only family."

"Maybe one of them dropped by after you were gone," Ivy suggested. "They could have left the door unlocked when they left."

"Would Mrs. Hagel answer the door after you left?" Holly asked.

"She could get around with her walker," Leonelle replied, "but she no hear so good. She sometimes no hear the bell."

Again, Holly was at a loss for what to ask next, and this time so was Ivy.

"Okay, Mrs. Gomez," Holly said. "Did the court appoint a lawyer for you yet?"

"No yet," she said. "They say maybe today."

"We can try to talk to your lawyer and see what he or she says," Holly offered. "Maybe the lawyer will have some more information that can help." She turned around. "Elena, can you call us once you have the lawyer's name?"

Elena nodded. "Of course."

Holly turned back to Mrs. Gomez and gave a weak smile.

"*Gracias. Muchas gracias,*" Leonelle said, her eyes locked on Holly's.

"*De nada*," said Holly, thinking grimly that their visit probably amounted to exactly that--nothing. She got up and handed the phone to Elena. "We'll wait for you in the lobby."

Ivy rose and the two sisters left by the door they had entered. Neither spoke as they walked down the corridor to the lobby. Holly wanted to run out of the building, race home, bury her head under the pillows and not come out of her room until this whole thing was over.

15 MANELLI REDUX

Out in the lobby, Holly pointed to a bench along the wall and said, “Let's sit a minute.” She sank down, pursed her lips and leaned back against the wall. “Listen, I agree with you. This woman didn't kill Mrs. Hagel, but I don't see how we can help her.”

“I know,” Ivy said, dropping down on the bench beside her.

“We can go see the lawyer. But I'm not optimistic.”

“Me, either.”

They both looked up and saw Elena Gomez approaching them from across the lobby. “I hope she can't read our minds,” Holly whispered as they stood to meet her.

“Thank you so much for coming,” Elena said. “I'll call you as soon as I get the lawyer's name. I feel so much better now that you'll go with me.”

Holly forced a smile. Ivy put her hand on Elena's shoulder. “We'll do what we can.”

“Thanks,” she said, looking at her watch. “Sorry. I have to go. I have just enough time to get to class.”

“Okay,” Ivy said. “We'll wait to hear from you.”

Once she was out the door, Holly sank back onto the bench. “Oh, this is the worst. That poor kid actually thinks we can help. What are we gonna do?”

“Maybe just by going with her we're helping,” Ivy said, also sitting back down.

Just then, a group of four men entered the lobby from the hallway to the right of where they were sitting. Holly blanched when she recognized Detective Manelli. She turned toward Ivy. "Look at me. That's the detective. I really don't want him to see us."

Ivy glanced up. "Too late. I think he's coming over here."

Holly took a deep breath, feeling irrationally nervous, as she turned back to see Detective Manelli heading straight at them.

"If it isn't Jessica Fletcher and her twin sister. What brings you two here? Thinking of becoming private eyes, girls?" Manelli asked.

Holly glowered at him. "No, Detective. We have complete faith in the police to solve crimes. Isn't that right, Ivy?"

Ivy looked up at Detective Manelli, gave a quick smile and turned her gaze to a bulletin board across the lobby, appearing to be very interested in the fliers posted there.

"Is that right? Then what are you doing here? May I be of assistance?" he asked, his tone mocking.

Holly hesitated. *Why not*? "If you must know, we just visited Leonelle Gomez."

"Really?" Manelli responded grinning.

"Really," Holly replied. "We don't think she did it."

At this Manelli threw his head back and laughed out loud. "Wow, what a shock! I didn't see that one coming."

"Look, Detective. We were right about Juan Alvarez," Holly returned.

"Even a blind squirrel finds a nut once in a while," Manelli snapped.

"Can I ask you a question?" Holly braved.

"Go ahead," Manelli said, seeming just a bit intrigued.

"Did you question the neighbors to see if anybody saw someone approach Mrs. Hagel's house after Mrs. Gomez left the night before the body was discovered?"

Manelli stared at Holly, not replying, the same stare he had given her when she asked him a question in her living room. The silence made Ivy look in their direction. She tapped her sister on the leg, but Holly remained totally focused on Manelli, unblinking.

Finally, Manelli replied, "You really are a piece of work. Look, Ms. Donnelly, just because you were right about Juan Alvarez, doesn't make you a detective. Forensics would have gotten to the truth without you. Why don't you just go home and leave the police work to the professionals before you or your sister gets hurt?"

Holly put her hands on her hips. "Is that a threat?"

"That's not what I meant," Manelli growled. He stopped, took a deep breath and continued more calmly, "Killers are dangerous, and unlike the police, they don't try to be fair, and they don't care who they hurt. Please, take my advice. Your guy got off. Go home and let us do our jobs." He turned and walked off before Holly could say another word.

As Manelli disappeared around the corner, Ivy stood up and said, "I think he likes you."

"Oh, shut up," Holly responded, grabbing her bag and heading to the door.

16 A CLUE

Holly fumed silently all the way home. When they got back she let Lucky out the back door and immediately went upstairs and changed to her gardening clothes. Out back she filled a watering can from the rainwater barrel beside the shed and headed to the front yard to see if the pots on the front steps needed watering.

As she doused the impatiens, she spotted Ira Breger coming out of the neighbor's and waved. He waved back and headed to his car. He opened the door about to get in, but then looked over at Holly, closed the door and walked towards her instead. Holly put down the watering can and went to the fence.

"Hi, Ira. What's up?"

"Look, I probably shouldn't be telling you this, but …" He paused, biting his lower lip.

"You can't stop now," Holly said.

"A lawyer friend of mine works for the Hagels." Again he stopped.

"C'mon, Ira. Don't keep me in suspense."

"All right. My friend violated attorney/client privilege by telling me this, but the Hagels aren't my clients, so technically I'm not breaching ethics here. He told me that Novardo Development wants to build a $30-million mixed-use development downtown. The last piece of property they need to move forward with the project is the Hagel Paper and Printing building. Mrs. Hagel wouldn't sell."

"Wow, Ira. That could definitely be a motive for murder, don't you think?"

"Yes, it could."

"You know Juan Alvarez was released. Turns out my sister was right. Mrs. Hagel died from a mix-up in her medication. She was already dead when someone plunged that gardening tool into her."

"What? So you and your sister cracked the case?"

"Not really," she laughed. "Forensics would have figured it out eventually."

"I'm not kidding when I say this. I know three firms that would hire you in a heartbeat."

"Stop!"

"Wait a minute. You mean, I just violated professional ethics unnecessarily?" Ira joked.

"Not totally." Holly explained how she and Ivy got involved in helping Leonelle Gomez.

The smile left Ira's face. "The information about the developer is public information--just not Mrs. Hagel's refusal to sell. Remember. You didn't hear any of this from me." He frowned. "Whatever you do, please be careful."

"Of course. Thanks so much for letting me know."

"I wish I'd known your friend got off before I told you though. I sensed how important it was to you to help the gardener. But now you're helping a total stranger. If anything happens to you because of the information I've shared, I'll never forgive myself."

"Relax. I don't know if there's anything I can do with it. What am I saying? I can share it with Mrs. Gomez's lawyer. Of course, I won't say how I found it out."

"Now that's prudent. Maybe you did learn something from working with us boring lawyers."

Holly laughed. "Maybe I did. Thanks."

"Sure. See you around." As Ira headed to his car, over his shoulder, he said, "If you change your mind about that job ..."

"Where's my hose?" Holly pretended to look around for it as Ira chuckled and got into his car. Picking up the watering can, she headed to the backyard where she found Ivy relaxing on the chaise, eating cherries and thumbing through *Plow and Hearth* catalogues.

"Where were you?" Ivy asked. "I was wondering if I had to send out a search party."

"Very funny." Holly frowned and grabbed a handful of the cherries and sat down on the loveseat. "If you must know, I was watering the pots in front and I just had a very interesting conversation with Ira Breger, one of the lawyers I sat on the Zoning Board with." Holly sat next to Ivy on the loveseat and summarized her conversation with Ira.

"What are you going to do? Are you going to tell Detective Manelli?" Ivy asked.

"And have him mock me again? I don't think so."

"What else can you do? That's important information. That's a clue, isn't it?"

"Yes, if you're interested in the truth. Manelli's a waste. When we see Mrs. Gomez's lawyer, I'll tell him. Even Ira thought that was a good idea."

"It is. A lawyer should know what to do with that information."

"Let's hope so."

17 JONATHAN GRABNICK, ESQ.

Elena Gomez set up a 9:00 a.m. appointment to meet with Jonathan Grabnick, her mother's lawyer, the next morning. Holly and Ivy were optimistic as they drove to meet her, armed with the information about Novardo Development.

Their optimism began to fade when they met Elena in front of a run-down, two-story commercial building. Grabnick's office was located on the second floor, directly above AAA Bail Bondsman. They had to enter through a door located in a litter-strewn alley.

Holly led the way through the unswept, poorly lit hallway that had a musty smell. Dust bunnies abounded and a Snickers wrapper lay in the corner. The three women climbed the stairs. At the top they faced a single door with the words "Jonathan Grabnick, Esq., Attorney at Law" printed on it, the "Esq." partially worn away. Behind Elena, Holly made eye contact with Ivy. Neither said anything.

Elena knocked on the door. A heavyset, older man with a bad comb-over opened the door.

"Come in, ladies. I'm Jonathan Grabnick. You must be Holly and Ivy Donnelly," he said looking past Elena from one sister to the other. "Are you twins?" he asked.

"No, just sisters," Holly replied sighing, weary of answering this question, and in no mood for small talk.

"And you must be Elena Gomez," Grabnick continued gravely. To Holly's horror, Grabnick adopted an almost funereal demeanor as he extended his hand to Elena. She feared he was about to offer condolences when he turned abruptly and said, "Won't you sit down, ladies?"

Grabnick appeared the opposite of Juan's lawyer. Holly estimated he was probably in his late sixties. He wore a gray pinstripe suit, shabby, wrinkled, and in need of dry-cleaning. By the looks of it, he did not have much of a practice at this late stage in his career. Holly wondered if he ever had much of a practice. Fighting hard against a sinking feeling, she began.

"Mr. Grabnick, yesterday we learned some important information that might help Mrs. Gomez's case. Did you know that Mrs. Hagel refused to sell her property to Novardo Development and that Hagel Paper and Printing is the last piece of property they need to go forward with a $30-million development?"

Grabnick just looked at her, then at Elena with a woeful expression. "I don't see how that information can help Mrs. Gomez. I'm very sorry, but the evidence against her is overwhelming. In order to avoid the death penalty, I have to advise her to plead guilty to robbery and voluntary manslaughter."

Elena gasped and quickly responded, "But my mother's not guilty. She could never kill anyone. What kind of lawyer are you?"

Ivy put her arm around Elena trying to calm her. Grabnick glared at Elena saying, "I assure you, Miss Gomez, that my reputation as a lawyer is impeccable. Why, I ..."

"Mr. Grabnick," Holly interrupted. "We believe Mrs. Gomez is not guilty. She had no motive. Why would she kill her employer?"

"Of course, she didn't plan to do it. The prosecutor is claiming that Mrs. Hagel caught her red-handed stealing her jewelry. In a desperate attempt to stop her from calling the police ..."

"What?" Holly cut him off again. "In a desperate attempt to stop her from calling the police, she mixed up her medication and ran out to the shed, past a set of butcher knives on the kitchen counter, and looked for a garden tool to come back and stab her with?"

"No," Grabnick snapped, caught himself and continued. "Ms. Gomez drugged her first and then decided to frame the gardener by using the garden tool."

"And she cleaned her fingerprints off the garden tool, but left them on the jewelry? That makes no sense. And what about the pills? If Mrs. Hagel caught Mrs. Gomez stealing and was about to call the police, would she really stop and take pills? Mr. Grabnick, do you believe Mrs. Gomez is guilty?"

Grabnick's cheeks reddened. He looked down grasping the edge of his desk with both his pudgy hands. After a moment he replied, "What I believe is insignificant. I'm telling you what the prosecution is saying."

"But can't you come up with a better defense?" Holly was now sitting on the edge of her chair. "Can't you poke a hole in the prosecution's case by asking the questions I just asked you, maybe introduce an element of doubt by suggesting another scenario, like someone else came to the house after Leonelle Gomez left and tried to frame either her or Juan Alvarez? Have you even for one minute considered the fact that someone else killed Mrs. Hagel, someone with a more powerful motive? A $30-million motive?"

"Ms. Donnelly, in my personal opinion, Mrs. Gomez will avoid a longer jail sentence and the death penalty, if she pleads guilty to the charges I've suggested," Grabnick replied, looking down at the papers on his desk, not making eye contact.

"Have the police questioned the neighbors about what they may have seen or heard the night of the murder?"

Grabnick shuffled the papers on his desk, located a file and read, "The police report states that the neighbors to the east and south neither saw nor heard anything. The neighbors to the west left town on vacation the morning the body was discovered and the police have been unable to locate them for questioning."

"Don't you think talking to them would be a good idea?" Holly asked.

Again Grabnick hesitated, grimacing. Holly couldn't tell if he was experiencing physical pain or simply refusing to answer. After a moment, he replied.

"Ms. Donnelly, I am a court appointed lawyer. As you can see, I have no staff. There is no budget for detective work. I have to rely on the police for that."

Holly suddenly realized that arguing with Grabnick was futile. She reached her hand across his desk and calmly asked, "Can I see the police report?"

Grabnick stared at Holly. "You know, you really have no rights here. You're not even a family member."

"But I am," Elena spoke up. She and Ivy had been silent during Holly and Grabnick's verbal ping pong match. "Whatever Ms. Donnelly wants, I want you to give it to her."

"Only your mother can authorize that." Grabnick said raising his chin a bit.

"Seriously?" Holly asked. "You're actually going to make this difficult for us? You know Mrs. Gomez will give permission for us to have access to whatever we ask for. All we want to do is help her if we can."

Grabnick stretched his neck and straightened his tie. "All right," he relented. "Here it is." Grabnick handed Holly the report.

"Can we make a copy?" Holly asked, eyeing a dinosaur of a Xerox machine in the corner.

Grabnick rolled his eyes, snatched back the report, got up and made the copy.

"Thank you, Mr. Grabnick," Holly said as she took the copy he handed her. He didn't say, "You're welcome."

"Shall we go, *ladies*?" Holly asked, echoing Grabnick's earlier use of the word.

Ivy and Elena rose from their chairs. At the door Elena stopped and turned back, looking directly at Grabnick. "My mother is not guilty, and Ms. Donnelly is going to prove it. You'll see," she said with an indignant toss of her head.

So much for understanding that we probably can't help her mother.

19 NOVARDO DEVELOPMENT

Back home Holly and Ivy sat down at the table on the back patio. Elena left for her Occupational Therapy class right after the meeting with Grabnick. In the parking lot before they parted, Holly once again reminded Elena that she shouldn't get her hopes up too high. Just because they had the police report didn't mean they would find anything. Elena said she understood. Holly was certain she did not.

Holly read the report, then handed it to Ivy. When Ivy finished, she looked up at Holly and frowned. "Gosh, I don't know. Nothing here jumps out at me. What do you think?"

"I think we're at a dead end, and we should drop this, just like we agreed. I'm really heartsick for Elena and Leonelle, but what can we do?" Holly asked.

"I know you're right, but every time I think of her and her little brother and sister…"

"There is one thing," Holly mused.

"What?"

"I used to know someone who worked at Novardo Development. That was a long time ago, and I don't know if she's still there. Even if she is, what do I do? Call her up and ask if she can think of anyone she works with who might have killed Mrs. Hagel?"

"You could always call Detective Manelli."

"Are you kidding me? Do you honestly think he'll react any differently than Grabnick?"

"Maybe not, but what can it hurt to at least tell him what you heard?"

"If you think that's such a good idea, you call and talk to him."

"Are you afraid of him?" Ivy grinned.

"Shut up!" Holly bared her teeth and waggled her head in Ivy's direction, her best imitation of a riled grizzly bear. "I'm not afraid of him, but I have no intention of speaking to that cretin and having him patronize me again. No way."

Ivy frowned, gazing down at the police report in her lap. "Can it hurt to call your friend?"

Holly rubbed her forehead and sighed. "Okay. Let me get my laptop and see if I can find her number."

She went inside and returned a few minutes later with her laptop and cellphone and launched an Outlook search. "Here it is. Teresa Nowicki. I'll be surprised if she's still there."

"How do you know her?"

"When I was Business Development Director at Meadowlands Architecture, we tried to get work from Novardo. I met Teresa at a networking event and she helped me get an appointment for the partners to meet Novardo's development group. She and I went to lunch and then out for drinks a few times. She was quite a character and very helpful to me. Once I started working in New York though, we just lost touch."

"So, you going to call her?"

Holly grabbed the cell phone and tapped in the number.

"Hello. May I speak with Teresa Nowicki please?" She looked over at Ivy. "I don't believe it. She's still there. They're transferring me."

Ivy gave Holly two thumbs up.

"Hello. Teresa? This is a voice from your past. I'm hoping you remember me. It's Holly Donnelly. Yeah. Well, I'm semi-retired now. I closed my marketing consulting business two years ago and I've been teaching English composition at Passaic County Community College." Holly smiled over at Ivy. "That's right. I can't believe you're still there after all these years. I'd love to get together to catch up. I was planning to do some shopping in Paramus this afternoon. Are you free for lunch today? Great. How's 12:30 sound? Where's convenient for you? Terrific. See you there."

Holly hit the end button on her cell and looked at Ivy, shaking her head. "What did I just do?"

"Sounds like you made a lunch date."

"Listen. I think that maybe I ..." Holly hesitated.

"Should go alone?" Ivy finished. "Don't worry about me. I'll make a burger and then Lucky and I will take a long walk. You know how I love to explore the neighborhood and see what's growing in all the gardens. I really haven't had a chance to do that since I got here."

"You're sure you're okay with this?"

"Of course."

Holly looked at her watch. "I better get moving if I'm going to get to Paramus by 12:30. I should be back by three. I'll call if I'm going to be any later than that." She stood up, retrieved her cellphone, but remained standing by the table looking at her sister.

Ivy made a shooing motion with her hands. "Go already. I'll be fine. I'm with you one hundred percent."

"What if nothing comes of this?"

"Hey, remember what Dave's mother said to him right before she died? Do the best you can and let the rest go."

"Yeah, but how do we know when to let go?"

"We'll know."

Holly nodded, picked up her phone and cellphone and went inside.

As Ivy heard the car pull out of the driveway, she went back inside and climbed the stairs to the guest room. She picked up the business card on the dresser, went over to the phone on the nightstand.

"Hello. Detective Manelli, please."

19 TERESA NOWICKI

Holly perused the Suburban Diner menu as she waited for Teresa. She wanted to select her order before Teresa arrived, so she could focus on their conversation. Pulling the paper end off the straw in her glass, she took a sip of the Diet Coke she'd already ordered, continuing to think over the subtle questions she'd rehearsed in the car to ask Teresa about Novardo's development plans for Pineland Park.

Holly looked at her wristwatch. Teresa was late. Taking another sip of soda, she looked toward the door. Was that Teresa? Holly hadn't seen her in nearly thirty years. Back then, Teresa was an average-sized brunette. The platinum blonde rolling through the door looked only vaguely familiar. Dressed in what appeared to be a black tent, the woman spoke to the hostess, who pointed in Holly's direction. "Holleee!" Teresa squealed as she ambled over. "I'd recognize you anywhere. You haven't changed a bit."

Holly smiled and braced for an effusive bear hug, unable to reach her arms around the woman embracing her.

"Hi, Teresa. It's so good to see you. Glad you were able to meet me on such short notice."

"Are you joking? I'd do anything to get out of that friggin' office," Teresa quipped. She smiled, dropping into the seat opposite Holly. The Diet Coke swished in the glass. "I can't wait to hear all about your new life."

"It's pretty good these days. I'm actually off for the summer."

"Good for you! What I wouldn't give to have a summer off. Of course, if I had to stay home with my kids, that'd make me nuts."

"How old are they now?"

"Brad is 28 and Linda is 27."

Holly hesitated, surprised and not quite sure what to say in reply.

"Do you have kids?"

"No, I never married," Holly answered.

"Unbelievable! An attractive woman like you! How did that happen? My kids are half your age and Brad is divorced twice and Linda once."

"You know me. Always fell for the wrong guy," Holly replied.

"Yep, I do remember that. Those Happy Hours at the Sheraton Sports Bar, you always seemed to pick the bad boys to talk to. What about now though? You still look so good. I know why I don't meet nobody. I just let myself go." Teresa's smile faded. "When my Bill died, I just ...I don't know. I didn't care no more."

"I'm sorry, Teresa. I didn't know."

"How could ya? How long has it been since we've seen each other?"

"I asked myself that same question while I was waiting for you. Can it be twenty-five years?"

"Unbelievable."

A waitress in a starched pink uniform and white apron came and took their order.

"I'll have the burger deluxe," Teresa said without even looking at the menu.

"Let me have the veggie wrap--no fries," Holly said.

As the waitress collected the menus and walked away, Teresa asked, "So the last time I saw you, you went to work for that engineering firm in New York. On the phone, you said you closed your consulting company. You were in business for yourself?"

Holly recounted her job history for Teresa and how she eventually opened her own marketing consulting firm.

"What I want to know is how you ended up teaching?" Teresa asked.

"I ran webinars as part of my business, and after I developed a writing webinar for marketers, I decided I wanted to end my working career teaching again. Besides I was tired of getting on planes and trains. Remember I was an English teacher before I started marketing."

"I forgot you started out as a teacher. Yeah, yeah, now it's coming back to me."

The waitress came over with two huge plates. Teresa and Holly ate their meals continuing to reminisce about old times.

As Teresa dragged the last French fry through a glob of ketchup on her plate, she looked directly at Holly. "So, it's pretty clear you don't need me to help you get appointments. Why'd ya get in touch with me after all these years? What'd ya want?"

Holly snickered. "Nobody could ever get anything past you, could they, Teresa?"

"Hell, no. Why d'ya think I'm still at this job with guys who chew up and spit out women just because they can?"

Holly looked down at her plate, then back up at Teresa. "You never changed. Always the straight shooter. So I'll be straight with you. Did you read about the murder in Pineland Park?"

"Yeah. Some old lady got stabbed by her gardener, right?"

"Not exactly." Holly told Teresa about how Juan was mistakenly accused of the crime, and eventually freed, and how she and Ivy were now trying to help Leonelle Gomez.

"That's some story, but why you telling me all this?"

"The woman murdered was Edna Hagel of Hagel Printing and Paper."

"Oh," Teresa said, nodding slowly, clearly making the connection between Hagel Printing and Paper and Novardo Development.

Holly leaned in. "I'm sorry if I'm putting you on the spot, and you can tell me to go to hell, but I don't believe Leonelle Gomez killed Mrs. Hagel. Her court-appointed lawyer, to borrow one of your famous phrases, 'couldn't find his butt in the dark.' Mrs. Gomez's daughter has asked Ivy and me for help. I'm just trying to find out if someone else could have had a better motive to kill Mrs. Hagel."

Teresa looked down at her empty plate and hesitated before she spoke. "I'll be honest with you. These guys are guilty of a lot of things. Tony is unethical. Paul can be underhanded and downright nasty. But murder? I don't think so." She shrugged and shook her head.

"Okay. Thanks for that. Your opinion means a lot to me. If murder is a line you think they wouldn't cross, then I accept that."

"I really respect what you're trying to do, but, like I said, murder's a stretch, even for these guys."

Holly signaled for the waitress to bring the check. She rummaged through her bag for her wallet and got out her credit card. "It's been great seeing you again, Teresa. I'm sorry to have had an ulterior motive."

"Hey, forget about it. Thanks for lunch. It was great to get out of that office."

After Holly paid the check, they got up and walked out to the parking lot. As Teresa hit the remote door opener, she turned to Holly and said, "Listen. I'm gonna check on a few things and if I find out anything, I'll let you know."

"I don't want you to do anything that might get you into trouble."

"Puh-leez! I know how to take care of myself. Don't worry about me."

"Thanks, Teresa." Holly gave her a hug. "It really was great to see you and remember the good old days."

"Yep," Teresa replied, getting into her white Lincoln Continental that had "Wash me" printed in grime on the back bumper. "We'll always have the Sheraton Sports Bar," she said, clicking her tongue, waving as she drove away.

20 THE BOATHOUSE CAFE

Ivy screamed, dropping her trowel.

"I'm sorry," Holly said. "I didn't mean to scare you."

"You really did though," Ivy said sitting down on the grass in front of the flower bed she'd been weeding. "I didn't hear you come out the back door." She got up and grabbed her knee pad and tool bucket. "So what did you find out?"

Holly sighed. "Not much. Did you eat?"

"Yeah, I had a late lunch."

"What do you say we skip dinner and go down to the Boathouse Café for some ice cream? I'll tell you all about my conversation with Teresa."

"Sounds good to me. Let me wash my hands."

Holly looked Ivy up and down. "I don't know how you do it."

"Do what?" Ivy's eyes widened. "I didn't do anything."

"What I meant was I don't know how you manage to work in the garden and not get a speck of dirt on you."

"Oh, that. I dunno," Ivy said, not making eye contact, as she headed inside.

****

At the Boathouse Café, Holly ordered vanilla ice cream with caramel sauce. Ivy selected a hot fudge sundae. They went out the back door and selected a spot on the patio deck facing the duck pond. From where they sat they could see Mrs. Hagel's house.

"It was great to see Teresa," Holly began. "But she said she doesn't believe the guys she works for would commit murder, and I trust Teresa's judgment. Looks like we're back to square one. I think it's time to pull the plug and tell Elena there's nothing more we can do."

"Probably," Ivy remarked, digging into her sundae.

"But, you know, there is one thing I wondered about. On the drive home I remembered the police report and the fact that the neighbors to the west of Mrs. Hagel left town the morning the body was discovered. It may be nothing, but doesn't that strike you as a little odd?"

"I don't know. Maybe we just want it to mean something."

"Look," Holly nodded her head in the direction of the Hagel house. "See how close that house is to Mrs. Hagel's. I bet they did see or hear something and just didn't want to get involved."

"Maybe the police will find out when they question them. They have to come home sooner or later."

"I wonder..." Holly ignored her sundae, and continued staring across the pond.

"Your ice cream is melting."

"You're right." Holly took a big spoonful, closing her eyes and savoring the taste. "This is really delicious. How's yours?"

"Yummy," Ivy replied, grinning the same way she did when they were little girls.

"Hey, when we were in Mrs. Hagel's backyard, did you notice what the side of the house facing Mrs. Hagel's was like?" Holly asked.

Ivy furrowed her brow, hesitated, then answered. "There was a bay window on the ground floor and two casement windows on the second floor."

"How do you remember that?"

"Because I was thinking I would have planted a privacy hedge to block the view from the downstairs window onto Mrs. Hagel's patio. I also thought a nice pergola would block the view from the second floor windows."

"I'm beginning to think my lawyer friend is right. With your powers of observation, you'd make a great hire for a law firm."

"Not me. You," Ivy laughed. "I may notice things, but you put two and two together."

"That's just great. How many old ladies does it take to make one good investigator?"

They laughed and then got quiet as they finished their sundaes, watching the Canadian geese glide by overhead.

"Uh-oh," Holly said as she put her plastic spoon inside the empty ice cream cup.

"What?"

"Don't look now, but Denise Archer is coming this way."

"Who's she?" Ivy asked.

"Remember Debby Downer from *Saturday Night Live*? That's her exactly. She's coming right over to us."

"Hi, Holly. Don't tell me. This is your sister. Holy cow! You look alike."

"This is my sister, Ivy. Ivy this is Denise Archer."

"Nice to meet you," Ivy said.

Denise eyed Ivy without smiling. Her A&R Auto Body t-shirt reached nearly to her knees and her faded denim cutoffs looked as if they might actually date back to the '60s.

"Hey, did you hear about my sister? She got in a car accident. Totaled her car."

"Sorry to hear that, Denise. Was she hurt?" Holly asked.

"She got whiplash. She's lucky though. She coulda been killed."

"How awful."

"What do you think about Mrs. Hagel?" Denise nodded twisting her mouth to the side. "I dunno. This neighborhood is really goin' to the dogs, isn't it?"

"It is a shame. She was a lovely person."

"Oh, yeah. They thought it was the gardener killed her. Now they say it's the nurse. If you ask me, I think they oughta check out that crazy neighbor of hers." Denise pointed in the direction of the Hagel house.

Holly exchanged a quick glance with Ivy. "Really?"

"Oh, yeah. He's as crazy as a jaybird. I been sayin' that for years. But ya know, he's got friends in high places."

"Who are you talking about?" Holly asked in as casual a tone as she could muster.

"Louie Brunetti. Ya know the councilman? That's his cousin. He lives on Ridge Road directly behind the Hagel House."

"You want to sit down, Denise?"

"No, no, I can't sit. My back is botherin' me. I went to the doctor's, but he couldn't find nothin'. They only want your insurance money, ya know what I mean?"

"It seems that way sometimes. So you really think Louie Brunetti killed Mrs. Hagel?"

"Oh, yeah. I bet you dollars to donuts before the summer's over he'll put a swimming pool in his backyard. Nothin' stopping him now. He hated Mrs. Hagel because she wouldn't sign off on the variance he needed to put a pool in. I seen him throw garbage over his fence into her garden. But you know me. I mind my own business. I dunno what this world is comin' to."

"You really don't want to get in the middle of someone else's fight," Holly said.

"No, no. Not me. Look. It was good seein' ya. I gotta go get my ice cream and get home in time to watch *The Bachelorette*. You watch it?"

"No, I don't."

"Oh, you should. It's so good." Denise looked at her watch. "Okay. See yas."

Denise turned abruptly and entered the boathouse.

"Waddaya think?" Ivy asked, her imitation of Denise spot-on.

"I dunno," Holly replied.

Both started laughing, covering their mouths, not wanting their laughter to be heard inside the café.

"C'mon," Holly said, grabbing both empty sundae containers and dropping them in a trash barrel. "Let's go before we really embarrass ourselves."

When they reached the front of Holly's house, Ivy stopped along the fence at the Gertrude Jekyll rose which was now in full bloom. She pulled a blossom towards her. "Ouch!" she exclaimed, looking at her finger, which started to bleed.

"These thorns can really tear your skin," Holly said.

"No kidding!"

"Here," Holly carefully pulled a branch close for Ivy to sniff a bloom.

"Now this is what roses are supposed to smell like. Hmm! What a heavenly scent!" Ivy gushed. Reprising her Denise Archer imitation, she said, "But they can kill you, ya know."

Both Holly and Ivy laughed, quite loudly this time. "C'mon." Holly grabbed Ivy's arm and pulled her to the front gate. "The neighbors will think we're crazy."

Holly opened the front door and Lucky barely greeted them as she headed directly outside.

"I'm going to just walk around the back with her and close up the shed," Holly said. "You better go put some alcohol on that scratch."

Ivy was waiting in the kitchen when Holly and Lucky returned. "You want to watch TV?" Holly asked.

"No, I'm going to bed. But I just wanted to say one thing. I really do think tomorrow we should tell Elena that we can't do anything more for her."

"You're sure? You don't think we should try to learn something about Louie Brunetti? Denise is a little flaky, but she could be on to something." Holly asked.

"No. Let the police do it."

"Okay then. Tomorrow we tell Elena we've done all we can and we re-start our vacation."

That night Holly dreamt she was weeding around her rose bushes. As she worked, the rose bushes started to send out giant branches that surrounded her. The thorns were huge and she got stuck no matter which way she turned. She awoke the next morning feeling quite unrested.

21 THE LOUIE BRUNETTI HOUSE

In spite of a restless sleep, Holly was up at 5:30. Lucky jumped up on the bed when she heard her stir. The dog lay down next to Holly and rolled on her back. "You do love your belly rubs, don't you?" Holly said, stroking the dog's furry underside. After a few minutes, Holly got up, pulled on a pair of jeans and a t-shirt and quietly opened her bedroom door. Sneakers and sox in hand, she tip-toed downstairs, not wanting to wake Ivy. In the kitchen she sat on a chair to put on her sox and Reeboks. Before she finished, she heard Ivy descending the stairs.

"Good morning," Ivy said. "Trying to sneak out without me?"

"No, but if you were asleep, I didn't want to wake you. It's so early."

"Couldn't sleep?"

"Off and on."

"I guess we'll sleep better after we tell Elena we're done with this whole affair once and for all."

Holly just nodded. She grabbed Lucky's leash and she, Ivy, and Lucky headed out the front door. At this hour, the neighborhood was quiet and peaceful, an unlikely setting for a murder. At the bottom of the street, Lucky turned left and the sisters followed. The Boathouse Café was closed. Only the lights of the reach-in refrigerator that held the sodas glowed from within the glass doors. Two women in spandex and neon sneakers jogged by.

When they rounded the duck pond, Holly headed up Ridge Road instead of continuing around the duck pond on Crescent Drive.

"Why are we going this way?" Ivy asked.

"I thought you liked to look at the houses and gardens on this street."

"I came this way with Lucky yesterday when you went to lunch."

"Lucky likes to go this way."

"You want to pass Louie Brunetti's house, don't you?"

"What if I do?"

"We agreed to get un-involved."

Holly stopped and faced Ivy.

"I don't get you. You were the one who insisted we help Elena Gomez. Now, suddenly, you want to stop. Why?"

"I don't get *you.* That's what we agreed to do if we felt we reached a dead end."

"But now we have another lead."

"A lead? Listen to yourself. You're talking like you're a detective. You're not. Face it. Besides, the ramblings of a neighborhood busybody don't exactly constitute a lead."

They continued walking.

"Shh. I think this next house is Louie Brunetti's," Holly said. As if she knew Holly wanted to linger, Lucky stopped to sniff the grass directly in front of the house in question. Holly peered into the backyard, but tall trees blocked any view of the neighboring yard beyond.

"If this is the house, you really can't even see Mrs. Hagel's," Ivy whispered.

Holly smiled. Ivy was in observation mode. "C'mon. Let's see if we can see through the backyard of the next house."

Stopping in front of the next driveway, Ivy confirmed, "This neighbor's house has a clear view through to Mrs. Hagel's."

The sisters continued walking in silence. Finally, Ivy asked, "We're going to tell Elena we're finished, right?"

"Yeah, yeah. Right after I make one phone call." Holly picked up her pace and Lucky got in step as she started running, leaving Ivy behind.

****

"One egg or two," Holly asked as Ivy entered the kitchen. Bacon was already frying in the pan. "With only ice cream sundaes for dinner, I figured we deserved a big breakfast."

"One," Ivy answered sinking into a kitchen chair. "Are you going to tell me who you're going to call or is it a secret?"

"No secret. I'm going to call my friend on the Zoning Commission for the past eight years. He'll know all about Louie Brunetti's request for a variance. He might even be able to provide me with an audio tape of the hearing. They tape everything, so absentee commissioners can review the hearing and not have to miss a vote."

"And what do you think you're going to get out of that?"

"Maybe Louie Brunetti made threatening remarks. Wouldn't that be great?" Holly asked as she sliced two bagels.

"And exactly what are you going to do if you find out he did? Denise Archer said Brunetti had friends in high places."

"I don't know," Holly replied, placing an egg and some bacon on a plate, handing it to Ivy. "Maybe I'll call Grabnick and push him to call the police. Or maybe I'll just call Manelli myself."

Ivy dropped the glass she'd just lifted to her mouth, spilling orange juice all over herself.

Holly grabbed a wad of paper towel and handed it to Ivy.

"Are you okay?" she asked. "Are you crying?"

"No--yes," Ivy sobbed.

"It's just juice, Ivy. Don't cry. I'll pour you another glass," Holly said, going to the refrigerator.

"It's not the juice," Ivy bawled.

"What is it then? Look, if it's going to upset you this much, I'll just drop the whole thing. I won't call anyone. Honest."

"It's not that either," Ivy sniffed. "Not exactly. I have a confession to make. You're going to be so mad at me."

"What could you possibly have done to make me mad at you?"

"I called Detective Manelli," Ivy blurted out.

"Oh?" Holly said dropping into her chair. "And?"

"When you left yesterday, I started to worry about you. I thought that if the developers did kill Mrs. Hagel, you could be in danger just asking questions. You know I wanted to call him with the information from the start."

"I know," Holly sighed. "What did Manelli say?"

"He said he appreciated the information, but that we needed to step back from the investigation, and I said we would."

"Okay, so what's the problem? As far as he's concerned, we have stepped away. Can I help it if people keep telling me things?"

"But there's more."

"More?"

"He asked to talk to you. I said you were shopping for groceries. I don't think he believed me."

"I still don't see the problem."

"He told me to have you call him."

"I'm not calling him. You could have forgotten to give me the message."

"There's more."

"Out with it already!"

"Last night when you went to close the shed and I came in there was a message from Manelli, asking you to call. I erased it."

"Great. Just great."

22 LYING TO THE POLICE

It took a while, but Holly managed to calm Ivy down and reassure her that she was not angry about her call to Detective Manelli. They finished breakfast and went out to sit on the patio, Holly with a mug of coffee and the crossword puzzle, Ivy with an orange cut in quarters and the latest issues of *Instyle* and *Martha Stewart Living.*

As she filled in the last word of the puzzle, Holly looked over at Ivy, who had fallen fast asleep on the chaise. She felt that guilty, remorseful ache she got whenever she was the cause of Ivy's distress. Maybe she shouldn't call Ira. Maybe she should just phone Elena and tell her there wasn't any more they could do.

Immediately, she remembered Jonathan Grabnick's swollen, self-righteous face. How could she abandon Leonelle Gomez to his incompetence? Why did Juan have to bring Elena to her for help? If she and Ivy and had never met Elena, they'd right now be getting ready for a day trip to some historic home on the Hudson River, instead of recovering from a sleepless night, worried about having to call the police. She couldn't just sit around. She had to do something.

Holly got up from her chair as quietly as she could and went inside. Upstairs she closed the door to her room, sat on the bed, reached for the phone and punched in Ira's number.

"Hi, Ira. It's Holly."

"Hi, Holly. Calling to apply for that job I told you about?"

"Not funny. But I am calling to ask you about a zoning variance case you probably heard about a year ago."

"Really? Which one?"

"Louie Brunetti's."

"Wow. I remember that one."

"Why is that?"

"Mr. Brunetti's brother-in-law is a city councilman. He sort of expected us to just rubber-stamp his application, but you know that's not how it works. Of course, one of the neighbors objected to the variance. Hey, wait a minute. I forgot that it was Mrs. Hagel. She was the lone neighbor who objected to the variance. Are you suggesting Brunetti killed her?"

"I didn't say that."

"You're playing with fire here, Holly. Brunetti and his brother-in-law, they're nasty characters. If they learn that you even hinted that Brunetti might have killed Mrs. Hagel, they will have building inspectors descend on your house and find code violations, whether or not they exist. They'll have police ticket you if you go a half-mile over the speed limit. I've heard horror stories from people who were harassed because they had the temerity to cross them."

"I'm not planning to cross them. I just want to suggest to Leonelle Gomez's lawyer, that there are other people who had motives to murder Mrs. Hagel, to introduce an element of doubt. After all, you jumped to the conclusion that Brunetti had a reason to kill Mrs. Hagel without my saying a word. Wouldn't a juror?"

"I hate to discourage you, but if Mrs. Gomez's lawyer is from Pineland Park, it is very unlikely that he'll point a finger at Brunetti without proof just to introduce an element of doubt. Everyone knows what Brunetti is capable of and no one wants to go up against him."

"I understand, but I need to know something. Did Brunetti actually threaten Mrs. Hagel at a hearing?"

Ira paused. "I, uh, I don't remember."

Holly recognized an evasive answer when she heard one. "Okay. Thanks anyway."

"Holly, as a lawyer and as a friend, I'm advising you to let this go. Whether Brunetti was or was not involved, you could end up entangled in a mess. Please, let the police investigate this murder."

"Oh, Ira," she sighed. "If only you knew how hard I have been trying to do exactly that. But last night someone from the neighborhood just happened to tell me about Brunetti's application for the variance. I just can't seem to shake loose from this thing."

"Is your sister still in town?"

Holly heard Lucky barking and looked out the front window. "Damn!" she said. Detective Manelli was getting out of his car parked in front of the house."

"Excuse me?"

"Sorry, Ira. That wasn't meant for you. Yes, my sister is still here with me."

"Why don't you two go away for a few days? Distance yourself from neighborhood gossip."

"That's not a bad idea. Listen, I have to go. Someone's at the door. Thanks for the advice. I really appreciate it."

"No problem. Send me a postcard from wherever you go."

"I'll do that," Holly laughed. "So long."

She replaced the phone in the charger and took a deep breath. What was she going to tell this detective? She took a look at herself in the mirror. *Ugh! No time for make-up now. Maybe just lipstick. Oh, forget it.*

She descended the steps quickly, going to the front door. But Manelli wasn't there. *Odd. Why isn't Lucky barking?* Holly went to the kitchen and through the window she could see Manelli seated on one of the patio table chairs, petting Lucky, talking to Ivy. *God help me! Here goes.*

Holly went out the back door onto the patio and with all the grace she could muster, smiled, and said, "Detective Manelli. Good morning. What a surprise! How nice of you to drop by. Can I offer you some coffee?"

A little out of breath, Holly realized she was gushing. Manelli stared at her, squinting, his mouth showing just the trace of a bemused smile.

"Holly," Ivy jumped in. "I was just telling the Detective that I forgot to tell you he wanted you to call him. He said he left a message on the machine, but remember? I hit the wrong button on the machine when we came in last night. I must have erased it." Ivy looked to Manelli. "I'm so bad with machines."

Holly knew that if she had sounded like Ivy just did, Manelli had to know they were lying. She just smiled and looked directly at him. He didn't say a word, and simply returned her gaze. She knew he was waiting for them to continue babbling.

Ivy looked from Holly to Manelli and started to fill the uncomfortable silence, "Holly, I explained ..."

"Why don't you go get the detective a cup of coffee?" Holly said.

"Sure," Ivy replied, jumping up. "Where are my manners?"

When Ivy went inside, Holly tilted her head to the side, grinned and asked, "So I don't suppose you're here to update us on the Hagel case, are you?"

"No, Ms. Donnelly, I'm not." Manelli leaned back in his chair, tilted *his* head to the side and asked, "Do you recall my cautioning you about letting the police do their jobs?"

"Yes, I do. And that's exactly what my sister and I want to do. Really."

"But?"

"No buts. In fact, I haven't told my sister yet. I was just on the phone making plans to go up to my friend's place in the Catskills for a few days."

Manelli just looked at her, as if waiting for the punchline.

"What, Detective? Don't you believe me?"

"What made you decide that? Yesterday you were investigating Novardo Development."

Now it was Holly's turn to stare. After a moment she said, "I don't know what you mean. I wasn't investigating. I just happened to hear about Novardo's desire to buy the Hagel property and Mrs. Hagel's refusal to sell. Ivy told you that."

"Who told you about the Novardo deal?"

"Um, I don't really remember," Holly dodged. Under no circumstances could she give Manelli Ira's name.

The kitchen door opened and Ivy came out with a small tray holding a mug of coffee, a sugar bowl and creamer, and a slice of bread covered with Nutella.

"Here, Detective. I don't know if you had breakfast, but this is a slice of Holly's home-made honey oat bread. It's just delicious with Nutella."

"Thank you," he said. To Holly's surprise he picked up the bread and took a bite. "Delicious," he nodded, unsmiling.

After a swallow of coffee, he looked back at Holly. "The Hagels' refusal to sell their property wasn't public knowledge. Who gave you that information?"

Holly squinched her nose, as if struggling to think. She remembered Ira's evasion technique. "Gee, I can't remember who told me. Ivy, I just assured Detective Manelli that we have no desire to interfere with police business, and while you were dozing, I was upstairs calling Kate. She said we should come up and stay with her for a few days. This is the weekend of the Trout Parade up there."

"Really? That's great."

Both Holly and Ivy looked over at Manelli, who was finishing the slice of bread.

"Would you like another slice, Detective?" Ivy asked.

"Yes, please."

Ivy took the plate. "Doesn't your wife make you breakfast, Detective?"

Manelli grinned. "I'm not married," he replied.

"Really? A handsome man like you must have lots of girlfriends to cook for you." When Manelli didn't take the additional bait, Ivy picked up the bread plate and as she turned to go inside said, "Holly makes great bread, don't you think?"

Manelli simply nodded, taking another gulp of coffee. As Ivy disappeared into the kitchen, he turned his full gaze on Holly.

"So you can't remember who gave you confidential information related to a murder case you've got an interest in?" he asked.

Holly, who had watched the exchange between Ivy and Manelli in total disbelief, sat frowning. She just wanted this visit to end, and he wasn't budging. She needed to get this over with before Ivy started taking lunch orders.

"Look. I've lived in the neighborhood for over twenty years. I know a lot of people. People gossip. I just heard it somewhere. I'll tell you something else I heard yesterday at the Boathouse Café and I'll tell you who told me. Denise Archer, whom I know through the Park Association, said she thinks Louie Brunetti killed Mrs. Hagel."

Manelli said nothing, so she continued.

"She said Mrs. Hagel was the only person who objected to his request for a variance to put in a swimming pool and that he made threats against her."

Holly felt as if Manelli's eyes were boring a hole through her.

"I wasn't investigating. Honest. Ivy and I went to the Boathouse Café for ice cream and Denise Archer came over and just started talking. That's why I want to get out of town, so nobody can tell me something else I don't want to know."

Ivy came back out and handed the replenished bread plate to Manelli, who immediately lifted the slice of bread and bit into it. "You finished your coffee. Would you like more?"

"Yes, please," he said, handing her the mug. She smiled, and turned once again to the kitchen door.

Holly glared, now beyond annoyed--with Manelli for not leaving and with her sister for happily waiting on him. She was determined to say nothing more, no matter how uncomfortable he made her feel.

"Really good bread," he said after what seemed like an eternity.

This time Holly just stared at him, arms crossed, saying nothing. Manelli didn't seem at all uncomfortable.

Finally, Ivy returned with the coffee.

"Thanks," Manelli said as he took it from her, smiling broadly, revealing beautiful white even teeth, perfect for a toothpaste commercial.

"You should smile more often, Detective," Ivy flirted. "Don't you think he's even more handsome when he smiles, Holly?"

Both Manelli and Ivy turned to Holly, the only one not smiling. Manelli's phone rang, and he got up abruptly as he viewed the Caller ID. "I have to leave now," he said, gulping down the coffee. " I'm glad you've decided to let the police do the investigation work and hope you have a good stay up in the Catskills."

He flashed his hundred-watt smile again at Ivy, saying, "Thanks for breakfast." Turning to Holly he said, "Could you walk me to the gate?"

Holly got up and followed Manelli. Lucky who was sitting in the shade in the front yard, got up, tail wagging. As Manelli bent to pet her, he said, "Do you understand that if Novardo Development or Louis Brunetti are involved in Mrs. Hagel's murder--and that's a big 'if'--you've put yourself and your sister in danger just talking about it?" He turned and looked directly at her, not a trace of a smile on his face.

"Yes," she answered after a moment, scratching the back of her head.

"You also understand that lying to the police is a crime?"

Again, the discomfiting silence, as his eyes burned her.

"Don't lie to me again, Ms. Donnelly." He turned, letting himself out the gate. Over his shoulder, he said, "Enjoy the Trout Parade."

Holly latched the gate behind him and walked to the back patio feeling unnerved. She couldn't remember the last time she'd been reprimanded by anyone. The fact that he was right made it worse. But she had to lie because she'd promised Ira she wouldn't reveal where she learned about the Novardo deal.

Had she endangered Ivy and herself? Ira was right. Getting out of town is exactly what they needed to do.

****

"What did he say?" Ivy asked, smiling as Holly reached the patio.

"Listen, Scarlet. I do believe you've lived in the South way too long. What was all that crap about his wife and his smile?"

"Hmm. What a smile! He's really gorgeous, don't you think?"

"What is wrong with you? For heaven's sake, he's a cop, not a gentleman caller."

"Cop or not, he's not married. Can't you flirt just a little?"

"You did enough of that for the two of us."

"I don't know. I think he's really into you."

"Stop! If he's into anyone, it's you, not me."

"So why did he ask you to walk him to the gate?"

"He wanted to make sure that I knew lying to the police is a crime."

"Did you ask him what the punishment for lying to him was?" Ivy giggled.

"Oh, shut up," Holly said, going into the house, slamming the door behind her.

23 THE WAKE

Holly went straight to the phone in the living room and called Kate.

"Kate. Holly. I have a favor to ask."

"Name it."

"Can Ivy and I come up to your place for a couple of days?"

"Of course. I was just thinking that I needed to find more excuses to walk downtown, because talking to the dog just isn't cutting it anymore. Speaking of dogs, you're bringing Lucky, right?"

"Yes."

"So when can I expect you?

"We'll pack today, take care of some odds and ends, and I thought we'd leave first thing tomorrow. We should arrive around noon. We can take you out to lunch."

"No, no. I'll make us lunch."

"Okay. We'll see you tomorrow around noon."

"Fabulous. Drive safe."

Holly hung up, turned and saw Ivy standing in the doorway.

"So you did lie to Manelli," Ivy chided. "Maybe I need to call him."

"Don't even joke about it," Holly cut her short. "Under no circumstances are you to call him ever again. I mean it."

Ivy laughed and turned around, heading back to the kitchen. Holly followed, shaking her head. As Ivy loaded the dishwasher and cleaned out the coffee pot, Holly tore a page off of the shopping list notepad that hung by a magnet on the refrigerator.

"Okay. I'll make a list of what we need to do before we leave," Holly said, sitting down at the table. "First, I have to call next door and ask them to pick up the paper. No point stopping it for just a day or two."

"Hey, speaking of the newspaper, could you check the lottery numbers? I bought a ticket the other day when you went to lunch with Teresa," Ivy said. "Let me just run upstairs and get it. It's in my purse."

Holly reached for the paper and started flipping through the pages. She realized she hadn't looked at anything but the "Better Living" section for the crossword puzzle.

"Wow," she said when she reached the obituary page and saw Mrs. Hagel's picture.

"What's up?" Ivy asked, as she came back into the kitchen, lottery ticket in hand.

"Mrs. Hagel's obituary is here. They're having the wake tonight at Maher's Funeral Home from 6:00 to 8:00. I've got to go."

"I'll go with you."

"You're sure? You don't have to."

"No, no. I don't want you to go alone."

"Okay."

Ivy took the paper and rifled through for the page with the lottery results. "Darn! Not even one number," she complained.

"What would you do if you won? Really?"

"Really?" Ivy hesitated, furrowing her brow in deep thought. "I know! I'd hire Leonelle Gomez a real lawyer and the best private investigator in New Jersey."

Holly grinned. "You always have your priorities straight, don't you?"

****

The parking lot of Maher Funeral Home was crowded. Holly managed to find one of the last spaces in the back corner. The sisters got out and walked around to the front of the building. A line of people trailed down the steps in front of the entrance.

"A lot of people," Ivy observed.

"Mrs. Hagel was in business in this town for I don't know how many years. She and her husband started their printing and stationary company in the 50s I think."

"Holly?" a voice queried from behind them.

Holly turned. "Hello, Doris. I'm so sorry about Mrs. Hagel." The woman's eyes filled with tears as she accepted Holly's embrace. "This is my sister, Ivy. Ivy, this is Doris Franklin. She's a member of the garden club and was a friend of Edna's, too."

Doris fumbled with the snap on her black patent leather handbag, searching inside. She pulled out a crisp linen handkerchief with crocheted edging, and dried her eyes before she extended her trembling hand to Ivy. "I just can't believe it. I can't believe she's gone."

"I know," Holly agreed, putting a supporting arm around Doris. "Had you seen her recently?"

"Just last week, I asked my son to drive me over. He dropped me off and we had a lovely visit. Who knew it would be our last?" She dabbed at her eyes and blew her nose.

Holly nodded, frowning. "It's good that you have that last memory."

"Yes. You know, they arrested Edna's nurse."

"I know."

Doris shook her head. She looked as if she were about to say something, but stopped.

Holly and Ivy exchanged glances. The line started to move. "Here, why don't you move up in front of us, Doris? Are you okay standing? Do you want me to ask if you could move to the front of the line? I'm sure no one will mind."

"Standing too long is a little hard on me."

"I'll go find the funeral director and he can escort you in," Ivy volunteered, excusing herself as she cut through the group of people and disappeared inside the building.

"I have to tell you something." Doris squeezed Holly's arm. "I don't think the nurse murdered Edna."

Holly's eyes widened. "Oh?"

"I've been to visit Edna many times. That woman was devoted to her. Edna herself told me she didn't know what she'd do without her."

"That's saying a lot."

"I'd believe that worthless grandson of hers killed her before I'd believe Leonelle did. God forgive me for saying that."

Ivy returned with the funeral director.

"Thank you girls so much." Doris smiled as the director took her by the arm.

"We'll see you inside," Holly said.

Ivy glanced at Holly and asked, "What's wrong?"

"Nothing. Why?"

"I don't know. Maybe because of that drained look on your face. Did that woman tell you something while I was gone? I know she looked as if she was about to say something, but then stopped herself."

"She said she didn't think Leonelle killed Mrs. Hagel."

"No way."

"And she said she'd suspect 'that worthless grandson of hers'--her exact words--before she'd suspect Leonelle Gomez."

"Unbelievable."

They stood silently as the line inched forward through the entrance hall, into the room where Mrs. Hagel's closed coffin lie in state. A picture of Mrs. Hagel, the one that had appeared in the paper, was displayed on a stand in front of a beautiful display of red roses with a white ribbon reading, "Dearest Mother" in gold lettering. Holly and Ivy filed past the coffin.

A couple in front of them was offering their sympathy to a middle-aged woman seated in a cushioned wing chair near the coffin. Her blonde hair coiffed in an elegant chignon, she wore a black suit accented by a strand of classic white pearls and matching earrings. She smiled graciously, accepting the condolences being offered. Standing beside her was a heavy-set young man, probably in his twenties. He, too, shook hands with the guests, but fidgeted impatiently, not making eye contact with anyone.

As the couple moved on, Holly approached the woman, extending her hand. "Hello. We've never met. I'm Holly Donnelly and this is my sister, Ivy. I've lived in the neighborhood for years and Mrs. Hagel and I shared an interest in gardening."

"Ah, yes, Edna, my mother-in-law, loved her garden. So very kind of you to come. I know she'd be happy you were here. This is my son, Phillip."

"So sorry about your grandmother, Phillip."

Phillip's hand was clammy and Holly detected a faint smell of alcohol. He said nothing, looking past Holly at the back of the room.

Holly turned and headed toward the rows of seats. She scanned the crowd and noted a few familiar faces from the neighborhood. On the far side of the room Doris Franklin sat alone. She waved Holly over. Ivy came up behind her and said she needed to use the ladies room, so Holly walked over to sit with Doris.

"The photo they selected is beautiful, isn't it?" Holly said.

"Yes, Edna was a real beauty," Doris replied

"How are you doing these days, Doris? I haven't seen you at the Garden Club meetings lately."

"Getting out at night is hard for me, you know. I can't drive anymore. Still, I really can't complain. My son is good about taking me places. He dropped me here and will pick me up later."

"That's nice," said Holly, glad the conversation had taken a personal turn.

Suddenly a loud noise startled them. They looked to the front of the room and saw that a flower arrangement had fallen to the floor. Phillip Hagel's face was flushed as he backed away from the display. He put his head down and quickly left the room, as the funeral director appeared and righted the display, rearranging some of the flowers that had been jostled by the fall.

"There. You see. He can't even conduct himself properly at a wake," Doris said with disgust. "I'm telling you, I'm just sick about Leonelle. Do you know her?"

"We met," Holly said, not volunteering any additional information.

"She didn't do it. I know she didn't do it. I read in the paper there were no signs of a break-in, so that's why they believe it was Leonelle, but I'm telling you, they should investigate that grandson. He had keys to the house. I know he did. The whole family did. Whenever I was there, they let themselves in. They never rang the bell. I hope the police talked to them."

Holly was relieved to see Ivy approaching. "Doris, my sister and I are leaving early tomorrow for a few days in the Catskills. We need to go home and finish packing, so we have to leave you. Listen, if you need a ride to the club meetings, call me. I'd be happy to pick you up and take you home."

"That's so kind of you, dear. If I'm up to it, I will call you. You have a safe drive tomorrow."

"Thanks, Doris." Holly stood up and turned to Ivy. "Let's go." As she took Ivy by the arm, she noticed a strained expression on her face. "Are you all right?" Holly whispered as they made their way to the door.

"I'll tell you outside," Ivy whispered.

In the hallway, Holly stopped. "Hold on. That's Mrs. Hagel's son. I've met him and I want to offer my condolences."

Steven Hagel stood conversing quietly with two men in the hall. His hand trembled slightly as he adjusted his horn-rimmed glasses. His baggy and wrinkled suit contrasted sharply with the chic and elegant attire of his wife. Holly waited a moment until one of the men made eye-contact with her, causing Steven to look over at her as well.

"Mr. Hagel, sorry to interrupt. I'm Holly Donnelly. I'm sure you don't remember me, but we met a few years ago when I was visiting your mother. I just wanted to tell you how sorry I am for your loss."

"Thank you. Donnelly, you say. That name sounds familiar. How did you know my mother?"

"Through the garden club. I bought the Jorgenson's house."

"Yes. My mother used to talk about you. Wait a minute. Aren't you the one who introduced her to that gardener?" he asked irately.

"Yes, but the gardener had nothing to do with …"

"But I heard from my lawyer that you're trying to help this Gomez woman now, too. You have a lot of nerve coming here," he said, his voice rising.

"I'm sorry, Mr. Hagel. I was just leaving."

"You should," he said coldly. "And please don't come to the funeral. If I find you trying to talk to my family, I'll call the police."

Holly turned, grabbing Ivy's arm, and headed to the door walking as quickly as she could. They stepped outside and closed the door. "That was humiliating."

Before they could descend the stairs, the door opened behind them and Steven Hagel's wife appeared. They felt like the proverbial deer caught in the headlights.

"Ms. Donnelly, I couldn't help overhearing and I just want to apologize for how my husband spoke to you in there."

"Please don't apologize."

"No, no. Steven is distraught. He loved his mother very much, but still it was rude of him to address you that way. No one is more shocked than I that the evidence pointed to Leonelle. If you are trying to help her, I'm sure you have your reasons."

"Thank you for understanding, Mrs. Hagel. I'm really sorry for your loss. We'd better go. Good-night."

Holly and Ivy turned and went down the steps, practically running to the car. Inside Holly immediately locked the doors.

"Ugh! I just can't believe that happened," Holly said. "While you were in the ladies' room, the grandson knocked over a flower display, and Doris started in again about how badly she felt about Leonelle. She read in the paper that there was no break-in, but she said she knew the grandson had keys to the house. The whole family did. Why do people keep telling me these things?"

"And the bad news is they're now telling me things because they think I'm you."

"Oh, no! That's right. I forgot you had something to tell me."

"When I was in the stall, two women came in the ladies' room, talking about the grandson knocking over the flowers. When I came out, one of them turned out to be Denise Archer. She thought I was you and started telling me about *The Bachelorette*, asking if I'd watched the show like she told us to. When the other woman left, Denise looked over at me."

Doing a dead-on imitation of Denise, Ivy continued, "You know, Holly, I've been thinkin'. Maybe it wasn't Brunetti who killed her after all. Those grandkids stand to inherit a bundle now Edna's gone. You notice the granddaughter's not here? They say she's taking care of the business. If you ask me, she's just a, well, it rhymes with witch, you know what I mean? The grandson's a klutz, but she's the one with the brains. If the brother had anything to do with Edna's death, she's the one who would have to tell him what to do, because he's not the sharpest tool in the shed. Ya know what I mean?'"

Holly grunted. "We can't get out of town fast enough."

24 A PHONE MESSAGE

Entering the kitchen, Holly noticed the light blinking on the answering machine.

"Aren't you going to check the message?" Ivy asked.

"And listen to someone provide me with another murder suspect, like a disgruntled employee of Hagel Printing and Paper or a spurned former lover or maybe a lost love child returned to claim her inheritance?"

"Okay," Ivy held her hands up in surrender. "Calm down. You go upstairs and I'll check."

"Fine. And if it's Manelli, you can call and confess that you lied about erasing his last message," Holly said as she headed to the stairs.

Ivy hit the play button.

"Hello. It's me. Elena." She sounded as if she'd been crying. "I tried not to bother you for the last few days, but I was wondering if you found out anything that could help my mother. She's been transferred to the county jail." Here Elena broke down, crying. "I'm so scared and worried for my mother. Please call me."

When the message ended, Ivy turned around. Holly was standing in the doorway. They just looked at each other. Holly dropped her handbag on the kitchen table and sank down onto a chair.

"What are we going to do?" Holly asked. "With everything that's been going on today, I actually forgot about her."

"Me, too." Ivy lowered her head. "I'm so sorry I convinced you to try to help this girl. We gave her hope, and now what do we tell her?"

Holly hesitated for just a moment, got up, reached for the phone, and said, "The truth."

"Hello, Elena? It's Holly Donnelly. I'm here with Ivy. I'm going to put you on speakerphone. Can you hear us?"

"Yes, yes. Thank you so much for calling me back."

"Elena, I'm sorry, but we don't have a lot to tell you. This morning Detective Manelli came here and told us we were interfering with a police investigation and that we had to stop. We told him everything we had learned, and now we have to just let the police do their jobs."

Elena started crying.

"Elena," Ivy cut in. "I think Detective Manelli will get to the truth. He listened to what we told him and I think he is going to keep investigating until they find the real murderer."

"You really think so?" Elena asked.

"Yes, I do," Ivy reassured her. "Holly and I are going to go away for a few days, but we'll call you when we get back, all right?

"All right."

"Try not to worry," Ivy said.

"I'll--I'll try," Elena sniffled.

"Good-night, Elena," Holly said.

"Good night."

Holly returned the handset to its cradle. "This is not any kind of a good night," she said, leaning back in her chair. "Do you really think Manelli will investigate what we told him, or did you just say that?"

"I don't know. Why did he come here today? Did he really need to do that?"

"Maybe he just wants to wrap this case up without any complications. Maybe he's worried that the police will look bad if we find out something they didn't."

"He doesn't impress me that way. He seems like a decent guy, not somebody who couldn't care less if an innocent woman goes to jail. Think about it. Maybe he came here because he was already investigating Novardo and he figured we could mess things up. Or maybe he thought we could get hurt and he needed to stop us."

"I don't know. I think you're just sweet on him because he's good-looking."

"So you admit he's good-looking?"

Holly stood up and said, "I'm going to bed."

"Yes, I guess we better try to get some sleep."

"'*Try* is the optimum word. I don't know what's worse, not being able to sleep, or the nightmares I'll have if I do fall asleep."

"Put the television on. Watch a sitcom. That might help take your mind off things."

"Okay. I'll give it a try."

In her room Holly turned on the television and searched the channel guide. She smiled when she saw *Bewitched* was playing. Thirty minutes with Samantha, the witch turned housewife, was exactly what she needed to clear her mind. She set the timer for thirty minutes. Before the first set of commercials finished, she was asleep. She dreamt that Gladys Kravitz, Samantha's nosy neighbor, came over and started telling her that she thought Abner, her husband, might have murdered Mrs. Hagel. When Samantha closed the door on Gladys, she turned to face Nick Manelli, dressed in a shirt and tie and a red cardigan sweater asking, "Who was at the door, Honey?"

25 REDDINGTON MANOR

At just about noon the next day, Holly drove up the steep, gravelly driveway to Kate Farmer's house at the top of Creamery Road in Reddington Manor, NY. As soon as they made the turn onto the property, Kate's dog, Amy, started barking. When Holly and Ivy got out of the car, Amy jumped up and down, her tail wagging like a metronome on steroids. Holly let Lucky out of the back seat and she joined in the excitement when Kate appeared on the front porch. After dog pats and hugs of welcome all around, the dogs' movements ratcheted down from fever pitch exhilaration to a lower grade of fidgety animation.

"Let's bring your stuff in right now, so we can really relax and have a leisurely lunch on the porch," Kate said.

Holly opened the trunk and they each grabbed whatever they could handle. Kate led them across the stepping stone path to the rambling white house. Forest green trim framed the windows and eaves, and a wide porch wrapped around three sides of the house. Wicker furniture lined the walls invitingly and a round table set for lunch nested in the corner with three chairs around it.

"Isn't this lovely!" Ivy exclaimed. "I've heard so much about this place that I feel as if I've been here before. I just adore this porch!"

"Yeah, the porch is what really sold me on the house," Kate said as she opened the door that entered into a huge country kitchen. A window opposite the door looked out onto the backyard and the farmland and mountain beyond.

"Wow! What a view. This is amazing."

Kate smiled and said, "Okay, let me show you to your rooms." She led them through the kitchen door that opened into the living room. The hardwood floors sparkled. Magazines and books were stacked in neat piles on the coffee table. They climbed the stairs and Kate took Holly's bag to the room straight ahead at the top of the stairs.

"Ivy, you're in there," she said pointing to the room directly to the right. "Why don't you settle in, use the bathroom if you need to and come back downstairs. I'll start plating up our lunch."

When they returned to the kitchen, Holly and Ivy found nicoise salad beautifully arranged on their plates. "Okay, what will you have to drink, Ivy?" Kate asked. "Holly, I don't have to tell you beer is in the refrigerator."

"Iced tea or water is good for me," Ivy replied.

Kate got out a jug of tea from the refrigerator, poured two glasses, and said, "Okay. Grab a plate and your drink and let's go outside. I can't wait to hear what you've been up to."

"Don't ask," groaned Holly as she opened a Blue Moon, placing the bottle directly in the iced mug Kate had waiting for her. She grabbed the mug by the handle, got her plate and followed Kate and Ivy outside.

"This looks delicious. I didn't realize it, but I'm actually starved," Ivy said.

"*Quelle* surprise!" Holly mocked. "You're always starved. She's just like you, Kate. The metabolism of a hummingbird. I don't know where you two put it."

They made small talk while eating, savoring the meal, the view and the company. After a dessert of ice cream and chocolate chip cookies, they carried their dishes inside, replenished their drinks and returned to the porch.

"Oooh, this is great," Holly purred as she sank into the comfortable cushions, pouring herself another beer. "I don't think I've felt this relaxed since ..."

"Since I arrived and we discovered Mrs. Hagel was murdered and Juan was the prime suspect," finished Ivy.

"Okay," said Kate, tossing her napkin on the table. "I've waited long enough. Tell me what's been going on."

"Let's see. When did I last talk to you?" Holly asked.

"Juan had brought Elena Gomez to you to see if you could help her mother."

"That seems like a lifetime ago now. Here's what's happened since."

Holly started by explaining how they agreed to go with Elena to visit her mother and her mother's lawyer and how their involvement snowballed from there. She ended describing the wake and the call to Elena the night before.

"Yesterday was just the worst. Can we stay up here for the rest of the summer?" Holly asked.

"Hey, don't forget I have a flight back to South Carolina next week," Ivy chimed in.

Kate turned to Ivy. "So, I guess this isn't exactly the vacation you were expecting? You even had a starring role there, saving Juan."

"I have to say it hasn't been boring, that's for sure. I'm glad I was able to help, but I think the police would have figured out that the pills killed her eventually. I have to tell you, though, Holly has left out one important character in the story. She hasn't told you about Nick Manelli."

"Nick Manelli! Who's Nick Manelli?" Kate asked, her eyes widening as she turned to Holly.

"Ivy, really?" Holly burrowed her head deeper in the cushions and closed her eyes.

"What?" Ivy laughed. "How could you leave him out of this story?"

"Tell me who Manelli is," Kate demanded turning back to Ivy.

Without opening her eyes, Holly said, "I didn't leave him out of the story."

"You described everyone else by name and in detail. Why not him?"

"C'mon, already, who's Nick Manelli?" Kate asked, spilling some of her tea, now on the edge of her chair.

"I just didn't think he was important."

Ivy laughed loudly, "Wow, are you in denial."

Kate stood up and shouted, "For heaven's sake, will one of you tell me who Nick Manelli is."

Holly opened her eyes and both she and Ivy looked at Kate, as if just noticing she was there.

"He's the hunky detective that has a crush on Holly," Ivy finally replied.

"You are just so ridiculous, I can't even believe it," Holly said, shaking her head and looking out into the garden.

"The Knight of Wands! I knew you were keeping something from me," Kate crowed, dropping back into her chair.

"The Knight of Wands?" Ivy asked.

Kate realized she'd made a tarot reference and exchanged a glance with Holly. She quickly covered, saying, "That's something from a book we read in book club and it's kind of become a code word for Mr. Right."

"I think Manelli is Holly's Mr. Right," Ivy said leaning against the porch railing. "You should see how he looks at her, but she just refuses to admit it."

"Unbelievable," Kate said shaking her head at Holly. She patted the chair for Ivy to sit back down and said, "So tell me all about him."

"I have to pee," said Holly, getting up and going into the house.

Unwilling to face the teasing about Manelli, Holly went up to her bedroom, closed the door, flopped down on the bed, and promptly fell asleep. The restless night before, the drive on winding roads, and the two frosty beers combined to make for the most restful two hours of sleep she'd had in a week.

26 A GAME OF CLUE

Holly awoke to the sound of dogs barking. She sat up, put on her sneakers and ran down to the porch in time to see the pack of four coming up the street, Ivy carrying several shopping bags. Released from their leashes once in the yard, the dogs ran over to greet her.

"You finally got up. Didn't want to talk about Manelli, huh?" Ivy taunted.

"Don't start," Holly warned as she bent down to pet the dogs.

"Don't worry," said Kate. "Ivy filled me in on all the details. I told her it's just your usual pattern. A guy's attracted to you, you deny it, you're unreceptive to his signals, he persists, you run in the opposite direction."

"Could we talk about something else?" Holly said. "I see you've been shopping."

"Yes. Kate took me on a tour of downtown Reddington Manor."

"The tour took all of 10 minutes," Kate joked. "The rest of the time we've been window shopping, or taking turns holding the dogs while one of us went inside stores to actually buy something."

"One of you? I'm sure you were the one holding the dogs while Ivy shopped," Holly said to Kate as they mounted the porch steps."

"These shops had the nicest things." Ivy sat down to open the bags and show Holly her treasures. "Look at this hand-quilted handbag. Isn't it beautiful?"

"It's okay. Kate shows me a new one every time I come up here. She buys them in seasonal colors. I don't know how you can keep everything from falling out without a zipper," Holly said.

"Didn't I tell you, Ivy?" Kate said, turning back to Holly. "She was going to buy one for you, Holly, but I stopped her," she added as she opened the door to the kitchen. "I'm going inside to start dinner."

After they ate and walked the dogs again, everyone settled in the living room. Kate located the remote control and plopped down in an armchair. "So, you want to watch TV?"

Holly's eyes darted from Kate to Ivy and back again. "Actually, I was wondering if we could maybe talk about Mrs. Hagel's murder," she said.

"I thought we were done with that." Ivy frowned.

"I know, but I just can't stop thinking about it. Can't we just talk, sort of theoretically?"

"You mean, like a game of Clue?" Kate asked sitting up like a dog who just heard the word "treat".

"Yeah, that's what I mean. Like a game. It doesn't mean we're going to do anything, Ivy, but maybe Kate can help us sort through the suspects."

"All right. I guess that couldn't hurt," Ivy conceded.

"Look at it this way," Kate said. "You're saving me from brain atrophy. I haven't had any mental stimulation in weeks. Let me get some pads and pens. This will be fun!" she giggled as she ran upstairs.

"Do you have an easel?" Holly called up to Kate. "We could create one of those boards like they do on all the crime shows."

"That would be great," Kate said as she came back down the stairs and handed them legal pads and pens. "Unfortunately, I didn't anticipate a murder mystery weekend. No easels."

"Okay," said Holly. "Why don't we start by listing the suspects? First is Novardo Development."

"How can a company be a suspect?" Kate asked.

"There are two owners. One or both of them could have committed the murder."

"Or one or both of them could have hired someone to do it for them," Ivy suggested.

"Good point."

"Hey, let's create two columns--suspects and motives," Kate suggested.

"That's good," Holly said.

After a few minutes, their lists consisted of the following:

Novardo Development: $30-million development

Louie Brunetti: Variance to build a pool

Phillip Hagel: Inheritance

Granddaughter Hagel: Inheritance

"What about Mrs. Hagel's son? What's his name? I'm sure he stands to inherit more than the grandchildren," Kate speculated.

"See, this is why it's good to do this with somebody new to the facts," Holly said. "I wouldn't have thought to consider him a suspect. I don't know why. What do you think, Ivy? He didn't impress me as a killer."

"Me either, but he did really fly off the handle when he realized who you were. *And* he was really defensive, saying he'd call the police if he caught us talking to any of the members of his family."

"He actually said that? I'd definitely put him on the list," Kate said writing on her pad.

"Maybe he suspects his own kids," Ivy mused. "He could just be covering for them."

"That makes him an accessory after the fact," Kate said.

"Listen to you," Holly hooted. "Did you get that from a *Bones* episode?"

"That or NCIS," Kate snickered.

"You know, there's something about that whole thing that bothered me at the time, and I just can't put my finger on it," Holly said.

"I know what," Ivy answered. "I wondered how Steven Hagel knew we were helping Leonelle Gomez. He said his lawyer told him, but how did his lawyer find out?"

"That's it! The police certainly wouldn't have told him."

"You mean Manelli?" Kate smiled.

"All right. Manelli. He's a jerk, but even I can't imagine him being chummy with a lawyer, or doing something as unprofessional as pointing us out to a suspect's lawyer."

"And why would Steven Hagel be lawyering up?" Kate asked.

"Lawyering up? Really, you have been watching too much TV," Holly laughed.

They all pondered the list silently for a few minutes, when Holly pounded the arm of her chair and spat out, "Grabnick! It had to be that sleaze ball. He's really the only other one who knew we were helping Leonelle."

"You're right," Ivy said looking glum. "What chance does Leonelle have if her own lawyer is unprofessional enough to reveal information like that to the victim's family?"

"It certainly shows he's not working in her best interest," Holly replied.

"You know, he could get disbarred for that," Kate interjected.

"But how could we prove it?" Holly asked.

"We could at least threaten to bring charges against him, couldn't we?" Ivy added.

Now it was Holly's turn to look glum. "That puts us right back in actual, not theoretical, mode."

"Okay, okay," Kate jumped in. "Let's not get off track here. Put Grabnick off to the side for a minute. Let's keep working. Steven Hagel is definitely a suspect, and if you ask me, he's got more possible motives than anyone else. One, he is the only son and so he probably gets the biggest inheritance. Two, if he didn't do it, but contacted his lawyer for advice because he suspects his kids might have, he's aiding and abetting criminals. Thirdly, if he's got his lawyer breaching ethics by soliciting confidential information from another suspect's lawyer--I don't know what that's called--but it's got to be illegal," Kate said, a triumphant grin on her face.

"You really are enjoying this, aren't you?" Holly laughed.

"Okay. I'm adding Steven Hagel to the list," Ivy said, putting her pen to paper.

"That's the spirit." Kate punched the air. "Okay, we've got all our suspects, now..."

"Wait," Holly said. "You know, another thing that bugs me is the fact that the neighbors next-door left town the morning after the murder."

"I forgot about them," Ivy said. "Does seem fishy."

"Who are they?" Kate asked.

"That's just it. I don't really know them," Holly answered.

"Let's add 'neighbors' to our list, motive unknown." Kate wrote the addition on her legal pad. "Now what is it they say about motive, means, and there's one more."

"Opportunity," said Ivy, finishing the addition to her list.

"You watch detective shows, too, Ivy?" Kate queried.

"Yep." Ivy nodded. "I've watched so many *Castle* re-runs on TNT, I could play Beckett's role."

"I told you this would be fun!" Kate wiggled in her chair.

"Yeah, but I'd be enjoying it more if it really was just a game," Holly said.

"Buzzkill!" Kate snarled.

"Back to work." Holly looked at her notepad. "We've got the motives. Anyone who got into the house had the means. Mrs. Hagel was murdered with her own pills which were right on the kitchen counter. But who had opportunity? This is where it gets hard because we're just guessing. We don't know the time of death and whether or not any of these suspects has an alibi."

"True, but we do know there was no break-in and that the family all had keys to the house. Novardo Development probably did not, and Louie Brunetti probably did not," Ivy said.

"The unknown neighbors, either," Kate added.

"Don't be so sure about that. My neighbors have keys to my house," Holly said.

"Okay, it's possible," Kate replied. "But I still think it's unlikely they'd have keys."

"You're right," Ivy said. "It looks an awful lot like one of the family did it."

"But which one?" Holly wondered out loud.

27 TAROT

Holly, Ivy and Kate studied their lists of suspects and clients. After a few minutes, Ivy looked up and asked, "Do you think that Manelli has reached the same conclusion? I mean, that it's probably a family member?"

"No, he believes Leonelle did it," Holly answered.

"I think you're wrong about that, but I can't argue anymore. I'm really tired and have to go to bed." Ivy stood up yawning, her eyes drooping.

"I'd have fallen asleep an hour ago if I hadn't had that nap after lunch," Holly said.

"And you do need to rest up so you're fresh for the Trout Parade tomorrow," Kate added. "I put towels in your room, and there's an extra blanket in the closet. If you need anything else, just yell."

"Thanks. See you in the morning," Ivy said as she climbed the stairs.

"Good-night." Holly turned to Kate. "She must be exhausted. I'm sure she didn't get much more sleep than I did last night."

"You realize she's as invested in this as you are."

"And it's killing me because I just wanted this vacation to be all about her and what she wanted to do. I'm afraid she'll never want to come visit again, let alone move in with me."

"Don't underestimate your sister. She's not as fragile as you sometimes describe her. Remember, you're cut out of the same cloth."

"I know. I forget that. Then I think of things she's done like joining the army and not taking her husband's last name when they got married, and I remember she's got a spine and a mind of her own."

"Good. Now let's get down to business." Kate jumped up. "Let me get my tarot cards."

Holly was clearing off the coffee table when Kate re-entered the room with the deck of cards and her notes for how to interpret them.

"Don't forget," she cautioned, "the cards don't lie, so you better not either. I still can't believe you denied that you'd met a man when the King of Wands came up in your reading."

Holly moaned. "You and Ivy are the same. If a single man comes within 25 yards of me, you swear he's interested in me. They never are or they're men that make me feel lukewarm at best."

Kate rolled her eyes as she shuffled the cards, "I don't know about you."

"Shut up and deal."

"What is your question for the cards?"

"I'm not entirely sure. You know, Ivy's right. We really don't have to do anything. The police ..."

Kate tilted her head, smirking.

"Okay. Manelli told us to back off. I have to admit I did get scared when he asked me if I realized that if Novardo or Louie Brunetti were guilty, that I put Ivy and me in danger just by talking about it. I hadn't thought about us being in danger. I talked to Ivy about how much I hate the fact that I used to be fearless about everything, and now I'm a chicken. If I see trouble, I want to run, not walk, in the opposite direction."

"That's normal, you know."

"Is it? That's what Ivy said, but when Juan was charged with the murder, I didn't even think about being scared. I just knew I had to help him if I could. Then when Ivy said she thought we should help Elena, I agreed, even though I didn't think it was such a great idea. I wasn't afraid until Manelli asked me that question."

"Nobody could blame you if you didn't do anything more."

"That's right. The hardest part was telling Elena and we did that. Okay, my question for the cards. Should we just forget about Leonelle Gomez and trust the police to find the real murderer? Can we just go home and start doing all the things we'd planned for this vacation because we've done all we can?"

"Here. Shuffle the deck and focus on your question."

Holly shuffled and handed the cards back to Kate who slowly placed the cards on the table one by one in a Celtic Cross spread. When she reached number ten, she put the deck down, and turned over the two center cards.

"The Six of Wands crossed by the Eight of Cups. That's the heart of the matter."

"What do they mean?"

"The Six of Wands signals victory or success."

Holly smiled. "Whew. Then I guess we're off the hook."

"Not so fast. That success is crossed by the Eight of Cups, a card about walking away, of deserting the source of your happiness or enterprise."

Holly's smile turned into a grimace. "So what you're saying is my walking away from this could block a successful outcome?"

"Maybe. Let's keep going." Kate turned over the remaining cards. "Oh, boy. In the Fears and Doubts position you have The Tower. That means things are out of control. There's instability and insecurity."

"Terrific." Holly leaned back, closing her eyes, resting her head on the back of the couch. "That is exactly how I feel."

"Hold on though. I know there are positive aspects to this card, too." Kate feverishly turned the pages of her notes. "Here.

It's about tearing down the present order to make way for something new. Could be a job or marriage."

Without opening her eyes, Holly barked, "Don't say it. Just keep going and finish this reading."

Kate shook her head and smiled. "Okay. In the Outside Factors spot, we have the Knight of Swords. I know he's all about rushing forward and riding into battle. Let's see. My notes say he's intelligent, forthright, courageous. Gee, I wonder if that could be ..."

"Bite me." Holly sat up and scowled.

"There is a negative here. It says he's eager to achieve his goals and maybe at the expense of others."

"A chink in his armor?" Holly sat up.

"You're admitting it's him?"

"How many more cards are there?" Holly snapped.

"Just two--hopes and wishes and the outcome." Kate turned over the next to last card. "The Sun. It's all about glory, triumph and victory."

Holly smiled and moved forward to the edge of the couch. "That's good, isn't it?"

"It doesn't get better than that. Look at the card. It practically glows. But it is hopes and wishes. The last card is the outcome card. Let's see what it is."

Kate turned over the card and both she and Holly gasped. The Three of Swords showed a heart pierced by three swords dripping blood.

"That can't be good, can it?" Holly whispered.

"Let me see." Kate read silently, then looked up at Holly. "Okay. I'm going to read this to you exactly. 'Need for clarification, need to see clearly. Emotions are clouding judgment. You're not dealing with the emotions of the situation. *Must accept the work.*'"

"No." Holly eyes widened, her skin turning pale.

"One more thing--here, you read it yourself because I don't want you to say I'm making this up." Kate handed Holly her notes, pointing at the line she wanted Holly to read. “Lesson: Take pain into our hearts and transform it with courage and love.”

“You can’t stop,” Kate said.

“How do I tell Ivy?”

“Tell me what?”

Holly and Kate looked to the stairs where Ivy was standing in her nightgown. Neither answered.

Ivy looked down at the coffee table. “Are those tarot cards?”

28 MUST ACCEPT THE WORK

Unable to deny the obvious, Holly looked at Ivy and said, “Yes, they’re tarot cards. Now before you …”

“Really?” Ivy quickly descended the stairs. “I’ve always wanted to have a reading, but I was afraid I’d get robbed if I went into one of those places with ‘Psychic’ flashing in neon over the front door.” She sat down directly in front of the coffee table facing Holly and Kate.

Kate burst into laughter. “Have you two met?” she asked looking over at Holly.

“Ivy, I thought you would consider this--I don’t know--sinful, I guess,” Holly said shaking her head in amazement.

“Why would you think that?”

“You still go to church almost every Sunday and I’m pretty sure your parish priest would tell you this is fortune-telling.”

“Oh, Holly! You’ve always been so literal, so all or nothing when it comes to the church.”

“That’s what I tell her,” Kate said.

“The Catholic Church is pretty clear about how it is all or nothing,” Holly replied.

“I just don’t see it that way.” Ivy turned to face, Kate. “You do readings?”

“Yeah, but I’m just an amateur.”

"She's pretty darn accurate," Holly broke in. "But before she does a reading for you, you need to know about the reading on the table."

"Okay." Ivy said looking from Holly to Kate.

"Tell her, Kate."

"No. You tell her."

"I asked the cards if we should we just forget about Leonelle Gomez and trust the police to find the real murderer. I asked if we could just go home and start enjoying our vacation."

"And what did the cards answer?"

"That we must, and I quote, 'accept the work.'"

"Oh."

"Yeah. Oh."

They sat quietly for a moment looking at the Celtic Cross spread on the table.

"The cards also say that love is the only power, and Holly needs to make way for marriage."

"Shut up!" Holly snapped, messing up the cards on the table as Ivy and Kate laughed.

"Well," Ivy said when she finally stopped chuckling, "if I end up with Nick Manelli as a brother-in-law, then I'm in."

Holly looked at her sister, her smile receding. "Seriously. We don't have to do this. We told Elena we couldn't do any more. We could get in trouble with the police. We could endanger ourselves."

"I know that. But I'm down here because, in spite of the fact that I'm exhausted, I could not fall asleep. I keep going over that phone call to Elena and it's tearing me up. I admit I'm scared, but will we ever be able to look at ourselves in a mirror again if we just go on our merry way, and Leonelle goes to prison?"

Holly sighed loudly. Ivy continued, "I'm not suggesting we actually investigate anything, but we can at least go with Elena to the lawyer again, can't we? Let him know we think his sharing information with the Hagel's lawyers is unethical, and maybe just go with Elena to visit Leonelle for moral support."

"I love you, sister. You have an unerring moral compass, and you're absolutely right. We can at least be there to show support and hope like hell the police..."

"Who?" Ivy asked, one eyebrow raised.

"Okay, we can hope Manelli does his job."

Kate had picked up the cards while they were talking. She handed the deck to Ivy. "Now think of a question you want to ask while you shuffle the deck."

29 BACK HOME

"Home Sweet Home," Holly said as they pulled into the driveway.

"The weekend was so much fun. After the Trout Parade, I'm not sure if I'm ready to face reality," Ivy said.

"Ready or not, here we are." Holly got out of the car and opened the back door. Lucky jumped down from her pop-up kennel on the backseat. "Would you take her around to the front gate and let her in? She loves to run around the yard and smell everything after we've been away. I'll get our stuff."

Ivy took Lucky around front and Holly popped the trunk. She grabbed as much as she could and brought it in through the garage to the basement. By the time she returned to the car, Ivy was there to help her.

They climbed the stairs to the first floor, and Holly stopped, noticing the light flashing on the answering machine. "Let's see who called. There will probably be 10 hang-ups. I can't believe the number of sales calls I get."

"I screen all my calls for that reason."

The first two calls were blank. The third call began with a sob. Holly and Ivy just looked at one another.

"Ms. Donnelly, this is Elena Gomez. I didn't want to call you, but I don't know what else to do. Mr. Grabnick, he called me, yelling something about a CD he got in the mail. He said, 'You tell that Donnelly woman that if she doesn't stop interfering, I'm going to go to the police. This is harassment.' Then he made it sound like this could hurt my mother's case. I didn't understand what he was talking about. I'm so sorry to bother you. Please call me. I'm so worried for my mother." Here Elena sobbed again. "Please. I have no one else."

Holly sank into a chair. "So much for weekend afterglow, huh?"

"We better call her right away."

Holly sighed, reached for the phone, located Elena's number, hit call and speaker.

"Hi, Elena. It's Holly and Ivy Donnelly. We just got back."

"Thank heaven. I thought you didn't want to talk to me anymore. I'm so sorry to bother you."

"It's okay, Elena. What CD was Grabnick talking about?"

"I don't know. I thought you would know."

"No, we don't. Are you home now?"

"No, I just got out of class."

"Meet us at Grabnick's office. We'll be there in ten minutes."

"Thank you so much."

Holly hung up, shaking her head. "What a creep Grabnick is!"

"Really. He didn't have to yell at her."

"He's nothing but a bully."

"What do you think this CD is?" Ivy asked.

"I don't have a clue, but let's go see the little pissant and find out."

30 GRABNICK REDUX

Elena was sitting in her car parked in front of Jonathan Grabnick's office. Holly pulled in behind her, and shut off the engine. Elena was out of her Honda before Holly and Ivy opened their doors.

"I am so relieved to see you," she said, rushing to hug Holly before she could even get out of the car.

Ivy came around to their side of the car and Elena held on to Holly's hand as she hugged Ivy.

"Elena, you have to calm down," Holly said. "Remember, the police told us not to interfere, so we must be very careful."

"I know," Elena replied, lowering her head. "But this man is... he should not have talked to me the way he did."

"No, he should not," Ivy confirmed. "Elena, Holly and I discussed things and we decided that we will continue to be with you and your mother for moral support, but we can't do more than that."

"We're here because this man issued a threat to us through you," Holly added. "We have every right to question him about that threat. Now when we go upstairs, you just relax and let me handle things, all right?"

"Okay."

The three women walked to the door leading upstairs to Grabnick's second floor office. The door stuck and Holly needed to lean her shoulder into it in order to get it open. The hall remained unswept since their last visit, the same Snicker's wrapper in the corner. At the top of the stairs, Holly knocked on the door. No answer. She knocked again.

"I hope he's here," Ivy said. "What will we do if he isn't?"

"Call for an appointment, I guess," Holly answered.

The door suddenly opened. Jonathan Grabnick looked startled. "I thought you were the deli delivery boy."

After an awkward moment, Holly sighed and asked, "Aren't you going to let us in, Mr. Grabnick?"

"I'm quite busy. This isn't a good time. You should have called for an appointment."

"We'll only be a minute," Holly snapped, pushing past him, Ivy and Elena following.

Grabnick huffed, shook his head and followed them in. He walked around his desk and remained standing.

"So why are you here? To harass me?" he asked.

"You're kidding, right?" Holly asked. "You called Elena, *harassing her* about some CD you got in the mail, threatening to go to the police about us, and suggesting it would hurt her mother's case, and you want to know why we're here?"

"I did no such thing."

"She's got a recording of your call. I think the police might not agree with you."

"You listen to me, Ms. Donnelly. You have no business ..."

"NO! You listen to me, Mr. Grabnick. If you had something to say to me and my sister, you should have called us, and not bullied this young woman. Now, what I want to know is what CD are you talking about?"

"You know very well what CD."

"No, I don't. If I did, we wouldn't be here. Show me this CD."

"You mean you didn't send it?"

"No. What's on this CD?"

Grabnick appeared genuinely baffled. He looked down at his desk and shuffled some papers. After a moment, he looked up, smiled and said, "Perhaps I was mistaken. Uh, Ms. Gomez, my apologies. Please just forget my phone call."

Holly, Ivy and Elena stared at Grabnick, appearing mystified by his change in demeanor.

"Will there be anything else?" Grabnick asked.

"Wait a minute," Holly said. "You got a CD related to Mrs. Gomez's case. What was on the CD?"

"As I said, I was mistaken."

"No, no. C'mon. You accused us of harassing you. You have to tell us what was on the CD."

"Now that I know you didn't send it I realize it had nothing to do with this case. It was just a matter of my jumping to the wrong conclusion. I now see it is related to another case. Please, accept my apology and just forget all about it. And Ms. Gomez, please know that I am doing everything I can for your mother."

Holly bit her lip, recognizing that they were not going to get anything more out of him. Beside her, Ivy moved forward to the edge of her seat. She looked straight at Grabnick and said, "Mr. Grabnick, I do hope you mean what you just said to Elena because Holly and I know that you shared information about this case with the Hagels' lawyer."

Grabnick's eyes widened. Before he could deny anything, Ivy continued.

"That's grounds for disbarment. Make no mistake about it. If we feel that you do not do everything you can for Leonelle, we will come after you. And if you bully Elena again, we will go to the police and bring harassment charges against you, you little pissant."

Ivy stood up, never breaking eye contact with Grabnick, who appeared stricken.

"Ladies, let's go," she said.

Ivy turned, opened the door and walked out. Struggling to keep the grin on her face from turning into a belly laugh, Holly followed without saying a word. Elena glowered at Grabnick, snapping her fingers at him and slamming the door behind her.

Out on the street, Holly started to laugh uncontrollably. Giggling, Elena hugged Ivy, who also began to laugh.

"Feel better?" Holly asked when she finally could speak.

"Yes. Yes, I do," Ivy said.

31 AN UNEXPECTED VISIT

When the three women stopped laughing, Ivy said, "How are we going to find out what was on that CD?"

"I don't know, but it's got to be important," said Holly. "It must be something that casts some doubt on Leonelle's being the murderer."

"Wouldn't that be great? Do you think it's possible?" Elena sounded hopeful.

"I don't know, Elena. Remember, we really can't do anything."

Elena's crestfallen expression made Holly want to go back upstairs and ransack Grabnick's office.

"Let Holly and me go home and talk this over, Elena," Ivy intervened. "We'll see if we can come up with an idea, okay?"

"Okay."

"Go home and we'll call you tomorrow or Wednesday," Holly said.

Elena looked at her watch. "I better hurry. I have to pick up my sister at school. She gets out early today."

Elena hugged Holly and kissed her on the cheek. She turned to Ivy, kissed and hugged her, saying, "You were wonderful up there. Thank you so much--both of you."

She got in her Honda and drove off. Holly and Ivy got in the Cadillac.

"You *were* wonderful up there," Holly said as she eased the car into traffic.

"I'm actually shaking a little," Ivy replied. "I'm not really sure what got into me."

"Whatever it was, I'm glad it did. I'd completely forgotten that we intended to confront Grabnick about talking to Hagel's lawyer. You so shocked him when you brought it up, he couldn't react fast enough to deny it."

"I guess that proves we were right. So it's looking more and more like someone in the Hagel family murdered Mrs. Hagel. What are we going to do?"

"I don't know. I really don't. But I'd love to know what was on that CD."

"Want to break into Grabnick's office tonight?"

"IVY! I'm shocked. You have got to calm down, girl," Holly teased.

"I'm only kidding, but short of breaking and entering, how else can we find out?"

"I honestly don't know." Holly put on her turn signal when they reached her block. As she rounded the corner, she caught her breath.

"Uh-oh! What's *he* doing here?" Holly asked. Detective Manelli was exiting their gate when he spotted them.

"Do you think Grabnick called him?" Ivy asked.

"No. Even if he had, Manelli couldn't have gotten here ahead of us."

"Stop the car," Ivy said.

Holly stepped on the brakes and lowered her window. Manelli walked over to the car and bent down to their eye level.

"Detective, we didn't expect to see you," Ivy said from the passenger side.

"Yeah, I didn't expect it, either. We need to talk."

Holly felt a tingling under her skin. "Okay. I'll park in the driveway and we'll meet you at the front door."

Manelli backed away from the car. Holly closed the window. "What could this be about? Why didn't we just stay at Kate's?"

Inside Holly went straight to the front door where Manelli was waiting.

"Come in," she said. Lucky came to the door, tail wagging at the sight of the detective. After he petted her, the dog continued outside. "Come this way, Detective."

Manelli followed Holly into the living room. "Have a seat," she said. He sat in the wing chair beside the fireplace and she sat on the couch opposite him. Ivy came in and sat down beside Holly.

"Why are you here?" Holly asked.

"You don't know why?"

"No. Look, we did what we said we would. We left Saturday morning for the Catskills and just got back a few hours ago."

"And you didn't mail me something before you left?

"No. What would we mail you? We just saw you the day before."

"Was it a CD?" Ivy asked.

Holly grabbed Ivy's arm. "What are you doing?"

"He needs to know, Holly. We should tell him everything."

Holly lowered her head and moaned, covering her face with her hands massaging her temples. Manelli sat silently, appearing to enjoy the interchange between the sisters.

"*Was* it a CD, Detective?" Ivy asked again.

Manelli smiled. "Why don't you tell me why you think it was a CD, Ms. Donnelly?"

"As Holly said, we got home about two hours ago. We were getting ready to go out to lunch--that reminds me, I'm starved. Holly, can we have pizza delivered? If not, what's in the fridge, I have to eat something or..."

"Ms. Donnelly," Manelli cut in, "could you just finish first?"

"Yes," she laughed. "I guess that's more important. I just get a little discombobulated when I'm hungry."

"So what happened when you got home?" Manelli asked.

"Holly saw the answering machine message light blinking, so she played the messages. There was one from Elena Gomez. Hey, it's still on the machine, right, Holly?"

"Yes." Holly sat up glaring at her.

"Let's go in the kitchen and you can hear it for yourself."

Ivy popped up and headed to the kitchen. Holly remained seated on the couch. Manelli stood up, waiting for her.

"You don't need me," she said. "She'll tell you everything you want to know and maybe even a little you don't."

"I'd like you to join us. You're part of this interview."

Holly sighed heavily, stood up and walked to the kitchen. Ivy had the refrigerator open. "There's some cheddar cheese in here. Do you have crackers, Holly?"

Holly went to the cupboard to get the crackers.

"Ms. Donnelly, could we get back to the phone messages?" Manelli asked, sitting down, placing his notepad on the kitchen table.

"Sure. Holly, would you hit the replay button? I don't want to hit the wrong button and erase anything. I'm so bad with machines. But I think you know that, Detective." Ivy smiled at Manelli.

Holly shoved the cracker box at Ivy, went over to the machine and hit replay.

After the message ended Manelli asked, "So what did you do next?"

"We called Elena, of course," Ivy answered. "Would you like a cheese and cracker, Detective?"

"For God sakes, Ivy!" Holly cut in impatiently. "We called Elena and told her to meet us at Grabnick's office. We went down there and told him that if he had something to say to us, he should have called us and not bullied Elena. We asked him what CD he was talking about. Like you, he said, 'You don't know?' I said no. All of a sudden he becomes Mr. Congeniality. He says he must have been mistaken. He apologizes to Elena, and he won't tell us what was on the CD. Now, if you got the same CD as Grabnick, it wasn't sent by mistake. And if you think we sent it, then it has something to do with Leonelle's case. But I don't suppose you're going to tell us anymore than Grabnick about what was on the CD, are you?" Holly stood glaring at Manelli, her hands on her hips.

"I'll tell you," Manelli said, looking up from his notepad. "The CD contains a recording of a Zoning Commission hearing."

Holly hoped her face did not betray her. *Good, old Ira.*

"A Zoning Commission meeting?" Ivy asked.

"Why don't you get out the fruit we bought at the parade yesterday?" Holly said, sitting down at the table.

"Oh--okay." Ivy walked over to the counter and started looking through the bags they brought back from Kate's.

Manelli flipped through his notepad. "Here it is. You told me that Denise Archer said Mrs. Hagel objected to Louie Brunetti's request for a zoning variance in order to put in a swimming pool. Isn't it something that two days later I get a recording of that Zoning hearing?

Feeling trapped, Holly said nothing. She sat quietly, looking down at her hands in her lap. Manelli continued, "Do you believe in coincidences, Ms. Donnelly? Because I don't."

After a few seconds, she inhaled deeply and asked, "Does Mr. Brunetti threaten Mrs. Hagel on that CD?"

Manelli didn't answer.

"Look, three days ago, I didn't even know who Louie Brunetti was," Holly said. "Based on what Denise told me, he has a lot of enemies. Maybe one of them sent the CD's. I sure didn't."

"But you know who did," Manelli said.

"Detective," Ivy cut in, returning to the table with a bowl of plums and nectarines, "since you spoke to us on Thursday, Holly and I have done exactly what you asked. Holly hasn't even made a phone call. We went away for the weekend. We are trying very hard to stay uninvolved, and we only got re-involved because Elena called us. What else could we do after we got that message?"

"You could have ignored the call," he answered.

Ivy stiffened, put down the fruit bowl and looked directly at Manelli. "We will not interfere with police work, Detective Manelli, but neither will we abandon this young woman to be intimidated by people not worth one half of her. Why, Jonathan Grabnick is not worth one-tenth of her! And by the way, we learned something else when we went to Mrs. Hagel's wake the night before we left."

Holly lowered her head and groaned.

"No, Holly. He needs to know this, too. When Holly offered her condolences to Steven Hagel, he jumped all over her because he said his lawyer told him she was helping Leonelle Gomez. Now how did Stephen Hagel's lawyer know that? The only ones who knew we had even talked to her were you and Jonathan Grabnick. And I'm sure you didn't tell him. Grabnick is supposed to be defending Leonelle, so talking to the Hagels' lawyer is unethical, which, of course, begs the question, why would Steven Hagel be talking to his lawyer about Leonelle Gomez in the first place?"

Holly stood up and turned to leave the room.

"Uh-uh," Manelli said, pointing to the chair she had just vacated.

"I told you, you don't need me. She'll tell you everything. I'm tired and I need to take a shower."

"I'm not finished with you. Have a seat, please."

Holly rolled her eyes, blew air through pursed lips and sat back down.

"Anybody else talk to you at the wake?" Manelli asked Ivy.

"Yes. What was that woman's name, Holly?" When Holly didn't answer, she continued. "I don't remember her name--Diane or Doris--an older woman, said she thought Mrs. Hagel's grandson killed her. And then Denise Archer saw me in the ladies room and she thought I was Holly. She said if the grandson did it, it was the granddaughter that told him to, so I'd be investigating the family if I were you, Detective."

Manelli looked up from the notepad he'd been writing in, smiled at Ivy and said, "Thank you, Ms. Donnelly. You've been most helpful. You call me if you think of anything else." He turned to Holly and said, "Could you walk me to the gate, please?"

Holly rolled her eyes, got up and headed to the front door. She opened it and went outside without looking back to see if Manelli was behind her. At the gate she stared at his car.

"I know you were on the Zoning Commission for two years, and I know you know who sent that CD. Whether or not you asked them to send it, you're the reason they did. I warned you before that you could endanger yourself. Now maybe you understand what I meant. Once you start mucking around in a murder investigation, you set things in motion that you don't control. That's why police conduct investigations. That's why we carry the guns."

Holly turned to Manelli. "Look, I took what you said seriously. That's why we went away. We don't want to be involved, but now we are, and I can't unsay what I said before. All we want to do is be there as moral support for Elena and her mother. That's all."

Manelli stared at her, as if trying to decide whether or not she meant what she said. Holly felt he was burning a hole right through her.

"You would do well to follow your sister's example."

Holly hated this. He made her feel like a school girl. "What's that supposed to mean?"

"When I ask you something, tell me the truth--the whole truth."

"You know the whole truth now that you've talked to Ivy."

"Yeah, but I suspect you keep things from her, too. Seriously. If you hold back information related to this investigation again, I'm going to find and bring in your friend on the Zoning Board for questioning. It won't take me long to identify which of those guys you talked to. That should splash some cold water on your network of 'informants'."

Manelli actually mimed quotation marks in the air when he said the word "informants". He reached inside his jacket pocket and fished out a business card. Clasping her right wrist with his left hand, he placed the card in her hand, pressing his right thumb into her palm. Holly tried to pull her hand away, but he didn't loosen his grip. "Keep this handy. I think you're going to need it."

"No, I won't," Holly objected.

"We'll see. I'm not sure why, but people seem compelled to tell you things. Call me if they do." He released her hand and Holly felt unmoored.

Manelli opened the gate, stepped onto the sidewalk and out onto the street around to the passenger side of his car.

"Don't count on any calls from me," Holly said. "I'm done talking to anyone about this case."

"Then you can call me just to chat," he said with a straight face. As he got in his car, he shot her one last look, and Holly could have sworn he winked at her.

32 STOPPING THE DONNELLYS

Could he believe her? Would she really stop talking to people about this murder? Would she call him if someone told her something related to the case? Those were the questions Nick Manelli asked himself as he drove off, leaving Holly standing at her front gate.

This case was starting to get to him. In spite of the evidence against Leonelle Gomez, his gut told him she didn't kill Edna Hagel. When he'd gone to arrest her, he found a cheaply furnished, but spotless apartment. Leonelle was calm and respectful throughout the questioning, as if she had nothing to hide. When he told her he was there to arrest her, her daughter started screaming at the patrolman who approached her mother with handcuffs. Leonelle quieted her daughter with a simple, "Silencio." He smiled remembering that she had reminded him of his own mother. One word from her was always enough.

Subsequent investigation of the Gomez apartment turned up no stolen jewelry and no hidden cash. Pictures of Leonelle Gomez and Mrs. Hagel's jewelry circulated at all of the pawnshops in Pineland County also turned up nothing. If Leonelle Gomez had stolen the jewelry, what had she done with it? Her bank account had a grand total of $557 in it--the result of $25 and $35 deposits made over a period of two years. If she'd sold the jewelry, where was the money?

No, he didn't believe Leonelle Gomez was guilty of theft or murder, but he didn't want anyone else to know that--especially the killer. This Donnelly woman was complicating things. He had to stop her interference. The problem was that within just a few days, she had figured out the key players in this investigation. If she worked for him, he would be ecstatic. But she wasn't a policeman. Having to look out for a meddling civilian only made an already hard job even harder. Besides, he was genuinely worried that she was going to stumble onto something that would get her or her sister hurt. He feared she may have already done that.

Manelli had never met women like these two sisters. On the surface they seemed like a couple of ordinary middle-aged women, mainstays of their neighborhoods, volunteer types, interested in their homes and gardens, and cutting recipes out of magazines. They were all that, but they were also very smart and unexpectedly fearless. Holly was more assertive, but Ivy was more observant. Together they had the qualities of a good investigator, and that, for him, was the problem. They had the smarts and the moxie to ask the right questions of the right people, but they weren't trained police officers and that was likely to put them in danger. Worst of all they were personally involved, committed to helping Leonelle and Elena Gomez. How was he going to stop them?

Suddenly Manelli remembered something. He pulled into a parking spot on Pineland Street and took out his notepad. What was it Ivy said about Steven Hagel? He flipped through his notes. There it was. Hagel knew the Donnellys were helping Leonelle Gomez. Ivy was right. If he and Grabnick were the only ones who knew the Donnellys were trying to help Mrs. Gomez, how did Hagel and his lawyer find out? It had to be Grabnick. What was a court-appointed lawyer doing talking about his client's case with the victim's family lawyer? Time to pay Grabnick a visit.

33 EXHAUSTED

Holly remained standing in front of the gate a few moments after Manelli drove off. She looked at his card. *What just happened? Was he flirting with me? No way. He was mocking me!*

Inside Ivy was waiting at the door. "Well?"

"Well what?"

"I saw him holding your hand, Holly."

"You're delusional. He wasn't holding my hand. He gave me his business card and just wanted to make sure I didn't throw it on the ground."

"Okay, Cleo."

"Cleo?"

"Yeah, Cleopatra, Queen of *Da Nile*. Say what you want. I saw him wink at you."

Holly brushed past Ivy and went to the kitchen.

Ivy followed. "Okay, explain to me about the CD. Who sent it?"

Holly looked at Ivy, stuck out her tongue and waggled her head. "I'm not telling you, Blabbermouth. What you don't know, you can't tell your new best friend. I thought you were going to tell him about our game of Clue and run upstairs and get your list of suspects. Maybe even give him Kate's number so he could get her take on things as well."

"C'mon. Tell me you honestly don't think it's better that he knows everything we know."

"It doesn't matter what I think now." Holly grabbed the cracker box and the cheese board and went out to the patio. Ivy followed.

As she sliced some cheese, Holly said, "I am sure of one thing. That CD has to have Louie Brunetti threatening Mrs. Hagel on it. That's why Grabnick freaked. He doesn't want to go up against Brunetti."

"Why not?" Ivy sat down across the table from Holly.

"Brunetti is brother-in-law to one of the city councilmen. Together they harass and make life miserable for anyone who messes with them."

"How do you know that? You said Denise Archer told you, but she didn't say any of that when she talked to us. And you told Manelli, you never heard of Brunetti before that."

Holly pointed the cheese knife at Ivy. "*Et tu, Brute*? So now, you're grilling me, too?"

"No, I'm just trying to understand."

"I'm not telling you who told me, so just drop it."

"Okay--okay."

Neither said anything as Holly finished the crackers and wrapped up the remaining cheese.

"What do we do now?" Ivy asked.

"You tell me," Holly replied.

"Should we go visit Leonelle? You know we only saw her once and maybe she's had some time to think about things and remember some other details that could help."

"She has to tell the police, not us."

"Hey, where's this coming from? What exactly did Manelli say to you?"

"He said he was going to find and haul in for questioning whoever sent that CD if we didn't keep him informed of anything we hear."

"Oh."

"Yeah. Oh."

"So what's the problem? We just tell him everything."

"I'm not convinced that telling him everything is a good thing."

"But..."

"Look, I'm just too tired to argue with you. I don't even want to think about this anymore." Holly grabbed the empty cracker box and stood up. Ivy lifted the cheese board and they returned to the kitchen.

"Uh-oh," Ivy said. "The message light is blinking."

"Please let it just be a sales call hang up." Holly hit the play message button.

"Holl-eee! It's Teresa. I need to talk to you. I found out something that may interest you regarding that matter we discussed at lunch last week. Gimme a call."

"This can't be good." Holly's shoulders sagged.

"Are you going to call her?"

Holly straightened up. "No. No, I'm not. I'm going to put my personal needs first. I'm going upstairs and take a shower and a nap. This can wait. I'll call her when I get up."

"Okay," Ivy shrugged. "I'll take Lucky for a walk." She grabbed the leash and went back outside.

Holly's shoulders ached and her neck felt as if it were in a vice. As she climbed the stairs, she struggled to keep her eyes open. In her room she took off her tee-shirt, then reached into her pockets to empty them before removing her shorts. In her right pocket, she felt Manelli's card and the feeling of his thumb on her palm returned. Though she would never admit it to Kate or Ivy, she was powerfully attracted to this man. This was the first time since her break-up with Brian, that she'd felt even remotely attracted to anyone. Manelli infuriated her. She hated his telling her what to do, but at the same time, she was drawn to him because he was strong and sure of himself, unlike any of the men she'd been out on dates with over the last ten years. And, as Ivy said, he was quite a hunk. She couldn't deny the combination was quite appealing.

She finished undressing and got in the shower. Really, what were the chances Manelli was interested in her? He must have a girlfriend. No man that attractive could be unattached. But he did wink at her. She wasn't imagining that. Ivy saw it, too.

Holly got out of the shower, put on clean clothes and collapsed on the bed. She wondered if Kate and Ivy were right. No. Impossible. It was much more likely that he was just playing with her to keep her in line during this investigation. He probably got his kicks teasing middle-aged women, knowing the effect he was having on them. She was not going to be made a fool of again. A lump formed in her throat as she remembered that suffocating sensation she felt when she learned Brian had been cheating on her. She pulled back the covers and got in bed. As she drifted off to sleep she tried not to think of how her wrist felt in Manelli's grasp.

35 MANELLI PAYS GRABNICK A VISIT

Manelli found a parking spot on Main Avenue near the office building that housed Grabnick's office. He looked at his notes again. Holly said that Grabnick became "Mr. Congeniality" when he found out she had not sent the CD.

He had to admit Holly was right. Clearly Grabnick had no intention of following up on Brunetti's threat against Mrs. Hagel or using it as part of Leonelle Gomez's defense. Even a court-appointed lawyer, with no resources to privately investigate, would contact the police with this evidence for them to investigate. Why hadn't Grabnick? There was only one way to find out.

Manelli put his notepad back in his pocket, got out of the car and walked to the side entrance of the building. The door stuck and he had to force it open. He climbed the shabby staircase and knocked on Grabnick's door. No answer. Manelli tried the door and found it open. A startled Jonathan Grabnick looked up.

"Can I help you?" he asked.

"Mr. Grabnick, I'm Detective Manelli with the Pineland Park Police Department." Manelli flashed his badge. "I'm investigating the Hagel murder case."

"Yes, of course. I saw your name on the police report," Grabnick said. "Have a seat. What can I do for you, Detective?"

Manelli sat down and stretched back in his chair, staring at Grabnick, smiling as he imagined the scene in this office earlier when Holly, Ivy and Elena had visited. He didn't respond to Grabnick immediately. *Will he squirm?*

Grabnick blinked almost instantly. He looked down at the papers on his desk, fidgeting in his seat. He checked his watch and said impatiently, “I'm rather busy this morning and quite pressed for time.”

Manelli pulled out his notepad, perused it for another second or two, looked up at Grabnick and asked, “Mr. Grabnick, did you receive something in the mail related to the Hagel case? Probably sent anonymously.”

“Something in the mail? Like what?” Grabnick asked, again looking down at the papers on his desk, not making eye contact.

Manelli disliked lawyers, and he especially disliked incompetent ones. “Like a CD recording of a Zoning Commission hearing.”

Now it was Grabnick’s turn to stall. He looked around his desk, and even reached over to his inbox as if he were really looking for the CD. "No, Detective. I don’t recall receiving such a CD. Why would anyone send me a copy of a Zoning Commission hearing?”

“Because I received one,” Manelli answered, becoming stony-faced.

Grabnick pulled his chair in closer to his desk, straightened his tie, pushed his glasses up on his nose, and shuffled some papers on his desk. “I don’t understand why you think I would have received this CD, simply because you did.”

“Mine came with a note that said a copy was sent to you.” That was a lie, but Manelli never felt any guilt about lying to a liar. Ironically, he found it one of the most effective means of getting at the truth.

“I didn’t receive it,” Grabnick said with an air of indignation.

Manelli’s face broke into a broad grin now. "Really, Mr. Grabnick? Because Holly and Ivy Donnelly tell me you accused them of sending you the CD.”

Grabnick grimaced, shaking his head. "Look, Detective. I did receive a CD, but it wasn’t related to the Gomez case. I explained that to the Donnelly women. Whatever CD you got is obviously not the same as the one I got.”

Manelli smiled, now really enjoying himself. “May I see the CD you received, Mr. Grabnick?”

“No, you may not. That CD is confidential information related to a totally different case. You'd need a warrant to see it,” Grabnick said, regaining some composure now that he was on solid legal ground.

“Don't you even want to know what the Zoning Hearing was about, Mr. Grabnick? Because it is related to your client's case.” Manelli taunted.

“Well, I...uh...yes, of course. But I don't know how a Zoning Hearing could be relevant?”

“It's relevant. It's very relevant because during that hearing Louis Brunetti threatens to murder Mrs. Hagel for causing his application for a zoning variance to be turned down.”

Grabnick licked his lips, scratched his neck, and again straightened his tie. "Um... that's...uh...that's information that, I suppose, could be helpful.”

“Yeah, I was thinking that myself. Playing that CD in court could definitely demonstrate that someone other than your client had a motive to kill Mrs. Hagel and, at the very least, introduce the element of doubt in a juror's mind, don't' ya think?”

“Yes.” Grabnick brushed some paper crumbs off his desk. “I suppose it could.”

“Maybe your copy got lost in the mail. I'll tell you what. Why don't I have someone in my office make a copy and hand deliver it to you? How's that sound?”

“That would be good,” Grabnick answered, sighing, staring at a coffee stain on his desk blotter.

Manelli got up to leave.

“Detective, will you be questioning Mr. Brunetti?” Grabnick asked, the bluster gone out of him.

“Count on it, Mr. Grabnick.” Manelli put his hand on the doorknob, stopped and turned back to face the lawyer. “One more question. You and I are the only ones who know the Donnellys are helping Leonelle Gomez. Any idea how Steven Hagel's lawyer found that out?”

Grabnick blanched. “I have no idea.”

Manelli grinned. "No? I didn’t think so. You know the American justice system is lucky to have men like you who do the job of defending the defenseless. Let me leave you to do your job, Mr. Grabnick. Have a good day.”

As he descended the stairs, Manelli shook his head. Taunting Grabnick was a kick. Unfortunately, he knew it was unlikely their conversation would motivate Grabnick to do a good job defending Leonelle Gomez. He had to find the real killer. He got in his car and headed to Louie Brunetti’s house for a visit he was dreading.

35 SECOND BLOOM

Holly woke up and went to the kitchen, saw the answering machine on the counter and remembered Teresa's message. She picked up the phone and searched the Call Log. Teresa's was the last call, so she hit "Talk". After seven rings, the phone went to voice mail.

"Hi, Teresa. It's Holly. Sorry I missed your call. I was away for a few days and had a hectic morning. I'm back now, so you can call this number. If you can't get back to me tonight, you can call me tomorrow. Bye."

Ivy walked into the kitchen as Holly hung up. "Didn't get her?"

"No."

"What do you think she wanted?" Ivy went to the refrigerator, got out the iced tea pitcher and poured herself a glass.

"I don't' know. Isn't it ironic though? Up at Kate's we decided only a family member could have had motive, means and opportunity. Since we got back, a Zoning Commission hearing recording that has Louie Brunetti threatening Mrs. Hagel surfaces, and now Teresa says she found something. It has to be related to the Hagels and their dealings with Novardo."

"Maybe," Ivy said taking a sip of the tea. "I passed the Hagel house walking Lucky before. The house next door still looks empty. I remember Manelli saying he didn't believe in coincidences. The fact that the neighbors left town the morning the body was discovered may be nothing, but doesn't that strike you as just a little too coincidental?"

“It does,” Holly replied, “But what’s their motive?”

“Just because we don’t know it, doesn’t mean they didn’t have one.”

“True. But now this is where the police have to investigate.”

“I’ll bet Denise Archer knows if they had a motive.”

“Listen to yourself. Didn’t I just hear you this morning tell Manelli that we, and I quote, ‘would not interfere with police business’?”

“Just kidding. But I’ll bet she does know.”

“Stop, before you get me in trouble. Let’s go outside and check the yard. I’m glad it rained while we were away. We won’t have to water, but I’m sure there’s plenty of weeding and deadheading to do.”

“Wow. Manelli really scared you, didn’t he?” asked Ivy.

“As much as I hate to admit he’s right about anything, I have to acknowledge that just the couple of conversations I had with people before we left set in motion a whole bunch of things I didn’t expect. More important, I don’t want Manelli hauling in a friend who gave me information confidentially. It could affect his job and I don’t need one more thing to feel guilty about.”

“All right. I get that,” Ivy said, heading out the door. Holly followed and they went to the shed to get gardening tools and gloves. Holly grabbed the long-sleeve pair.

“I thought you were finished pruning the roses,” Ivy said.

“I got rid of the deadwood, but I noticed a lot of deadheads when we pulled in the driveway. If I clip them now, I may get a second bloom later in the summer.”

“A second bloom.” Ivy grinned. “Wouldn’t it be wonderful if people could get a second bloom? Like in your fifties you’d become as beautiful and vibrant as you were in your twenties. You know, taut skin, no wrinkled neck and puckered underarms.”

“Throw in boundless energy, 20-20 eyesight, and no hearing loss and I’m with you,” Holly laughed putting on her gloves.

"How about increased libido and no need for lubricants?" Ivy giggled.

"You're killin' me," Holly chortled as she picked up her tool bucket and walked to the front yard.

An hour later, Holly decided she had done all she could for one night. She grabbed the bucket filled with deadheads and walked to the backyard, where she found Ivy had completely weeded the vegetable garden.

"That's it for tonight. I think I need another shower and I'm ready for bed."

"Me, too."

Back inside the kitchen, Holly looked over at the answering machine. No blinking light. She picked up her cell phone from the counter.

"Any message from Teresa?" Ivy asked.

"No. I'm sure I'll hear from her tomorrow."

That night Holly dreamt that Teresa came to visit, but it wasn't the platinum blonde, overweight Teresa whom she'd met for lunch a few days ago. It was the slim and sexy, brunette Teresa she knew almost 30 years ago. "Yeah, Holl. The doctor said it's my second bloom. As soon as you start yours, we'll hit the Sheraton Sports Bar. Just like friggin' old times!" she howled.

36 A VISIT TO LOUIE BRUNETTI

Manelli pulled up in front of Louie Brunetti's house on Ridge Road. He lingered, looking at the house a moment. Letting out a heavy sigh, he shut off the ignition, got out of the car and walked up to the front door. He only had to ring the bell once. Louie Brunetti himself appeared at the door. He stared at Manelli a moment, then opened the door, wide, breaking into a smile.

"Nicky, c'mon in. Gosh, it's good to see you. Me and Nina was just talkin' about you the other day, sayin' how we wished you'd come see us once in a while, and now here you are."

Manelli stepped inside, and extended his hand to Brunetti, who grasped it and pulled Manelli in for a bear hug.

"Nina's out shoppin'. She's not gonna be happy, when I tell her she missed you. You know she loves you, Nicky."

"I'm here on business, Louie."

"Business? What business?"

"The Hagel murder investigation."

"Oh, brother. I didn't have nothin' to do with that. C'mon. You know me better than that."

"I know, Louie, but I'm just doin' my job. I have to ask you a few questions."

Brunetti raked his fingers through his thick gray hair. Shaking his head, he said, "Awright. Let's go sit down." He led the way to the living room and sat down in the armchair Manelli knew no one else dared to sit in. "Siddown," he growled pointing to the chair across from him.

"Louie, you threatened to kill Mrs. Hagel because she opposed your application for a zoning variance."

"I wasn't happy about it, but I didn't threaten to kill her."

"There's a recording of a Zoning Board hearing where you're clearly heard threatening to kill Mrs. Hagel."

"Dammit!" Louie swore. He shook his head, then looked directly into Manelli's eyes. "I hate this modern technology. Nothin's off the record no more."

Manelli had to smile. "No, Louie, nothing's off the record."

"Okay, so's I threaten to off the dame. That don't mean nothin'. I just figured if I scared her, she'd give in. You know me. Murder's not what I do. As a matter of fact, I remember how happy me and Joe was that you got transferred from vice to homicide. We considered ourselves lucky that we wouldn't have to worry about you investigatin' us no more. You could even ask him."

Manelli just shook his head. "Where were you last Friday?"

"Last Friday? Let's see." Brunetti looked up at the ceiling then broke into a smile. "I was at Bally's casino in Atlantic City. Me and Nina went down. We got a free, two-night stay. That proves it wasn't me, Nicky, don't it?"

"If it checks out, it proves you didn't do it, but folks might say you had somebody do it for you."

Brunetti sat back in his chair, and looked directly at Manelli. "I had nothin' to do with it. I swear it on my daughter Anna Marie's grave."

Manelli looked down and said nothing.

After a minute, Brunetti asked, "Nicky, how you doin'? You datin' anyone? It's been two years now."

Manelli looked up at Brunetti, swallowed hard and then looked away.

"You know Anna Marie would want you to be happy. No father loved his daughter more than I loved her, but son, you got to move on." When he got no reply, he said, "Hey, whaddya hear from Nicky Junior? How's he doin' up there in Boston?"

At the final question, Manelli looked up, smiled and answered, "He's doing great. He called me on Sunday. Just got another promotion."

"That's terrific. He's a smart kid."

"Yeah. He got that from his mother." Manelli looked down again.

"You tell him to call his Grandmother, would ya?"

"Yeah, I'll do that, Louie."

"So, we're good here? You believe me don't you, Nicky?"

"Yeah, Louie. I believe you." Manelli stood up, and Brunetti followed him to the door.

"Please, come back and visit Nina. I'm tellin' you she worries about you and Nicky, Junior and it kills her that you don't come around no more."

"Okay, Louie. Tell Nina I'll be by. Here's my card. Tell her to call me the next time she's makin' ravioli."

"If I tell her that, she'll start cookin' tomorrow," Louie laughed.

The two men shook hands and parted.

Manelli had known this visit would bring back painful memories, emotions he'd worked hard to keep buried. As he drove away, he forced himself to go over his conversation with Louie. He was relieved to learn he had an airtight alibi. No, murder was not Louie's style, not even by proxy. Steven Hagel was next on his list.

37 LOST CONTROL

The next morning as Ivy read the newspaper, Holly glanced over her coffee mug at the front page. Without her glasses she couldn't read more than the headlines. A picture of a mangled Lincoln Continental caught her eye. She squinted to read the caption, but all she could make out was a capital "P". She got an uneasy feeling, put down her mug, and reached for her reading glasses. Leaning across the table she read the car accident photo caption and gasped.

"What's wrong?" Ivy asked, lowering the paper.

Holly grabbed the paper from her and pointed. "That's Teresa's car."

Ivy looked at the photo. "That's why you didn't hear back from her last night. She was in a car accident."

"What if it wasn't an accident?" Holly bit her lip. "What have I done?"

"Don't jump to conclusions. The caption says the driver lost control of the car."

"And that she's in critical condition at Hackensack Hospital," Holly burst into tears.

"I'm so sorry, but you can't blame yourself."

"Well, I do," Holly sobbed.

Ivy sat quietly for a moment or two. "You know what you have to do?"

"What?" Holly sniffed.

"You have to call Manelli."

Holly groaned.

"You have to." Ivy went over to the refrigerator where she had affixed Manelli's business card with a guardian angel magnet she'd gotten Holly on a visit to St. Patrick's Cathedral. She got the card and the phone and handed them both to Holly, who heaved a deep sigh, looked at the card and began to punch in the number.

38 STEVEN AND ELAINE HAGEL

Detective Manelli had only spoken to Steven Hagel the day of his mother's murder. Hagel had appeared genuinely distraught, and unable to think of anyone who might want to harm his mother. Still, destined to inherit millions, he, his son and his daughter, all had much stronger motives to kill Edna Hagel than Leonelle Gomez. They also had means and opportunity.

Manelli pulled up in front of the Steven Hagel residence located just a few blocks from Edna Hagel's home. Compared to Edna's modest colonial, Steven's home was palatial. Four, two-story white pillars fronted the sand-colored brick façade. A huge chandelier hung just above the second-story, wrought-iron railed terrace positioned over the front entrance. Large urns filled with lush plantings framed the double-door front entrance. Edna Hagel's home whispered wealth. Steven Hagel's home screamed money.

Manelli rang the doorbell. A tall woman in a gray maid's uniform with a white-starched apron answered the door.

"I'm Detective Manelli. I have an appointment to see Steven Hagel."

"Yes, sir. Come in," the woman said, a trace of a West Indian accent in her voice. "This way, please," she said, leading him into the living room. "Have a seat. Mr. Hagel will be with you in a moment. Can I get you something to drink, sir?"

"No, thank you," he answered.

As the maid glided out of the room, Manelli surveyed his surroundings. The spacious room had a palette of only two colors, blue and white. Robin's egg blue walls contrasted sharply with plush white rugs. White satin upholstery covered most of the furniture. Accents included azure pillows and cobalt blue vases. Worried he might soil something, Manelli wondered how anyone could actually enjoy spending time in this room.

Before he could decide where to sit, Steven Hagel appeared. He extended his hand to shake Manelli's.

"Have a seat, Detective. I'm hoping you're here to tell me you have definitive proof that the Gomez woman killed my mother."

"I'm afraid not, sir. You and I spoke only briefly before, and I just want to clarify some things. I have a few additional questions I wanted to ask you."

"Ask me? Why?"

"Perhaps if I can refine the timeline of when and where everyone was, I might be better able to come up with definitive evidence."

"I guess that's understandable. Okay. Let's sit down." Hagel pointed to the two white sofas that framed the fireplace. Once they were seated, he asked, "So what do you want to know?"

"Were there any deliveries, any repairman scheduled at your mother's the day before or the day her body was discovered?"

"No. Not that I scheduled. If the Gomez woman scheduled anything for my mother, you would have to ask her."

"Okay," Manelli said looking at his notepad. "Now, the day your mother's body was discovered, you, your wife and your daughter dropped by your mother's in the morning. Is that correct?"

"Yes. But I told you all that before."

"Yes, sir. Where was your son?"

"Phillip was at the store."

"What time did he leave for the store?"

Steven Hagel's eyes widened. He stood up. "Are you suggesting my son may have killed his grandmother?" Hagel sputtered.

"No, sir. As I said, I just need to know when and where everyone was at the time of the murder."

Hagel stood staring at Manelli. "My son left for the store after breakfast, around nine o'clock."

"Who can I talk to at the store to confirm his time of arrival there?"

At this Steven Hagel stood up. "This conversation is over," he shouted. "You get out of my house."

"Steven? What's going on?"

Both Manelli and Steven Hagel turned to see Elaine Hagel standing in the doorway. Dressed in crème-colored pants and a royal blue blouse, she matched the room perfectly Manelli thought.

"I'll tell you what's going on here, Elaine. Instead of building a case against that Gomez woman, the detective here is investigating us, that's what," Hagel said waving his arms. "He's asking questions about Phillip. Can you believe it?"

"Steven. Steven, please calm down," Elaine Hagel said in a soothing tone, patting his arm. The gesture seemed to have a calming effect on him. "Darling, your tea and biscuits are ready in the dining room. Why don't you go in and I'll speak to the detective?"

Steven Hagel stroked his wife's hand. "Okay. You're right, as always, love." He turned and glared at Manelli. "And you! Don't come back here again. You can talk to my lawyer from now on."

"Now, Steven…" Elaine Hagel sounded more like an indulgent mother than a wife. "Go ahead to the dining room, dear, and I'll be right there." She gently turned her husband around and with her hand on his back, she firmly guided him out of the room. She stood watching as he walked down the hall, and then turned back to Manelli.

"I'm so sorry, Detective. I'm Elaine Hagel." She extended her hand and smiled as if he were a welcomed guest in her home. "You have to excuse Steven. This has been so difficult for him. He's just not himself."

"I'm sorry, too, Ma'am, but I'm just doing my job and I do have some questions."

"Perhaps I could answer them for you. Why don't you have a seat?"

"Okay. Mrs. Hagel. Can you tell me where you were the day Mrs. Hagel's body was discovered?"

"I remember the day very well. I insisted Steven take the day off so we could go pick out a graduation present for our daughter, Dina. She graduated from Princeton cum laude. We're very proud of her," Elaine said flashing Manelli a smile. "Anyway, we got up, had breakfast, and then around ten o'clock Steven, Dina and I went over to Edna's house. You see, Steven was devoted to his mother. He visited her almost every day. So that morning, he wanted to visit her first before we went shopping. We dropped by there, then went to the jeweler's. After that we had lunch at Buco. We came home around three."

"And where was your son?"

"Phillip? Phillip was at the store all day and came home around 5:30. We all had dinner at seven and watched TV until..." Elaine Hagel hesitated, lowering her head. After a moment, she lifted her chin and looked directly at Manelli, "until we got the call from the police."

"So you, your daughter and your husband were all home after 3:00 PM. Your daughter didn't go out again?"

"No."

"How can you be sure? This is a big house."

"The children always tell us when they're leaving. I know they're not really children, but they are *my* children. Just out of simple courtesy, they always let us know when they're going out and when to expect them back. They learned from their teenage days that was much easier than having us hunt them down and embarrass them." Elaine Hagel giggled and fluttered her eyelashes. She was charming and quite beautiful, and Manelli suspected she knew it.

"Thank you, Mrs. Hagel. I appreciate your cooperation. I will need to speak to Dina and Phillip myself. Are they home?"

"No, they're at the store downtown taking care of the business. They're such good kids, Detective. Steven's been so distraught. They've really stepped up and taken on responsibility for the business since my mother-in-law's death. Would you like me to call them and tell them you'll be dropping by? We all certainly want to assist the police in any way we can."

"Thank you. Yes, please tell them I'll be down to the store this afternoon," Manelli said standing up.

Elaine Hagel walked Manelli to the door. She placed her hand gently on his arm and gave him a warm smile. "Again, Detective. My husband is just not himself right now. Please don't hold it against him."

"I appreciate your help, Mrs. Hagel. Have a nice day."

As he walked to his car, Manelli wondered what this gracious and beautiful woman was doing with the rather boorish, homely Steven Hagel. He turned to look at the house again. *I guess money does change everything.*

In the car, Manelli checked his phone, saw there was a message and recognized Holly Donnelly's phone number. He doubted she was taking him up on his invitation to chat. Immediately, he called his voice mail. Expecting to hear Ivy's voice, he was surprised to hear Holly's.

"Detective Manelli, this is Holly Donnelly. Something has happened that I think you need to know about. Could you please call me?"

Manelli hung up and turned on the ignition. If she broke down and called me herself, something must be really wrong. He pulled away from the curb and headed straight to Holly Donnelly's house.

39 NO COINCIDENCE

When Holly heard the doorbell, she thought Ivy must have forgotten the key when she took Lucky for a walk. In the hall she stopped when she saw Detective Manelli through the glass panel. *Why didn't he just call me back?* She took a deep breath and opened the door.

"Hi. I didn't expect you to come over," she said.

"I was just a few blocks away when I got your message."

"Come in. Let's go in here," Holly said, leading the way to the kitchen.

Manelli followed her. She gestured to a chair and sat down herself. He sat and took out his pad and pen without saying a word. She exhaled deeply and began.

"Last week I had lunch with an old friend of mine who works for Novardo Development." She picked up the newspaper from the table and pointed to the picture of the demolished Lincoln Continental. "That's her car. She's in critical condition at Hackensack Hospital."

Manelli looked from the newspaper to Holly. "Why did you think you needed to tell me your friend had a car accident?"

"You said you don't believe in coincidences. Listen to this." Holly hit the replay button on the answering machine. When the recording ended, Manelli looked at Holly, but said nothing, so she continued. "Ivy and I went out to lunch after you left yesterday, and that message was waiting for me when we got back. By the time I returned the call, she'd left work, and now she's in the hospital."

"Tell me about the conversation you had with her," Manelli said jotting something in his notepad. After Holly finished summarizing her discussion with Teresa, he looked up. "Anything else you can think of?"

"No," Holly answered.

"If you do think of anything, you know what to do," Manelli said as he got up and headed to the front door.

Holly followed him. As he approached the door, she asked, "No lectures? No I-told-you-so's?"

"No. I probably can't make you feel any worse than you already do."

"What will you do now?"

"My job." He opened the door, hesitated, then turned back around to face her. "You did the right thing by calling me. If this wasn't an accident, you could be in real danger. Don't go anywhere alone. Anything else comes up, you call me."

Holly just nodded. Manelli turned and walked out the door, pulling it shut behind him. Holly breathed in deeply, struggling to find air in the vacuum left by his departure.

40 DINA HAGEL

What has she stumbled into? Manelli wondered on his drive to Hagel Printing and Paper Company. No, this could not be a coincidence. He was relieved that Holly was shaken by the car accident. Up to this point he hadn't been sure if she was just paying him lip service when she said she was done meddling in this investigation. He hoped her tear-stained face and dispirited demeanor meant she would not discuss the case with anyone else. But now he had a nagging worry that she actually might be in danger. Did Mrs. Hagel's murderer cause Teresa Nowicki's accident, and if so did he or she know Teresa was talking to Holly?

Did this murder really tie back to the Novardo development deal? From the beginning, Manelli felt this murder had a personal motive behind it. It did not feel like a murder orchestrated by a corporation. The framing of Juan Alvarez and Leonelle Gomez had to have been planned by someone who knew the day-to-day workings of the house. When he got back to the office, he would have his assistant start researching Novardo and its two partners.

Manelli found a parking space directly in front of Hagel Printing and Paper. The four-story brick building had a store at its base. He pulled open the glass door and entered the cramped storefront. To the left, an antique desk and chairs retained some of their former elegance, reminiscent of an earlier time when women actually bought personalized stationery that was printed for them. Manelli would bet that Mrs. Hagel had picked out the furniture herself. Behind the counter, a young Hispanic woman was working at a computer terminal, the one item in the storefront not purchased in the 1950's.

"I'm Detective Manelli here to see Dina and Phillip Hagel," he said to the keyboarder.

The young woman picked up her phone and punched in three digits. "Detective Manelli to see you." She put down the phone and pointing to the antique chairs said, "Have a seat. Ms. Hagel will be right out."

Manelli remained standing. It was just a minute before the young woman appeared. Extending a well-manicured hand, wearing a hard-to-miss diamond ring, she said, "I'm Dina Hagel. My mother told me you'd be stopping by. Why don't we go to my office?"

Manelli followed her through a doorway that led to the printing shop. Machinery whirred as they passed by printers that were spitting out color brochures. Two men appeared to be examining the color quality. The printing shop seemed to be more modernized than the front retail store. Dina led Manelli to a corner office that was clean and uncluttered.

"Have a seat," she said. Not as beautiful as her mother, she was, however, as poised and well-mannered and appeared to be as crisp and sharp as the Armani suit she wore. "Now, how can I help you, Detective?"

"Ms. Hagel, could you tell me your whereabouts the day your grandmother's body was discovered?"

Dina pursed her lips as if in pain, sighed and began. "Yes, of course. My father and mother and I were going to the jewelry store. They wanted me to pick out a piece of jewelry as a present for my graduation from college. We visited my grandmother..." Here Dina broke off, reached for a tissue, and dabbed at her eyes. "I'm sorry. That was the last time I saw her."

"I'm very sorry for your loss, Ms. Hagel," Manelli offered and waited for her to continue.

Again, she sighed audibly, and said, "We were at Grandma's for about half an hour. Then we left, went to the store, had lunch and came home. We all had dinner together, Mother, Daddy, Phillip and I. After dinner, I went upstairs and viewed my Facebook account and texted some of my friends. I was about to go to bed when the phone rang." Dina lowered her face, bringing the tissue to her eyes again.

"Can you think of anyone who would want to kill your grandmother?"

"No. Absolutely not," she snapped. "Grandma was a tough business woman, first and foremost, but a real professional. Everyone respected her."

"Anything unusual happen during the last few weeks? Did your grandmother confide any worries or concerns to you?"

"No. Not really."

"Is your brother here, Ms. Hagel?"

"No, Phillip had to visit one of our clients. He probably won't be back today."

Manelli took out a business card and handed it to Dina. "Would you have him call me please?" He stood up. "Thank you for your time. If you think of anything that might have some bearing on the case, please call me."

"Of course, Detective. We all certainly want to assist the police in any way we can," Dina said, getting up.

"No, need to get up," he said. "I can see myself out. Good day, Ms. Hagel."

Manelli turned and re-entered the print shop. The workmen looked up at him. When he made eye-contact, they quickly returned to their printing jobs. Back at the storefront Manelli walked over to the young woman who was typing at her keyboard. He took out a business card and handed it to her.

"What's your name?" he asked.

"Maria Colon."

"Maria, what time did Phillip Hagel come to work last Thursday?"

Maria Colon's eyes widened. "Uh--I--I can't say."

"Why not?"

"Everyone comes in through the back door from the parking lot. I don't really know when anyone gets here." Maria looked over at her computer screen.

"Okay, Maria. I gave my card to Ms. Hagel, but I want you to give the one I just gave you to Phillip. Could you be sure he gets it? And please tell him I need to talk to him to find out if he was aware of anything suspicious that might help us solve his grandmother's murder." The typist just nodded.

From out on the street, Manelli looked back through the plate glass storefront windows and saw Dina Hagel walking over to the typist's desk. *That was some performance.* In spite of all the sobbing, Manelli hadn't seen any evidence of genuine tears--no smeared mascara, no streaked face make-up. Dina Hagel even used her mother's exact words--*we all certainly want to assist the police in any way we can.* He couldn't wait to speak to Phillip Hagel.

41 GROUNDHOG DAY

After Manelli left, Holly moped around the house the rest of the day and went to bed early. When she awoke the next morning, she discovered all of her pillows, as well as the comforter, on the floor. She looked at the clock. 5:12 AM. She got dressed and as she headed downstairs she heard Ivy.

"I'm up. I'll walk with you."

An occasional jogger and a few couples passed them as they walked. Because there were so few people in the park at this time of the morning, Holly let Lucky off the leash. They circled round the back end of the park reaching Crescent Drive. As they neared the Hagel residence, Lucky picked up her nose, sniffed the air and took off at a run. Too late, Holly spotted a brown ball of fur lumbering up the Hagel driveway.

"Oh, no! Not again," she shouted, running after Lucky, already in hot pursuit of the fur ball. She stopped at the foot of the Hagel driveway in front of the yellow police tape.

"What was that?" Ivy asked coming up along side her.

"A ground hog. They're overrunning the neighborhood and with this property pretty much abandoned for over a week, they've probably moved right in here. The bad news is that Lucky caught one in my yard a few weeks ago and she actually killed it. I'm afraid she thinks it's great sport now. What am I gonna do?"

"You can't cross the police barrier."

"I should never have taken her off the leash," Holly said, looking up the driveway. "I've got to get her. Squirrels are one thing, but I'm always afraid those bigger animals will bite her." She looked at her watch, then back at Ivy. "Look, it's five thirty in the morning. I haven't seen a patrol car in or around the park since they made cutbacks to the police department a year ago. No one will even know I was back there. You wait here."

"Holly, don't do this," Ivy pleaded.

"I'll only be a minute." She looked around and as soon as she was sure no one was in sight, she moved up the drive quickly, leaving Ivy on the sidewalk.

When she reached the back patio, Holly looked around. It occurred to her that she was trespassing, and just in case someone was staying in the house, she better let them know why she was in the yard. She knocked loudly on the back door. When no one answered, she peered in the back kitchen window. The place looked the same as the day she and Ivy had discovered Mrs. Hagel's body. Relieved to find the house unoccupied, she turned around and scanned the backyard. She didn't see Lucky anywhere. Not a weed or shrub moved. She stepped down from the back stoop, walked over to the shed and up the two steps to the start of the garden path.

As she surveyed the property, she understood why the neighbors to the south and east wouldn't have seen or heard anything the day of the murder. The arborvitae separating the Hagel's from Louie Brunetti's property and the dense foliage of the trees between the Hagel house and the split level to the east completely screened the Hagel property. The only house with a clear view was the house to the west, the house belonging to the neighbors who left the day of the murder. Maybe Ivy was right. Maybe their leaving was not happenstance.

Holly started down the gravel footpath. Suddenly, in the opposite back corner of the yard she spotted a bush wriggling sporadically. She didn't want to call Lucky. Even though the neighbors couldn't see her, they could be in their backyards and she didn't want to draw attention to herself. Besides, if Lucky had the groundhog cornered, she was unlikely to come on command.

Holly struggled with her footing, but managed to make her way through some tall weeds to the shimmying bush. Lucky started barking when she saw her. She had the ground hog cornered between the bush and the back fence. She lunged at it, and the groundhog reared up on its hind legs, swinging its front paws at Lucky. Holly was relieved to see the groundhog was not a fully grown adult, but she knew better than to get any closer.

As she pondered what to do, the ground hog got back on all fours, and in one rapid motion, Lucky sprang, grabbed it in her teeth by the nape of the neck, and gave it one sharp shake. She released the ground hog, which landed belly up, remaining motionless.

Holly shivered, then called Lucky to her. The dog came right over, tail wagging. She sat down in front of Holly, waiting for her treat, clearly pleased with herself. "No more off-the-leash for you?" Holly said shaking her head. She connected the leash to the dog's collar and dug in her pocket for a treat. "I guess I should be happy that at least you don't eat them," Holly said grimacing. Lucky chomped the treat with relish.

Turning to face the house, Holly realized she'd never been this far back in the yard. Relaxed now that she had Lucky on the leash, she stood admiring the property. She decided to take the path that branched off through the opposite side of the yard and see if that would lead her back to the patio.

She and Lucky made their way past perennial beds in varying degrees of bloom. As they rounded a turn, Holly stopped and held Lucky back. The path was blocked with some serious overgrowth, most of it from the Gertrude Jekyll rose, the one with the wicked thorns.

"C'mon, Lucky. We can't go this way." They turned retracing their steps leading to the back corner of the yard and climbed through weeds returning to the footpath that led back to the patio. As they passed the shed, Holly looked over at the red shrub rose bush she and Ivy admired the day Mrs. Hagel died. Just a week later, the bush needed deadheading. As she got closer, she caught a glimpse of something on the ground beneath the bush--something red, but definitely not a rose.

"Sit, Lucky," she said, as she knelt down and carefully parted the branches to see if she could tell what it was. *A matchbook cover.* She controlled herself as she reached for it, trying to avoid any contact with thorns. She carefully retrieved the matchbook by its edges, not wanting to get any fingerprints on the front or back.

She stood up and examined the cover. The name, Evergreen Construction and a phone number appeared on the front, a fir tree logo stamped on the back. That logo seemed familiar, but she wasn't sure where she'd seen it. When she opened the matchbook, she got really excited because inside was a hand-written phone number. Holly put the matchbook in a plastic bag she had in her pocket for collecting dog poop and headed back around the side of the house to the driveway.

At the corner of the house, Holly stopped. She spotted Ivy across the street watching the Canadian Geese swimming in the duck pond. She gave a whistle and Ivy turned, appearing relieved at the sight of Holly and Lucky. She walked back from the edge of the pond to the curb directly across from the house. Holly mouthed the word "Clear", pointing first to the left, then the right. Ivy scanned the street and the park. When she was sure that no one was around, she nodded and waved for them to come out.

"Don't ever do that to me again," Ivy said as they headed home. "You're lucky no policemen were patrolling. Why are you smiling?"

Holly increased her pace as she said, "Let's get home. I think I found a clue."

41 FACEBOOK

“Good Morning, Detective,” said Officer Yolanda Rivera from her desk in front of Manelli’s office.

“Morning, Rivera,” he answered. ”Have you solved the case yet?”

“No,” she replied, chuckling. “But I have a few things for you that might help.”

“C’mon in,” he said, opening the door and walking over to his desk.

The uniformed Rivera picked up her Microsoft Surface Notebook and followed. Her thick brown hair was pulled back in a ponytail. She wore no jewelry and no make-up, except for a light coat of lip gloss.

Manelli hand-picked the no-nonsense, 28-year old to be his assistant two years ago, when her computer skills helped solve a case he was working. A rookie, not even assigned to his case, she’d read his reports and did some research on her own. When she approached him with what she’d learned, Manelli immediately set out to have her assigned to his department. He knew initiative was one thing you couldn’t teach someone. Either you had it, or you didn’t. Yolanda Rivera had it.

“What ya got?” he asked leaning back in his chair.

Yolanda’s unpainted finger nails tapped her screen. “First of all, I contacted the Paramus Police Department. Turns out one of my fellow cadets from the Academy just started working there. He told me the Nowicki car crash was no accident. A witness called the day after it happened. A woman who’d been driving a few car lengths in front of Nowicki’s

Continental reported that as she was driving, she happened to look in her rearview mirror. She saw a white box truck veer into her lane, and it looked to her like the box truck cut the Continental off. She didn't think too much of it until she saw the paper the next day. She, of course, didn't get the license number of the truck, but the Paramus police found a white box truck abandoned on a Paramus side street later that day. The truck was reported stolen that morning by Franklin Plumbing in Paramus."

"Anything on the driver?"

"Just that he was a white male. The witness said she couldn't identify him."

"Too bad, but at least we now know the crash was no accident."

"Looks that way."

"What else?"

"I spent a little time on Facebook yesterday and found something I think you're going to like."

"What?"

Yolanda slid her finger across the screen, then entered some rapid keystrokes. She turned the tablet so Manelli could see the screen. A group shot of about fifteen twenty-somethings with their glasses raised in a toast filled the screen.

Manelli shrugged. "What am I looking at?"

"You see the boy in the center? That's Phillip Hagel. This photo was posted on his Facebook page the day of Edna Hagel's murder. It could provide him with an alibi."

"Then why did his father, mother and sister say he was at the store?"

"That's the question I asked myself."

"Anyone tell you, you're going to make a good detective?"

"You, sir, thank you." Rivera smiled and continued. "I called Phillip's cellphone all afternoon yesterday and since I got here this morning. It's going straight to voicemail. If he has an alibi, why wouldn't he want to talk to us and get cleared?"

"Also, a good question," Manelli mused. "Keep trying to reach him."

"I will. One more thing. I can't find anything to suggest that Novardo Development or the two partners have been involved in anything remotely criminal. The partners don't even have a parking ticket between them."

"Nice work, Rivera."

"Thank you, sir." Rivera stood up, sliding her fingers across her notebook as she returned to her desk.

Manelli's cellphone rang. He looked at the screen. A number he didn't recognize.

"Manelli," he answered.

"Hello, Detective?"

"Yes."

"This is Maria Colon. You gave me your card yesterday when you came to see Dina Hagel."

"Yes, I remember you."

"I don't know if I should be calling, but..." The woman hesitated.

"Ms. Colon, you must have information that you think is important or you wouldn't have called me. Anything you tell me will be held in the strictest confidence."

"I heard Dina talking on the phone after you left. They don't know where Phillip is."

"The family?"

"Yeah. It sounds like he just disappeared or something."

"When?"

"I'm not sure. He hasn't been to the office since the day before Mrs. Hagel was murdered. All of us from the office--we went to the funeral. I saw Phillip drive away from the cemetery, but he wasn't at the repast luncheon. That's the last time I saw him."

"Ms. Colon, thank you. You did the right thing by calling me. This is important information. My advice to you is don't tell anyone, not even your mother, that you talked to me, okay?"

"Okay," she giggled.

"And if you learn anything else, you call me."

"All right. I will. Good-bye."

That explains it. With Phillip missing, the Hagels don't know he had an alibi. They may even be afraid he did kill his grandmother, so they're covering for him. Or, maybe he left the party and actually killed Edna Hagel.

"Rivera," Manelli shouted. He refused to use the intercom buzzer.

Officer Rivera appeared in the doorway.

"You think you can do your Face Page thing and find some likely places Phillip Hagel might be hanging out."

"That's Facebook, sir, and I'll get right on it," she said. The phone rang and Rivera turned to see which line was lit. "That's your line, sir. You want me to pick it up?"

"No, I'll get it." Manelli picked up the handset. "Manelli."

"This is Steven Hagel. I want that Donnelly woman arrested," Hagel snarled.

"On what charges, Mr. Hagel?"

"Trespassing. I just emailed you a picture of Donnelly in my mother's backyard this morning. That woman had no business being there. I want something done about her."

"Okay, Mr. Hagel. I'll take care of it."

"You better!" The phone clicked in Manelli's ear. He checked his email and opened the one from Steven Hagel. Next he clicked on the attachment. No doubt about it. Holly Donnelly was standing on Mrs. Hagel's patio, and the time stamp on the photo showed today's date.

Manelli shook his head, got up, grabbed his jacket and stopped at Rivera's desk. "Have a patrol car meet me at 7 Park Place."

43 BUSTED

"Okay," Ivy said once inside the house. "What did you find?"

Holly pulled the plastic bag containing the matchbook out of her pocket.

"Where'd you find that?"

"Near the shed in Edna's yard."

"But what makes you think it's a clue?" Ivy sat down at the kitchen table.

"Look," Holly giggled. She pulled the matchbook out of the bag by its edges, careful not to touch the cover. Opening the matchbook, she pointed to the phone number written on the inside.

"Anyone could have dropped that, even Juan. You said he sometimes does day work for other landscapers."

"Maybe, but he doesn't smoke," said Holly, returning the matchbook back to the plastic bag. "And maybe--just maybe--that number belongs to the murderer."

Ivy frowned. "Why didn't the policed find it?"

"I thought about that." Holly sat down, dropping the plastic bag in the center of the table. "The day of the murder the rose bush was still in full bloom. The red matchbook cover probably blended with the red roses. A week later the blooms are spent. Any flowers left on the bush are dark and faded."

"Okay, but what if it was dropped after the murder?"

"How could it be? The place is cordoned off."

"Right. So you're going to call Manelli, right?"

Holly sighed. "I guess I have to. But I'd love to know whose phone number that is inside the matchbook."

"Why don't you call it?"

"What if it's Steven Hagel's?"

"So? Just hang up."

"Ivy, you do know what caller ID is, don't you? If he sees my name on his phone screen, he might make good on his threat to call the police. I already have to admit to Manelli that I crossed the police barrier. I don't want Steven Hagel calling him to say I'm harassing him."

"Maybe Steven Hagel doesn't have Caller ID."

"Unlikely. Most all phones do."

"Really?"

Holly shook her head. "You have to be the most technologically unsavvy person on the planet."

"Guilty. But I don't think it's hurt me," Ivy sniffed. "So call Manelli."

Holly frowned. "Wait. I know what. I'll do a reverse lookup on the Internet." Holly placed the matchbook on the plastic bag, picked up the bag and headed downstairs to her office.

"What's reverse lookup?" asked Ivy trailing after her.

"The opposite of the phone book. You enter the number and reverse look-up tells you who the number belongs to."

"How do you know these things?"

"How do you not know these things?"

Holly sat down and turned on the computer. She located the reverse look-up site and typed in the number. "Here goes," she said as she hit the enter key.

"Aha," Holly said. Ivy peered over her shoulder and saw "Hagel Printing and Paper" on the screen.

"So a landscaper had the Hagel number on his matchbook? That doesn't prove anything."

"At the very least it means that a landscaper was in Mrs. Hagel's backyard."

"But like I said before, maybe Juan did some work for them and he dropped it there." Ivy walked over to the armchair opposite the work station and sat down.

Holly squinched her nose and looked up at the ceiling. "Why would Juan have the Hagel's company number? He was working for Edna. What if an Evergreen landscaper dropped it? What was he doing there?"

"Maybe Mrs. Hagel just called that landscaper and asked him to come over and give her a price. Maybe she realized that working with a guy like Juan was too much for her, and she just needed a crew to come in once a week and take care of everything."

"You're probably right." Holly started the computer shutdown and looked over at Ivy. "I guess this wasn't much of a clue after all."

"So go call Manelli."

"What for?" Holly shrugged. "We just concluded this matchbook probably doesn't mean anything."

"I think you should call him about it anyway."

"You just want me to talk to him."

"That's not it," Ivy moved forward to the edge of the chair. "You haven't already forgotten about Teresa's accident and the fact that you may be in danger, have you?"

"No." Holly swallowed hard and closed the laptop.

"Call Manelli. Let him decide if the matchbook is a clue or not."

"Yuck. That means I have to admit I crossed a police line and listen to another lecture. Let's just forget it. Pretend it never happened."

"But what if it is a clue, and it can save Leonelle?"

"Oh, brother!" Holly jumped up. "You're making this really difficult. I'll tell you what. Let's go upstairs, have breakfast, and see if there are any vegetables to harvest out in the garden. After that, *you* can call Manelli. You didn't cross the police tape."

"Deal," Ivy said smiling. "I forgot about breakfast until just now. I'm starved."

"Really?"

Ivy just rolled her eyes and went upstairs. Holly looked at the matchbook sitting beside the laptop and frowned. *Just in case*. She placed the matchbook inside the plastic bag and took it upstairs.

After breakfast, the sisters went out to the shed. Holly handed Ivy the watering can. "You water the pots in front. I'll check the back bed for zucchini."

Holly had just reached the vegetable patch when she heard Lucky barking furiously.

"Holly!"

Holly turned to see Ivy running towards her, pale-faced and unsmiling.

"What's wrong? Is Lucky all right?"

"Yes, Lucky's fine. But Manelli's here."

"Did you tell him about the matchbook?"

"No. I didn't even think about it."

"What? Why?"

"He says he needs to talk to you."

"So? He's been here to talk to me before."

"This is different. He's here with a squad car and they have their lights flashing."

"Where is he?"

"Waiting at the front door."

As she reached the hallway, through the glass panels of the door, Holly could see Manelli's face wore a dour expression. She opened the door and saw a uniformed policeman standing on the walk a few feet behind Manelli. The flashing lights on the patrol car unnerved her. *Ivy's right. This can't be good.*

"We were going to call you," she said.

"Really?" Manelli said.

"Would you like to come in?"

"That won't be necessary," he replied.

Ivy came up behind her. "Detective Manelli, we were just talking about you this morning. Can I get you a cup of coffee?"

"No," he replied, barely looking at Ivy. "Ms. Donnelly, do you recall our last conversation?"

"Yes," Holly answered.

"And what did I tell you at that time, Ms. Donnelly?" he asked, looking skyward.

Holly's apprehension turned to annoyance. Why didn't he just say what he came to say and quit with this supercilious banter?

"Detective, you know what you told me," Holly began.

"Yes, I know what I told you, but I don't think you do, so I was wondering if you could tell me what I said."

Holly rolled her eyes and said, "That I could be in danger."

"Very good, Ms. Donnelly," Manelli said with an exaggerated smile. "What else did I say?"

"Not to go anywhere alone and to call you if anything came up."

"Right again. Now what part of that didn't you understand?"

"Look, Detective, we already said we were planning to call you today..." Holly started to explain.

"Isn't that something?" Manelli cut her off. "You were going to call me, and here I've come calling on you. Don't you think that's quite a coincidence, Ms. Donnelly? Wait. You don't believe in coincidences do you?"

Holly glared at Manelli. When she didn't reply, he continued. "Do you think that my being here might have something to do with your crossing a police barricade at a crime scene and trespassing on the Hagel property this morning?"

Busted. Holly put her hands in her pockets to hide the tremor that started in her fingertips. How did he know she was there? She was positive no one had seen her. When Holly didn't respond to Manelli's question, Ivy stepped forward. "Detective, this morning Holly and I were walking the dog when Lucky spotted a groundhog and ran into the Hagel yard. Holly just went in the yard to get Lucky."

"Seriously?" he said to Ivy in a more gentle tone than the one he'd used with Holly. "You really expect me to believe that out of all the yards you walked past, your dog picked the Hagel yard to run into?"

"Yes--yes," Ivy stammered. "With the property unoccupied, the groundhogs ..."

"Nice try," Manelli stopped her. "I won't arrest you for lying to a police officer because I know you're just trying to cover for your sister."

"Are you here to arrest me?" Holly asked, her eyes widening.

"Yes."

"Arrest me?" she exclaimed. "I haven't done anything."

"How about trespassing, obstruction of justice, interfering with a police investigation, maybe tampering with evidence?" he asked.

"Well, when you put it in those terms...."

"Wait a minute," Ivy objected. "Please don't do this, Detective. Honestly, we were planning to call you and tell you..."

"And," Holly pushed Ivy behind her, "tell you that I crossed the police tape."

"A confession?" He raised his eyebrows.

"I just went to get the dog," Holly replied, feeling like a mouse in the paws of a cat, a rather large cat.

Manelli laughed out loud and got his phone out. "So you're not denying it's you in this photo taken this morning in the Hagel backyard?"

Holly looked at the photo. "Yes, it's me."

"All alone and no dog in sight?"

Holly sighed. *What's the point of answering?*

"Officer Jensen, cuff Ms. Donnelly and read her her rights."

"You're kidding, right?" Holly hoped this was a joke and that he would say he just came by to scare her.

"Wrong," he said.

The young patrolman approached and Lucky growled. He hesitated.

"Ivy, take her inside, please," Holly said.

Ivy got the dog by the collar and guided her inside closing the door. Officer Jensen stepped behind Holly and gently placed the cuffs on her. "You have the right to remain silent..."

"Did you hear that Ms. Donnelly?" Manelli cut in. "I suggest you exercise that right."

Holly's cheeks burned. She turned her head, refusing to even look at him. *And I was actually beginning to think I could trust you.* At that moment she hated him.

Manelli set off down the walk and opened the gate. Officer Jensen continued to read Holly her Miranda rights as he guided her behind Manelli. She didn't say another word. She knew she'd screwed up, and there was nothing she could do but go along quietly.

44 HOPELESS

On the drive to the police station Holly's mind was racing. She had so many unanswered questions. Who took that photograph of her in Edna's backyard? If someone was inside the house, wouldn't they have called the police right then and there? If the police had been called, they would have arrived before she left, and she would have been caught red-handed.

She was sure no one in the houses to the east and the south could see into the yard. That meant someone had to have been in the house to the west. That was the only possibility--the only place with a clear view of the Hagel backyard. Had the vacationing neighbors returned? Did they call the Hagels?

The car transporting Holly pulled into the Pineland Park Police station lot and parked. As Officer Jensen assisted her out of the car, she shouted to Manelli who had parked a few spaces away. "Detective, can I talk to you?"

Manelli grimaced, but walked over to her anyway. Holly looked at the patrolman and said, "Privately?" Manelli laughed under his breath, looked over at Jensen and said, "Give us a minute, would ya?"

"All right, what is it?" he asked looking at his watch.

"Look, I know I wasn't completely honest with you in the beginning," Holly began.

"Another admission? This just keeps getting better and better," Manelli taunted.

"When I went in Mrs. Hagel's backyard, I knocked on the door. No one was in that house. The only house with a view into the backyard was from the house next door on the west side, the house supposedly vacant because the neighbors left on vacation the morning of the murder."

"How do you know that?" Manelli asked.

Holly decided further lies were futile. "Leonelle Gomez's lawyer gave me a copy of the police report." Manelli just shook his head, gritting his teeth.

"Who called you?" she asked. When Manelli didn't answer, she continued. "Because if it was the Hagels, someone called them and let them know I was there. The only place a picture could have been taken from is the house that's supposed to be vacant."

Manelli started to walk away. "Wait," Holly pleaded. "I know you think I'm just enjoying playing amateur sleuth. I'm not. This isn't about me. It's about Leonelle Gomez. No matter what the evidence shows, I know she didn't kill Mrs. Hagel. Her lawyer is a total waste. He just wants her to plead guilty. She's got no one on her side, and she's got no chance if *you* consider this investigation closed."

"You're right," he said. Holly held her breath. Manelli turned back to face her. "I do think you're enjoying playing amateur sleuth. Maybe a night in our holding cell will cure you of that."

Holly closed her eyes, leaning back against the patrol car, feeling any hope she was clinging to exit with the breath she exhaled. When she opened her eyes, Manelli had already walked away. Officer Jensen came beside her and escorted her into the building where she was handed over to a policewoman for booking.

45 CLUE CONFIRMED

Back inside, Ivy returned to the kitchen, uncertain what to do. She'd felt a bit relieved after Manelli told her she could come down to the station the next day at 9:00 AM to pick Holly up. He actually winked when he said Holly would be safer downtown at police headquarters. *I knew he liked her.*

The empty house itself seemed subdued without Holly. Ivy sat down at the table and Lucky came over to her resting her head on Ivy's knee. "Don't worry, girl. Everything will work out. You'll see." Lucky's tail thumped the floor.

As she continued to pet the dog, Ivy spotted the matchbook inside its plastic cover on the counter. She remembered how excited Holly had been just a few hours ago, reveling in her discovery of a "clue". That was Holly--always enthusiastic--ever the optimist. Her enthusiasm was contagious.

Wait a minute. Why had Holly cut her off when she was about to mention the matchbook? If they had turned it over, maybe Manelli wouldn't have arrested her. It didn't make sense. Maybe she should call Manelli and tell him about the matchbook. *No, maybe not.* Holly had warned her never to call him again.

Enough. Ivy jumped up. She'd go crazy just sitting around. The best thing she could do was keep busy. She went outside and spent the next few hours puttering around the flower beds. The work took her mind off Holly and the case--for a while at least. When her stomach started gurgling, she went inside. The clock said 4:17 PM. No wonder she was hungry. She'd skipped lunch.

After she ate, she took a shower. The cool water relaxed her. As she dressed, she pondered what to do next. She really wanted to put on her nightgown, get in bed and pull the covers over her head, but it was too early. Whenever she felt like this, she always called Holly for advice. Without her to call, she felt quite lost.

Ivy slowly walked downstairs, wondering how Holly was doing. Was she in a jail cell? She felt certain Detective Manelli wouldn't put her in danger. But spending a night in jail, in the best of circumstances, couldn't be pleasant. The more she thought about it, the more mixed her emotions became. What if she was in there with some tough women? Could she get hurt?

All of the feelings she'd managed to keep at bay all day while she was gardening came crashing in on her. And it was starting to get dark. The phone rang, causing Ivy to jump. She crossed the kitchen and picked up the cordless phone, hoping it was Holly.

"Hi, Ms. Donnelly. This is Elena."

"Oh," Ivy replied. "Hi, Elena."

"I just wanted to know if..."

"Elena, Holly was arrested this morning."

"Dios Mio!" she gasped. "Why? What for?"

"She went into Mrs. Hagel's yard and the police charged her with trespassing and obstruction of justice. I'm sorry, but I don't think there is anything more we can do for you."

Elena sighed. "How could this happen? My mother and your sister are such good people. I'm so sorry."

"I know," Ivy replied. "I'm sorry, too."

"Are *you* all right? Is there anything I can do for you?" Elena asked.

Fighting hard not to start sobbing, she replied. "I'm okay. You just take care of yourself and your brother and sister."

"Okay," Elena answered. "But you call me if you need anything. Really. You have been so kind."

"I have to go," Ivy said. "Good-bye, Elena." Ivy hung up before Elena could say anymore and burst into tears. "What are we going to do, Lucky?" The dog had come over to her and put her head full in her lap. As Ivy patted her, the phone rang. *I can't talk to that girl again. But what if this time it is Holly?* She inhaled deeply, not wanting to sound as if she'd been crying, and picked up the phone.

"Hello."

Ivy was chilled when she heard a man's voice say, "I saw you in the Hagel yard this morning."

All day Ivy had felt alternately anxious and sad. Now she felt fear--paralyzing, agonizing fear. Her hands started trembling and her muscles turned to jello. After a moment, she managed to ask, "Who is this?"

"You don't need to know that. All you need to know is that I want what you picked up in the Hagel backyard."

"I didn't pick up anything," Ivy answered truthfully.

"Look, if you don't want to get hurt, you'll just give me what you found."

"Sorry, but I gave it to the police," she said.

Ivy heard the phone disconnect. "No, no, no!" she said aloud, placing the handset back in its cradle. She stood up, put her left hand on her forehead and started pacing. She had to do something. This was a direct threat. This meant the matchbook cover was a clue. And not just a clue, but an incriminating clue. Holly was right. *Damn her. She's always right.*

Suddenly what she had to do became clear. She lifted the plastic bag with the matchbook cover from the counter and ran downstairs. Turning on the computer and the scanner/printer, she said aloud "Think, Ivy, think!" She actually laughed picturing how annoyed Holly would be with her right now.

Holly had shown her how to scan and save documents more than once, but every time she sat down at a workstation, she couldn't remember the steps. She looked at the small screen on the front of the printer, relieved when she located the icon for scanning. She placed the matchbook face down on the printer/scanner and pressed the icon, following the directions that appeared. "Thank you, God," she said when the word "scanning" appeared in a box on the screen. The next message said, "Document Saved." "I'm going to have to trust you on that one," she said to the computer.

She repeated the process with the inside of the matchbook. After the "Document Saved" message appeared again, Ivy lifted the lid of the printer/scanner and carefully retrieved the matchbook returning it to the plastic bag. She shut off the computer and printer, and returned to the kitchen where she found Manelli's card. When she called his cellphone number, it went straight to voice mail.

"Detective, this is Ivy Donnelly. I have to talk to you about something Holly found in the Hagel backyard this morning. Please call me."

She scratched the back of her head. What should she do while she waited? How long should she wait before she called him again? F*orget this.* She picked up the phone, looked at the business card and tapped in the other number listed.

"Pineland Park Police Station."

"Detective Manelli, please," Ivy said.

"Sorry, Ma'am, the Detective isn't here. Can I help you?"

"Yes. This is Ivy Donnelly. Could you please let the Detective know that I'm coming down to the station right now with a piece of evidence related to the Hagel murder?"

"Ma'am, the detective won't be back until tomorrow morning. Can it wait until then?"

"No, it can't. I received a threatening phone call, and I want to get this evidence to the police as soon as possible. I'll be there in just a few minutes. Good-bye."

Ivy put the plastic bag in her pocketbook and got Holly's car keys off the key rack in the hall. Lucky looked at her expectantly. "You stay here, girl. I'll be back," she said and headed to the garage. She got in the car, hit the automatic door opener on the visor, and backed the car out. "Damn!" she said, realizing she had left her driver's license on the dresser in the guest bedroom. Turning off the ignition, she opened the car door, and heard Lucky barking ferociously. She got out of the car and that's the last thing she remembered.

46 THE NEIGHBORS

After arresting Holly, Nick Manelli spent the afternoon testifying in another case at the courthouse in Paterson. At six o'clock he got in his car and checked in with Officer Rivera. She'd come up with a list of possible places Phillip Hagel could be staying. He told her he was on his way back to Pineland Park, and not coming back to headquarters. Phillip Hagel could wait until tomorrow. Instead he wanted to stop at the Hagel property and then go home.

He'd been too focused in court to think about the Hagel case all day. On the drive back to Pineland Park, he started mentally clicking through his "to do" list. He had to see the Hagel backyard. What had Holly Donnelly really been doing there this morning?

Manelli thought the Nowicki car crash had finally sidelined her. But then he also thought she'd begun to trust him to investigate this case and not just accept the trumped up evidence against Leonelle Gomez. Manelli was used to being misjudged by both suspects and victims. When the case was solved, she'd know the truth and, he hoped, change her mind about him. In spite of what she thought, he took no pleasure in arresting her. Well, maybe a little. Fat chance she was going to cooperate with him after this. But she'd left him no choice. Besides, she was safer in jail.

Manelli parked in front of Mrs. Hagel's, walked up the driveway and followed the walk along the west side of the house. Once in back, he followed the footpath and as he neared the back of the yard, he noticed a weed patch that appeared to have been trampled. He left the footpath and made his way through the weed patch, stopping at the dead groundhog. "Good girl,

Lucky," he said aloud. *So they weren't lying about the groundhog.*

Manelli returned to the footpath and followed the same route Holly had, stopping at the Gertrude Jekyll rose overgrowth. He turned around and headed back the way he came. At the back of the yard, he stopped and surveyed the surroundings. *She was right.* The only way someone could have seen her was from the house to the west.

Manelli retraced his steps and walked back to the front of the house. In spite of the fact that he had no backup, he decided to go over to the neighboring house, and knock on the door. No answer. He was about to return to his car, when he saw someone coming out of the house next door to the vacant house. A woman in a hurry headed to the mini-van in the driveway. Manelli took out his badge.

"Ma'am, excuse me. I'm Detective Nick Manelli. Could I ask you a few questions?"

She clicked her tongue. "Sorry, I don't have time," she said. Looking over her shoulder, she grunted as a boy who looked to be about eleven years old, clad in jeans that hung below his considerable butt, came out the front door, shouting, "Wait for me!"

"Now see what you've done?" The woman glared at Manelli. "I was trying to leave before he realized I was gone."

"Sorry, Ma'am. I just want to know if you've seen anyone enter the house next door during the last few days, in particular, yesterday or this morning."

"No," the frazzled woman replied, as her chubby son opened the door. "Didn't I tell you to stay home? I'm just going to get milk."

"I know, but I want ice cream."

"You're not getting any. You've had enough to eat today."

"Ma'am," Manelli cut in. "You're sure you saw no one enter or leave the house next door last night or this morning?"

"I already told you no," she answered, addressing Manelli in exactly the same impatient tone she'd spoken to her son.

"I did," the son said as he struggled to stretch the seatbelt across his wide belly.

"What?" both his mother and Manelli asked simultaneously.

"Yeah," he said. "I saw a guy go in the back door last night."

"What time?" asked Manelli.

"I think it was around…" The boy hesitated looking at his mother who was just staring at him.

"What time, son?" Manelli prompted.

"Uh--I'm not sure," he said.

Manelli recognized the dodge. "Son, could you step out of the car. I'd like to ask you a few questions."

The boy looked at his mother. "You heard the officer," she said. "Get out of the car."

As the boy fumbled with the seat belt, his mother turned to Manelli, mouthing the words, "Thank you." After he got out, she put the car in reverse and shouted out the window, "You go right back in the house as soon as the policeman is finished with you, you hear? I'll be back in ten minutes."

Manelli actually felt sorry for the boy whose mother rushed off, leaving him alone to talk to a policeman.

"So now that your mother's gone, tell me. What time did you see the man go into the house last night?"

Pouting, the boy stood staring at the back of his mother's car as it sped down the street. He looked up appearing confused, almost as if he'd forgotten Manelli was even there.

"What?" he asked.

"What's your name, son?" Manelli asked.

"Bobby," he answered.

"Bobby, you said you saw someone enter the house next door last night. Do you know what time it was?"

"You won't tell my mother, will you?" the boy asked.

"No. I won't tell your mother. This is just between you and me."

"It was around two o'clock in the morning."

"That's pretty late to be up. You sure you weren't dreaming?"

"I wasn't dreaming," Bobby replied puffing out his chest. "I stay up late all the time. After my mother falls asleep, I turn the TV on in my room."

"If you were watching TV, how did you see the man go into the house?" Manelli asked.

"'Cuz I had to go to the bathroom. Before I got back in bed, I looked out the window and I saw the man goin' in the back door."

"Can you show me which window is yours?" Manelli asked.

"Sure," he answered, leading the way to the side yard, where he pointed to a second-story window that had curtains with spaceships on them.

Manelli looked from the window over to the neighboring yard. The window had a clear view of the neighbor's back door.

"How can you be so sure it was around two o'clock," asked Manelli.

"'Cuz I was watchin' Sponge Bob Square Pants," Bobby answered.

"What was that?" Manelli asked, certain he hadn't heard the name correctly.

"Sponge Bob Square Pants," Bobby repeated, slowly and more loudly.

Manelli got out his notepad and wrote it down. He'd check the TV schedule to confirm the timing. He shook his head as he wrote, "Sponge Bob Square Pants."

"Bobby, did you recognize the man who went in the house?" Manelli asked.

"Yeah. It was the brother of the lady who lives next door, Mrs. Stiles." Bobby started walking back to the front of the house.

"You're sure it was her brother?"

"Yeah," Bobby said, kicking a stone down the driveway.

"Do you know his name?"

"No. I just know he's a creep." Bobby turned his gaze from the stone to Manelli.

"Why do you say that?"

"Cuz one day me and my friends were playin' Frisbee back here and the Frisbee went in their yard. He took it and wouldn't give it back to us."

"Yeah, he's a creep," Manelli confirmed. "Do you know what kind of car he drives?"

"He drives different things. Sometimes he comes in a truck. Sometimes a car. Look, can I go in now? I'm gettin' kind a hungry and…" he broke off looking out to the street.

Manelli guessed he wanted to get back in the house and grab a snack before his mother returned.

"Okay, Bobby," Manelli said. "Here's my card. If you see that man again, you call me, you hear? And if you get another policeman when you call, you tell him Manelli told you to call. Okay?"

"Okay." Bobby looked at the card. "Can I go now?"

Manelli nodded and watched the boy waddle to his front door, disappearing into the house. He walked down the driveway and got in his car. *It had to be this neighbor's brother who saw Donnelly in the backyard and took her picture.* What was the connection between the Hagels and this brother? The neighbors' leaving the morning of the murder was not a coincidence.

A cellphone chirp interrupted his thoughts. "Manelli."

"Detective, it's Desk Sergeant Watson. I thought this could wait until tomorrow, but a woman called earlier and said she received a threatening phone call and she was on her way down here with a piece of evidence in the Hagel case. That was about an hour ago and she didn't show. I thought maybe you'd want to know."

Manelli felt an adrenaline surge as he asked. "Who was she?"

"Let's see--the name was Donnelly," Watson replied. "Ivy Donnelly."

"Send a squad car to 7 Park Place," Manelli said as he turned on the ignition and pulled out into the street. As he drove up Park Place, he saw the garage door of the Donnelly house wide open and the car in the driveway. He parked, jumped out of his car and ran to Holly's parked car. He heard Lucky barking inside the house. On the pavement beside the car, he found Ivy unconscious, her pocketbook beside her, the contents spilled on the pavement. He bent down and put his hand on her wrist, relieved to feel a healthy pulse. He pulled out his phone. "Get an ambulance to 7 Park Place ASAP."

He slipped the phone back in his pocket. "Ms. Donnelly," he said squeezing Ivy's forearm. "Ms. Donnelly," he repeated a little louder. No response. A squad car pulled up and a patrolman got out.

"Over here," Manelli yelled.

At the sound of his voice, Ivy's eyelids fluttered. "Ohhh," she moaned, her eyes still closed.

"Ms. Donnelly, it's Detective Manelli. Talk to me."

After a moment, Ivy opened her eyes. She tried to get up, but Manelli restrained her gently, saying, "Don't move. An ambulance will be here in a minute. Can you tell me what happened?"

"I don't know," she said placing her hand on her forehead.

"You called the police station. You said you were coming down with some evidence. Do you remember that?"

Ivy tried to get up. Again, Manelli prevented her from moving. “My pocketbook. Where is it?” she asked.

“It’s right here beside you.”

“Get out the plastic bag with the matchbook in it,” Ivy said.

Manelli looked at the scattered contents and inside the bag--tissues, sunglasses, a wallet, Tic Tac’s. No plastic bag. “No matchbook.”

“Oh, no,” she groaned, as the ambulance pulled up. Two EMTs came over and Manelli got out of their way. He walked down the driveway, and called headquarters.

"I want an unmarked car stationed in front of 14 Crescent Drive,” he said. “That’s right. The house next to the Hagel house. I want anyone who even hesitates while walking past that house brought in for questioning.”

As he finished with the call, he turned and was relieved to see that Ivy was up and walking to the ambulance with the help of the EMTs. The patrolman told him that she had suffered a severe head injury, and they were taking her to St. Francis Hospital to get checked out. They’d probably keep her there overnight. Manelli walked over to the ambulance, looked inside and said, “Tomorrow morning I’ll release your sister and bring her to the hospital.”

“Okay. Thanks,” said Ivy. “Detective, a man called and said he’d seen Holly in the Hagel yard this morning. He said he wanted what she found.”

“And that was the matchbook you were bringing me?”

“Yes,” Ivy answered.

An EMT came up alongside Manelli. “We’re ready to go, Detective.”

“Wait a minute,” Ivy said. “Lucky’s in the house alone. I need to get a neighbor to take care of her.”

“I’ll do it,” Manelli offered.

“The keys should still be in the car,” Ivy said. “Thank you.”

As the ambulance pulled away, Manelli got back in his car, which he'd left blocking the driveway. He banged on the steering wheel. How did he let this happen? He parked and went back up the driveway to Holly's Cadillac.

Removing the keys from the ignition, he locked the car and entered the garage. He looked at the key ring. More store tags than keys. Two tries and he was in. The door opened into the laundry room where Lucky was sitting. She remained still when she saw him, putting her ears back and her head down.

"It's okay, Lucky. Let's go upstairs and let you out." The dog stood up, tail wagging and headed up the stairs.

As Manelli followed her across the laundry room he noticed a refrigerator against the wall. Feeling thirsty, he wondered if there were any cold drinks inside. When he opened the door, he was greeted by three full shelves of Blue Moon and Michelob Ultra beer bottles. One bottle of wine was lying on the bottom shelf, and just a few assorted soda cans filled the door shelves. *What do you know! Holly Donnelly drinks beer.*

"I owe you one," he said out loud, smiling as he grabbed a Blue Moon.

Through the laundry room he entered Holly's office and looked around. The desk was well-organized, though the bulletin board was cluttered. He didn't stop to read anything, feeling as if he were the trespasser this time. He continued upstairs through the hall to the kitchen. Lucky was already waiting at the back door. He flipped on the patio light switch, turned the deadbolt, opened the door and followed Lucky outside. The dog headed to the front. Manelli sat down on the patio chair he'd occupied the day Ivy served him Holly's honey oat bread. He opened the beer and took a long draught.

This was not how this day was supposed to end. He'd arrested Holly Donnelly to protect her. He hadn't thought Ivy was in danger. At least she'd be safe in the hospital tonight.

And what was this matchbook she mentioned? He couldn't believe Holly found something his police crew had not. And again, she'd withheld evidence from him! At this moment, he wasn't a bit sorry he arrested her, and he hoped she was having the most miserable night of her life. He laughed out loud thinking of her in the holding pen.

Lucky returned, went over to Manelli and sat down in front of him waiting to be petted. Manelli scratched behind her ears.

"You had a pretty exciting day, too, didn't you? I saw that groundhog. Glad I don't have to arrest you for murder." He stopped petting the dog and she batted his hand with her nose. He smiled and resumed petting her. "You like that, huh?" Taking another swig of beer, he leaned back in the chair, and wondered what, besides beer, Holly Donnelly liked.

47 LOCK UP

In spite of the circumstances, Holly was slightly amused that she would no longer be able to glibly check the "no" box on forms that asked if she'd ever been arrested. Officer Rodriguez, a policewoman in her late twenties, took her through the booking process. Totally business-like and efficient, the officer was respectful, but not friendly. When the fingerprinting and paperwork were complete, Officer Rodriguez said, "Okay. Let's go."

Suddenly Holly's bemused attitude deserted her. This wasn't a game, and she was really being escorted to a jail cell. As they walked through a metal security door and down a short corridor, Holly caught her first glimpse of the jail cell bars. Inside were five women, who seemed to look up in unison as if they were part of a synchronized dance team. They appraised her silently as the officer unlocked the door to let her enter.

Holly stepped inside, scanning the faces focused on her. By their clothes, Holly guessed that at least four of the women were prostitutes. A tall, young woman, dressed in a hot pink, micro mini skirt, torn fish-net stockings and matching pink stilettos, was sitting alone to Holly's left. Her face wore a scowl and anger seemed to be seeping out of her pores. No surprise she was off by herself. In the right corner of the cell three woman were sitting together. One wore silver spandex pants and silver stilettos. *Clearly the shoe of choice for women of the evening.*

The woman in the middle was about Holly's size and very pretty. She had on a deep-cut, v-neck red dress that hugged every curve of her body. The smaller woman was dressed in blue jeans and a denim jacket. She had a tomboyish air about her that made Holly wonder what she was in for.

Finally, a woman in her late thirties or early forties was sitting, or rather lounging on a bench by herself. She was dressed in a black dress with spaghetti straps, a perfectly good LBD, maybe just a little too short for her age. She looked quite relaxed, as if she were just waiting for someone to call her seat number so she could board a plane.

Holly tried to appear unafraid in spite of the pounding in her chest. The door closed behind her and Officer Rodriguez left. Holly headed to an empty spot on the bench occupied by the young woman in pink. The woman stretched her long legs to block Holly's path. *Great. Here we go*. She stood still, uncertain what to do. Stepping over the young woman's legs didn't seem like a good idea. Turning around and retreating? Not an option.

"What's the matter, girlfriend? You want to sit down?" the woman asked.

"Yes, I'd like to sit down." Holly replied. A few snickers from the other women caused Holly's heartbeat to spike. Apparently, confrontation served as spectator-sport here.

"You can't just come in here and sit down," the woman continued, lifting her legs onto the bench, taking up the seat Holly had hoped to sit on.

"What you in here for, Blanca?" the woman in the red-dress asked.

"It sure ain't for soliciting. Not in those clothes," the woman wearing the LBD chimed in. All five of the women broke into laughter.

Holly looked down at herself and realized she was dressed in her dog-walking/gardening clothes--blue jeans with grass stains at the knees, a tee- shirt dotted with specks of mud, and the blue work shirt she wore as a jacket. She had to laugh herself at the woman's remark.

"Hey, look, Keesha. Whitey's got a sense of humor," the LBD woman said, directing her remark to the woman in hot pink.

"So what?" Keesha snarled. "Claudette, you stay out of this. A sense of humor doesn't earn you a seat here," Keesha said, returning her focus to Holly.

Everyone got quiet again. "I asked you a question, bitch," Keesha said, glaring at Holly. "What did you do?"

"Hurto en tiendas, probablemente," said the tomboy as she eyed Holly.

"*Sí, Sí.*" nodded the woman in red.

"No, I wasn't shoplifting," Holly replied.

"Ayeee!" squealed the lady in red. "Habla Español."

Keesha stood up and shouted, "Shut up." She turned and charged at Holly backing her against the wall with her forearm up against Holly's throat. None of the women moved or uttered a sound.

"Now, bitch, for the last time, what are you in here for?"

Holly coughed as she tried to speak. The arm in her throat prevented any words from coming out. As if it made no difference to her, Claudette said, "Maybe if you got your elbow out of her throat, she could answer you, Keesha."

Keesha glared at Holly, and after a moment eased up on the pressure she was exerting on Holly's larynx. Holly swallowed hard, coughed, looked directly into Keesha's eyes, and said, "Trespassing, obstruction of justice, interfering with a police investigation--maybe tampering with evidence."

Keesha hesitated for a moment, released her hold on Holly, and exclaimed, "What!" Then she burst out laughing. "I'll give it to you. You really are a comedian. What do you think, Claudette? You think we got Ellen Degeneres here?" Keesha looked at Claudette, who had a relaxed smile on her face.

Holly hadn't moved a muscle since her release from Keesha's lock hold. She didn't trust that Keesha was genuinely amused.

"If you were black, I'd think you was Wanda Freakin' Sykes," Keesha continued. A malevolent expression returned to her face, as she pinned Holly against the wall again. "You expect me to believe a white- bread bitch like you is guilty of all that shit?"

"Why would I lie?" Holly replied.

"Maybe you're just stupid. Is that it? Are you stupid, White Bread?"

"Yeah, I'm stupid," Holly answered, feeling for the second time today like a mouse in the paws of a cat. She knew it never ended well for the mouse.

The sound of the metal security door opening outside the cell caused Keesha to release Holly. She returned to the bench she'd marked as her territory. As the door opened, Holly saw Officer Rodriguez entering with a young woman. She gasped when she saw it was Elena Gomez.

Officer Rodriguez said something quietly to Elena, who nodded her understanding. The officer stood by the door and Elena approached the cell, looking mournfully at Holly who came forward to meet her. "Ms. Donnelly, I am so, so sorry this has happened to you," she said starting to cry.

"Elena, what are you doing here?" Holly whispered.

"I called your house. Your sister told me what happened. My neighbor is a cousin of Officer Rodriguez. She asked her to get me in to see you. I want to know what I can do to help you."

"Elena, there's nothing you can do. I'll probably be released tomorrow. You should just go home."

"*Chica, que paso? Que hizo esta mujer?*" the tomboy asked Elena from where she was sitting.

"*Ella ayuda a mi madre*," Elena replied.

"*Quien es su madre*?"

"Leonelle Gomez," Elena answered.

Holly shook her head. "Elena, go home and don't worry about me. I'll be all right." Elena looked bereft, unwilling to leave. Holly looked at Officer Rodriguez. The policewoman came over and said, "Okay. Time's up."

Elena squeezed Holly's hand through the bars. "Don't you do anything that could get you in trouble, okay?" Holly cautioned.

Elena just nodded, lowering her head as tears streamed down her face. The officer put an arm around her as she led her back through the security door.

Holly turned around to see all eyes on her. She bit the inside of her lip, unsure whether or not to move. The woman in red said, "*Venga aqui, Señora y siente*." The woman moved to make space for her on the bench."

"Wait a minute," sputtered Keesha. "I'm not finished with her."

"Oh, yes you are," said the tomboy, jumping up and putting herself between Keesha and Holly. Keesha was a full head taller than this girl, but that didn't seem to matter to her.

"Listen, you little runt, who do you think you are?" Keesha demanded.

"I'm the little runt who's gonna cut you up when I get out of here and get my knife back. When I'm finished with you, only blind *viejos* will buy what you're selling."

For the first time since she entered the cell, Holly saw Keesha's face register fear. She didn't know if that was a good thing or a bad thing. Fear could make her more dangerous. While Holly was grateful to no longer be the focus of Keesha's anger, she certainly did not want to see her young defender get hurt. If Keesha didn't back down, this could turn ugly very quickly.

After a moment Keesha stretched her neck and lifted her chin with a regal air. "All right, punk. This piece of trash isn't worth my time anyway. You just keep her over there." With that, Keesha returned to her bench, stretching her form to fill the full length of it.

"*Gracias*," Holly said, as the tomboy returned to her seat with a bit of swagger in her step and a satisfied smile on her face.

"Hey, *de nada*. They call me Peppy. Juan Alvarez is my cousin. I know what you did for him. If I knew you were the one who helped him, I would have shut that *puta* up long ago."

Holly laughed quietly. She felt much safer now, but she certainly didn't want to do anything that might antagonize Keesha.

"*Me llamo Maria. Mucho gusto, Señora,*" said the woman in red, smiling graciously.

"*Me llamo Holly,*" said Holly. "*Hablo Español solo un poco. Podemos hablar in Ingles?*"

"*Sí*. I mean yes. I speak English," Maria replied.

"I'm Barbara," said the woman in silver. "So, you're in jail because you're trying to help Leonelle Gomez?"

"Yes," sighed Holly. "I found some evidence in the backyard of the woman who was killed, but someone saw me there and the family called the police to say I was trespassing. They charged me with obstruction of justice and all the rest because I crossed the police tape and entered the scene of the crime."

"We all know about Leonelle. She's no murderer. You think you can you help her?" Maria asked.

"I don't know." Holly shook her head frowning.

"You don't think Leonelle did it, do you?" asked Peppy.

"No, of course, I don't, but the evidence is against her. Finding who really did kill Mrs. Hagel is the only chance she's got, but I'm not sure I can do that."

"Can we help?" asked Peppy.

The women spent the rest of the night talking about the case, until one by one, they fell into uncomfortable sleep, sitting upright with their backs against the wall.

48 FREE AT LAST

Holly awoke to the slam of the jail security door. For a moment, she didn't remember where she was. One look around and it all came back to her. She was jolted out of her grogginess when Officer Rodriguez said, "Donnelly."

Holly glanced at Rodriguez and then bent down to tie her sneakers. Before she finished, the ladies of the cell block seemed to come alive as if someone hit a cosmic "on" button. Holly looked up to see what was causing the stir. Standing behind Officer Rodriguez was Nick Manelli.

Claudette stood up, straightening her LBD. "Why, Detective Manelli! Aren't you a sight for sore eyes?"

"*Si*, Detective. You look *muy guapo esta manana*," Maria flirted as she tugged her red dress into place.

"Yeah, Nicky," Keesha added in a cheerful voice that made Holly turn and stare. "What's the matter? Since your promotion, you don't have time for us girls no more? We got the time for you, baby."

The comments were followed by an assortment of sounds--the feminine equivalent of the taunts workmen direct at young women passing a construction site. Holly remained seated, just watching. Apparently Manelli had worked vice before homicide because each one of these women knew him by name. Manelli didn't crack a smile and she wondered if he was enjoying the fuss.

"Donnelly, let's go," he said. The women groaned in disappointment.

"What's the matter, Manelli? Lost your taste for brown sugar?" Claudette teased.

Holly's eyes widened and she put her head down to conceal the grin that spread across her face.

"When you graduate to homicide, Claudette, I'll be back for you," Manelli replied. His tone was stern, but his choice of words made the women shriek like school girls. "Donnelly, move it," he commanded.

Holly scrambled to get up. She'd been so entranced by the spectacle of Nick Manelli being flirted with by a cell block of hookers that she hadn't moved. As she approached the cell door, Peppy called out, "Hey, Manelli, you better treat this woman right. She's no criminal. *Comprende*?"

"*Sí,*" Maria added. "She only tries to help a good woman, Detective."

Manelli glared down at Holly as she came face to face with him in the doorway. She lowered her head and quickly moved past him into the hall.

"Señora, *recuerde. Llámenos si usted nos necesita*," Maria called after her.

"You know where to find me," Peppy said.

Holly turned and said, "I do, and I'll call you with that information about how to get your GED."

"Move it," Manelli said impatiently.

"*Gracias. Adios*," Peppy called after her.

****

Holly couldn't stop grinning as Manelli led her to his car. She was surprised when he opened the front passenger door and gruffly said, "Get in." Without looking at her, he walked over to the driver's side of the car, got in and turned on the ignition. He pulled out of the parking lot, and they drove silently for a block or so. Holly finally broke the silence. "So you worked vice before homicide, Detective?"

Staring straight ahead, Manelli said, "You really enjoyed that scene back there, didn't you?"

"C'mon. You have to admit, it was pretty funny, *Nicky*. May I call you Nicky?"

"No, you may not," he replied.

Holly laughed loudly. "Seriously? Don't you ever laugh?"

"No," he replied again.

"Okay, be that way. I honestly don't know why those girls seemed to like you," Holly mused, turning to look out her passenger window.

"And what about you, Donnelly? Are you some kind of 'felon whisperer'? Friend to man or beast?" Manelli asked. "You got a cell block of hookers telling you to call if you need them."

Holly was taken aback. She suddenly realized that, aside from Manelli's generally dour disposition, this morning he seemed particularly annoyed. Was it because she had made friends with her cellmates? *Maybe he really did just do this to scare me*. But something else surprised her.

"You speak Spanish?" she asked.

"We're not all racist cretins," he replied.

"I never thought that," Holly said, a bit chastened. That is exactly what she'd thought. After a minute she continued, "Look, maybe we both formed opinions of each other that were not entirely accurate."

"Maybe," he replied, still looking straight ahead.

Holly wasn't sure what to say after that. For the first time since she met him, she wondered what it must be like to be him--to do his job. If you had any empathy or compassion for the people you dealt with, you couldn't show it. Had she misjudged him? Was the tough guy persona just an act?

At Lafayette Street, Manelli put on his turn signal and made a right-hand turn. "Where are we going?" she asked. "Please. I've learned my lesson. I just want to go home. My sister is probably frantic by now."

"I'm taking you to see your sister," he replied.

"What?" Holly asked, bewildered. "This isn't the way to my house."

"Your sister is at St. Francis Hospital," Manelli said

Holly felt as if the air had been sucked out of the car. She couldn't breathe. Her heart started pounding in her chest and she felt her muscles quivering.

"What happened?" she managed to croak out.

"She was mugged in your driveway yesterday. She had a concussion, but she's okay."

This is my fault, completely my fault.

For the first time, Manelli glanced over at her. This time she looked straight ahead as the tears rolled down her cheeks. He pulled up in front of the hospital and Holly opened the car door and ran to the front entrance not looking back. At the desk, she asked for her sister's room number. The nurse handed her a visitor's pass and she ran to an elevator where a couple was just coming out. As she pressed the fourth floor button, she looked up and saw Manelli coming towards her. She pressed the "Close Door" button, leaving him in the lobby. *This is your fault, you jerk. If you would have just listened to me instead of arresting me, my sister wouldn't be here right now.*

She was shaking by the time the elevator reached the fourth floor. When the doors finally opened, she rushed off and asked an orderly the way to room 403. She tore down the hallway and as soon as she saw her sister with a bandage on her head she started sobbing. "Oh, Ivy. I'm so sorry. So sorry."

Ivy, who was sitting up, opened her arms in invitation and the two sisters embraced, Holly now weeping uncontrollably.

"It's okay, Holly. Stop crying. I'm all right. I had a concussion, and they just kept me here for observation. I think Detective Manelli thought I'd be safer here overnight. He really was very concerned about me."

Holly pulled back angrily and said, "Seriously? He was concerned about you? If macho man had listened to us in the first place, none of this would have happened. I hate him."

Ivy looked over Holly's shoulder and saw Manelli standing in the doorway. She grimaced and said, "Hello, Detective. Holly's just a little upset."

Holly turned and glared at Manelli. "What are you doing here? We don't need you now."

Manelli looked at Ivy and asked, "How you doing?"

"I'm fine. The nurse said I could leave as soon as you arrived," Ivy answered.

"You mean as soon as *I* arrived, don't you?" Holly snapped.

"Holly, Detective Manelli is just trying to protect us," Ivy began.

Holly's eyes widened and she felt as if the top of her head was about to blow off.

"Protect us?" she yelled, looking from Ivy to Manelli.

Before she could say any more, Manelli looked at Ivy and said, "I'll wait for you in the lobby." He turned and left.

"Don't bother," Holly shouted after him. "We'll take a cab."

"Calm down, Holly," Ivy urged.

"No, I won't calm down. What's wrong with you? He's the one who wouldn't listen to us. He's the one who arrested me just for the kick of seeing me behind bars with a bunch of prostitutes. He's the reason you were home alone, and he's the reason you're here. Don't you see that?"

Ivy sighed. "Holly, don't forget that you're the one who wouldn't turn over the matchbook to him yesterday, and if you had done that, he might not have arrested you. That matchbook is why I'm here. Besides, whoever did this to me, didn't mean to do it to me. They meant to do it to you."

49 BACK HOME

A nurse arrived with a wheelchair and Ivy said she'd explain everything when they got home. She didn't think she was up to waiting for a cab, so Holly reluctantly agreed to get back into Manelli's car. She held open the front passenger door for Ivy, got in the back seat behind her, and didn't say a word during the short drive home. When Manelli parked in front of the house, Holly jumped out, opened Ivy's door and tried to help her out of the car.

"Really, Holly, I may not be up to weeding the garden, but I can get out of a car by myself."

Holly held the gate open for Ivy and closed and latched it behind them. Manelli followed, unlatched the gate and let himself in. At the front door Holly realized she didn't have keys. She turned to Ivy. "Do you have the keys?"

Ivy glanced at Manelli. He reached in his pocket, pulled out the keys and held them out to Holly. She turned to Ivy and scowled at her.

"You gave him the keys to my house?"

"Calm down. Detective Manelli was kind enough to offer to take care of Lucky when I went to the hospital."

Holly bit her lip and reached for the keys, careful she didn't touch Manelli's hand. Turning she opened the door and reached down to pet Lucky who was waiting, tail wagging. Lucky accepted the pat, then brushed past Holly, going straight to Manelli, ears back, butt wiggling flirtatiously.

Holly glared at Lucky, turned and ran up the stairs to her room.

Ivy said, “Come in and have a seat in the kitchen. I’ll go up and get her to come down.”

“She has to talk to me,” Manelli said.

“I know. Just give me a minute.”

******

Upstairs Holly undressed and jumped in the shower. When she came out of the bathroom, Ivy was waiting.

“Holly, you have to come downstairs and talk to Manelli.”

“No, I don’t.” She walked over to the dresser and started to brush her hair.

“Yes, you do. He’s a policeman, and if you don’t come down to answer his questions, he can have you brought downtown again. Is that what you want?”

Holly stopped brushing her hair and pivoted around to face Ivy. “Did he threaten to arrest me again?”

“No, he didn’t, but you listen to me. I got a phone call last night. Whoever saw you in Mrs. Hagel’s yard saw you take the matchbook. He said he wanted it back. He threatened me--well, you, really. That’s when I decided I had to take the matchbook down to Manelli. I called his cellphone and when he didn’t answer, I left a message. Then I called the Police Department and said I was coming in with evidence and they should let Manelli know. I got in your car and backed out of the garage, but I realized I’d left my driver’s license upstairs. The last thing I remembered was getting out of the car. Manelli found me and got an ambulance to take me to St. Francis. And all that happened, not because of him, but because you were right. The matchbook was incriminating evidence. Whoever talked to me on the phone and knocked me out thought I was you. You’re in danger. Now get downstairs and talk to Manelli, or I’m going to call the airline and take the next plane home, and he can put you in jail until this murder is solved for all I care.”

Holly stood for a moment, then sank onto the bed, and started to cry. “You could have been killed.”

“You, too.”

“What are we gonna do?”

"I'm going to go downstairs and make coffee. You're going to get out of that bathrobe and into some clothes and follow me. Then we're going to put ourselves in the hands of that policeman. I trust him completely, and you have to, too. So get a move on."

50 THE MATCHBOOK

When Holly entered the kitchen, Ivy and Manelli were sitting at the table eating honey oat bread smothered in Nutella. Lucky was lying on the floor at Manelli's feet. She went over to the cupboard, got a mug and poured herself some coffee. Sitting down, she grabbed a slice of bread, smeared on some Nutella and took a bite. Manelli waited until she'd eaten a few bites and drunk some coffee. He got out his pad and pen and began.

"Your sister said she explained to you what happened last night. I got the phone number of the caller from your caller ID. We'll check it out. Now I want you to tell me exactly what you did when you entered Mrs. Hagel's backyard yesterday."

Holly put her mug down on the table. "I looked for Lucky. When I reached the backyard, I realized, besides crossing the police barricade, I was trespassing, so I decided to knock on the back door of the house just in case someone was there. Nobody came to the door. Then I saw a bush moving in the back corner of the yard and figured that had to be Lucky, so I headed straight back there."

"Through the weeds?"

"Yeah. That's when I saw Lucky had a groundhog pinned between the bush and the back fence." Holly scratched the back of her head, picked up her mug and drank some more coffee.

"After she killed the groundhog, what did you do?"

"I called Lucky and put her on the leash. When I turned to walk back to the footpath, I stopped for a minute and just looked around. That's when I understood why two of the neighbors didn't see anything the day of the murder. Only someone in the vacant house could see Mrs. Hagel's yard and house."

"Then what did you do?"

"I followed the path away from the shed, but couldn't get through because the rose bush has overgrown the path. I headed back to the shed, and that's when I spotted the matchbook under the rosebush beside the shed. I picked it up, put it in a plastic bag and walked out the same way I came in."

"Why did you find a matchbook, when my forensics team didn't?" Manelli asked, looking at his notepad.

"Because when you were there the rose bush was in full bloom and the red matchbook cover would have blended with the rose blooms. Since then the buds have started to fade and drop."

Manelli stared at her for a few seconds, then wrote something in his notepad. "You didn't see or hear anyone?"

"No."

Manelli looked up. "Why didn't you give me the matchbook yesterday?"

"Ivy and I talked and sort of agreed that it probably wasn't a clue. She was going to call you."

"But why didn't *you* give it to me when I came to arrest you?"

"You kind of just answered your own question. You came to arrest me. I was angry and I wasn't thinking straight."

Manelli looked at Ivy. "So the matchbook was taken from your bag last night?"

"Wait a minute!" Ivy exclaimed, jumping up from her chair. "I almost forgot. Holly, you're going to love this. I scanned the matchbook. It should be on your computer downstairs." She got up and headed to the basement. Holly and Manelli stood up simultaneously and just looked at one another. "After you," he said.

Downstairs Holly turned on the laptop. "I think I did it right," Ivy said to Holly. "It said 'Scan Saved' when I finished."

Holly went to her scan folder and opened the most recent document. The red matchbook cover appeared on the screen.

"I did it right, huh?" Ivy grinned looking at Holly.

"You did it right," Holly confirmed smiling back. "Uh-oh."

"Something wrong?" Ivy asked.

"The scan of the inside is blank. We lost the phone number."

"Too bad." Ivy frowned.

"But I did a reverse lookup and the number was registered to Hagel Printing and Paper," Holly said, looking at Manelli.

"Can you print the cover for me?" Manelli asked.

Holly reached over, turned the printer on and sent the document to print.

"Will this be of any use to you, Detective?" Ivy asked.

"We'll see," he answered.

When the scan printed, Holly looked carefully at the red cover. "Is it possible to get a print off a scan?" she asked as she handed the sheet to Manelli.

"I don't know about the printout, but I want you to email the scan to Officer Rivera. You still have her card?"

"Yes." Holly turned back to the computer and opened her Outlook. Manelli's phone vibrated. He looked at it and stepped into the laundry room to answer the call.

Ivy smiled at Holly. "Gosh, I hope this helps. I'm so sorry I lost the matchbook."

"You're kidding. I almost got you killed, and you're sorry?

Ivy smiled and squeezed Holly's shoulder, as Lucky started barking upstairs. "I'll go let her out," Ivy said.

Holly turned back to the computer, typing in Yolanda Rivera's email address. As she hit 'Send', Manelli came back into the room. He pulled up a chair and sat down facing her.

"I arrested you because, in addition to an irate phone call from Steven Hagel, the Paramus police confirmed the Nowicki car crash was no accident. Your friend had been forced off the road by a box truck, which was reported stolen that morning, and found abandoned in a parking lot later that day. With no direct threat made against you, I couldn't justify police protection for you. We don't have that kind of manpower. I figured the only way I could keep you safe was to lock you up in a jail cell."

"Really? Exposing my sister, who's practically my twin, to danger instead?"

Manelli looked down. "I forgot how much you look alike."

"Forgot?"

"Yeah." He looked up at Holly. "When I first met you two, I thought you looked identical. The more I got to know you, I didn't see it anymore." He hesitated. "I'm sorry your sister got hurt."

Holly looked down at her keyboard. After a moment she looked up and asked, "How did you know Lucky killed the groundhog? I didn't tell you that."

"I'm a homicide detective. All the evidence pointed to her," he replied straight-faced.

Holly couldn't help laughing out loud. Manelli's phone vibrated again. He looked at the screen, then back at Holly. "I have to go. Promise me, that you and your sister won't leave this house today."

"We can walk the dog, can't we?"

"On a leash and not after dusk," he replied.

"Okay."

"And record all your calls."

"All right."

"If you get any calls, any hang ups, email the numbers to Officer Rivera. I'm serious. Dead serious."

"I'm taking you seriously," Holly said, no longer smiling.

Manelli gave her that searing look she hated. She knew he had good reason not to believe her. After a moment, he nodded and said, “Just stay put. Relax on the patio. Have a beer.”

He turned and took the steps two at a time before Holly could react.

51 PHILLIP HAGEL

"You're gonna love this." Officer Rivera followed Manelli into his office.

"You found Phillip Hagel?" he asked.

"Maybe." She grinned waggling her eyebrows. "In addition to two million dollars, he inherits his grandmother's house down the shore."

"You got an address?"

"Do fajitas sizzle?"

Manelli turned without even sitting down. "Grab your gun and badge and let's go." He paused at her desk as she got her gear. "Can you use that Notebook thing in the car? Mrs. Stiles has a brother and I need you to find out his name and address. He was in the Stiles' house yesterday, and he may be the one who mugged Ivy Donnelly last night."

"I can search on my phone." Rivera collected her phone, badge and gun and scrambled to catch up with Manelli who was already out the door.

****

"Three hours to go less than 70 miles! Ah, the NJ Parkway in June," Rivera said as Manelli made a left onto Jefferson Avenue in Point Pleasant.

"Where do we go from here?" Manelli asked. "If we go much further, we'll be in the Atlantic."

Rivera looked down at her phone for directions. "Here. Make a left onto Ocean Avenue. It should be this block. Yep, it's the one behind that next house, the one facing the ocean."

Manelli pulled up and parked. They both sat a moment looking at the two-story, clapboard colonial. Much like Mrs. Hagel's home in Pineland Park, this home was at least a hundred years old. It could have been a beach home for a movie set anywhere on the East Coast, anytime during the twentieth century. Located a comfortable enough distance from the boardwalk, the oceanfront property had its own private beach.

"What's the value of something like this?" Manelli asked.

"About a million and a half, two million," Rivera answered.

"Yeah, a bit above my pay grade."

"Your pay grade? I think renting it for a week would be above mine."

"Okay. Let's go," Manelli said. "I'll knock on the front door. You go around the ocean side. When you get to the edge of the house, draw your weapon. Be ready for him to bolt out the back."

They got out of the car and walked casually toward the house, splitting up at the front walk. Manelli waited for Rivera to reach the edge of the house, then walked up the three wooden steps and knocked on the door. No answer. He knocked again. He felt his phone vibrating in his pocket, but before he could check it, he heard Rivera shout.

"Detective Manelli."

Manelli tensed, pulled out his gun, and moved quickly around the side of the house opposite the side Rivera had taken. He stopped and lowered his weapon when he saw Rivera on the back deck, her weapon down, facing a hapless-looking Phillip Hagel, stretched out on a chaise lounge, clad in red swim trunks and white tee-shirt, an orange, iced-drink in his hand.

"Backup?" Phillip asked, looking from Manelli to Rivera. "Really unnecessary. I'm a lover, not a fighter. Now, my shister, I mean, my shisister...ssshe's the fighter," he slurred, taking another sip.

Manelli holstered his gun. "Mr. Hagel, I'm Detective Manelli and this is Officer Rivera from the Pineland Park Police Department."

"Yes, the lovely ossifer introduced hershelf already," Hagel smiled, raising his glass in a toast to Rivera. "Nice to meet you, Detective...what was your name again?" he asked, taking another sip.

Rivera walked over and reached for the glass. "Mr. Hagel, we need to ask you some questions. Do you think you could finish your drink after we're done?"

"Anything for you, darling," he said, gulping down what was left of the drink, handing her the empty glass.

"Okay, Mr. Hagel, could we go inside, please?" Manelli asked, wondering how productive this interview was going to be.

"Ssshure," Phillip said, struggling to get out of the chair.

"See if you can find some coffee and maybe some food for him," Manelli said to Rivera, as he bent to help Phillip get up from the chaise.

"I like Irish coffee," said Phillip, unsteady on his feet.

"Yeah, maybe later, pal," Manelli said, guiding Phillip through the sliding doors inside. "Maybe you'd like to wash up before we talk."

"No. No, I don't do that anymore. I just swim in the ocean. I mean what difference does it make now anyway?"

Manelli looked at Rivera through the cut-out opening into the kitchen, rolled his eyes and shook his head as he continued to steer Phillip toward the staircase. "It does make a difference, Mr. Hagel, so let's get you upstairs and into a shower."

Half an hour and a pot of coffee later, Manelli reached in his pocket for his pad. He remembered his phone had signaled before. Checking it and saw a number he didn't recognize. *This'll have to wait.* He put the phone on the glass and chrome coffee table and began. "Okay, Mr. Hagel. We'd like to start with our questioning."

"Mr. Hagel is my father," Phillip said, no longer as genial as he'd been on the deck. "You can call me Phillip."

"Okay, Phillip. Your mother, father and sister all say you were working at the store the day your grandmother's body was found."

Phillip laughed, rubbing his eye with his right hand, his left arm stretched along the back of the plush white couch. "Really? So they thought they had to cover for me?"

"Where were you, Phillip?" Manelli asked.

"At a birthday barbecue for a friend in Montclair."

"Were you there all day?"

Again, Phillip laughed. "Your guess is as good as mine, Detective. I don't know. I just know I woke up in my car about midnight and drove home. That's when I found out--what happened."

Phillip closed his eyes a moment, then jumped up. "Look. Would you like a drink? I really need one."

"No, thank you," Manelli said. "Please sit down."

Phillip sank back onto the sofa.

"Could you give us the names and numbers of the people who were with you at the party?" Officer Rivera asked.

"Here," he said, handing his I-phone to Rivera. "Just take all the numbers from the missed calls list."

"You said your family thought they had to cover for you. Why would they think that?" Manelli asked next.

"I don't know. I guess just because I wasn't at the store."

"Did they have reason to believe you might have murdered your grandmother?" Manelli asked.

"God, no!" Phillip exclaimed. "Kill Gran? Me? I'm the only one who..." Phillip's eyes teared up. He looked from Manelli to Rivera, covered his face with his hands and started sobbing.

Manelli and Rivera exchanged glances.

"Phillip, you're the only one who what?" Rivera asked gently.

Phillip looked up, tears streaming down his face. "I loved my grandmother, and I know she loved me. If you think I could have killed her. . ." Again, he broke off and put his head in his hands.

"Your family doesn't seem to know you're here, Phillip. Why are you here?" Rivera continued.

Phillip sat up. "Without Gran around, there's no reason for me to be in Pineland Park anymore. Gran left me this place. It's the only place I was ever really happy. She'd bring me here and we'd spend the day on the beach and at night she'd take me to the boardwalk and…" Phillip drifted off, staring out at the ocean through the floor-to-ceiling glass wall that faced the deck. Suddenly he stood up. "Let me fix us some drinks."

Manelli sighed. "Sit down, Phillip. We still want to know why your family felt they needed to provide an alibi for you."

Phillip's shoulders sagged and he sank back down on the sofa. "Look, I'm the family screw-up. I never do anything right. I was lousy in school. I stunk at sports. I'm no good down at the print shop. And I'm just not good-looking enough to land myself the trophy wife my mother and father want me to marry to bring even more money into the family. That's my sister, the golden girl. She's smart, she's got a head for business and now she's engaged to Leonard Biggs, the third. They're all about planning a wedding. They sure don't want any scandal that might jeopardize that."

Phillip bit his lower lip, looking from Manelli to Rivera. "Look, I don't know why my dear family thought they had to cover for me. They're all so freaking smart, they didn't think to look for me here. You found me and you don't know anything about me." Phillip teared up again.

"Can you think of anyone who would want to kill your grandmother?" Manelli asked.

"Not Leonelle Gomez, that's for sure."

"Why do you say that?"

"If you saw Leonelle care for my Grandmother, you'd say the same thing. She didn't do it. Period."

"Okay. But somebody did kill her. Again, you have any ideas who?" Manelli pushed.

Phillip shook his head. "No. I don't know anyone who would want my grandmother dead. If you think I did it, arrest me. Why not? I've got nothing now Gran's gone."

Manelli got out his card, placed it on the glass coffee-table top, and picked up his phone. "If you think of anyone who might have wanted to harm your grandmother, or remember anything suspicious leading up to her death, please call me."

Manelli and Rivera left Phillip Hagel staring out at the ocean.

51 CONSCIOUSNESS

Holly came in from the patio and froze when she saw the light blinking on the answering machine. *Who could that be?* They'd talked to Elena Gomez this morning and caught up with Kate earlier this afternoon. She hit the "Play Messages" button.

"Hello. Ms. Donnelly. My name is Brad Nowicki."

Holly caught her breath. D*ear God, please don't let this be bad news!*

"My mother, Teresa, asked me to call you. She re-gained consciousness last night, and the doctors say she's going to be all right. She said she needs to talk to you. Visiting hours at Hackensack Hospital are from 1:00 to 4:00. She's in Room 555. Mom's really anxious to talk to you, so I hope you can drop by. So long."

Holly called out, "Ivy!" as she ran up the stairs.

"What is it?" Ivy asked coming out of the bathroom.

"There was a message from Brad Nowicki, Teresa's son. She's regained consciousness and wants to see me."

"That's great news, but don't you think you need to call Manelli?"

"I'll go downstairs and call him. His card is on my desk," Holly said going into her room, switching from bedroom slippers to sandals."

"If Manelli says it's okay for you to go, I'm coming with you. You can't go alone."

"You need to rest."

"If you go, I'm going with you."

"All right." Holly grabbed her sweater and bag. "I'll be downstairs calling Manelli."

In the office, Holly sat down at her desk, located Manelli's card and tapped his number into her cellphone. The call went to voice mail.

"Detective, it's Holly Donnelly. I know you told us not to leave the house, but I got a call from Teresa Nowicki's son saying his mother is conscious and wants to talk to me. It's almost three o'clock and if we don't leave now, we'll miss visiting hours. Please call me if you get this message."

"I brought Lucky in," Ivy said as she descended the steps. "Do you think it's wise to leave without hearing back from him?"

"No, but you heard what I said. How can I say no to someone who nearly died because of me?"

Ivy sighed. "Okay then. Let's go."

****

It was 3:35 when they arrived at the Hackensack Medical Center parking garage. At the front desk, Holly pulled out her phone. Manelli still hadn't returned her call.

"Cell phones not allowed in the hospital. You'll have to turn it off," the woman at the desk said as she handed them the guest passes. Holly turned the phone off and she and Ivy walked to the elevator. She was practically vibrating by the time they reached the fifth floor.

When they reached Room 555, Holly squeezed Ivy's hand, took a deep breath and walked in the room.

"Holl-eee," Teresa said, but in a much weaker voice than the last time Holly heard her on the answering machine.

A lump rose in Holly's throat as she looked at Teresa. Her face was badly bruised, her head bandaged, and her left arm was in a cast.

"Teresa, I'm so sorry this happened to you. Can you ever forgive me?"

"Just prepare yourself. The payback on this favor is going to be fierce," Teresa said, trying to smile, but only managing a slight pull of her lips.

"I don't know how you can joke at a time like this." Holly gently clasped Teresa's free hand.

"Drugs," she smiled, squeezing Holly's hand. "I'm really doped up, so I got to tell you this before I drift out again. The morning of the accident, I had to go back in my boss's phone log to locate the phone number of a banker for him. That's when I saw a phone message from a D. Hagel. I googled the Hagel murder and saw the message was left the same morning they found the body. Now, ain't that a coincidence, I thought. So I called the number and asked for D. Hagel. They put me through to Dina Hagel. I made up a story that the boss was out of town, and I was doing some back checking to see if her call was returned or if there was anything I could do for her. Get this. She denied ever calling and leaving a message. I thought that was some facocta story, so that's when I called you."

"That call to Dina is what put you here," Holly said.

"Duh? I kinda figured that. You better be careful. You're dealin' with some dangerous cookie there."

"Tell me about it. My sister spent last night in St. Francis Hospital with a concussion. Somebody mugged her in my driveway." Holly turned and motioned to Ivy, who'd remained in the doorway, to come over. "Teresa, this is my sister, Ivy."

Teresa squinted. "Wow, you two look identical."

"That's what put me in the hospital. The mugger thought I was Holly." Ivy said.

"Damn, Holly," Teresa said. "You better go tell the police what I just told you."

"That's exactly what I plan to do," Holly agreed. "I'm so sorry, Teresa. I..."

"Get outta here." Teresa waved her good arm towards the door. "Let me sleep. I want to dream up some ways for you to make this all up to me."

Holly gave Teresa's hand a gentle squeeze. "Whatever you want. Name it."

Teresa just closed her eyes, a trace of a smile on her battered face.

53 DISCONNECT

How could a young woman kill her own grandmother?" Ivy asked, once they were back in the car.

"I don't know, but it sure looks like she did," Holly said putting the key in the ignition.

"You should call Manelli, right now."

"Okay, get out my cellphone."

Ivy dug through Holly's enormous pocketbook and finally found the phone, handing it to Holly. She turned the phone back on and it rang almost immediately.

"Hello."

"This is Detective Manelli."

"I was just getting ready to call you."

"Really?"

"Yes, Ivy and I are just leaving the hospital. I spoke with Teresa. She said that the morning of her accident, she found a phone message from D. Hagel. She called Dina Hagel and said she was following up to make sure all old messages had been replied to. Dina denied ever having made the call. That's what made Teresa call me. On the drive home that night she was forced off the side of the road by the box truck."

Manelli didn't respond. Holly thought maybe the call got dropped.

"Detective?"

"So, what you're telling me is that all your friends are as crazy as you," Manelli finally replied.

"Look, I know you told us not to leave the house..."

"So you drove to Hackensack Hospital? Do you have a death wish or something?"

"No, of course, not. Look. Teresa asked to see me. She almost died because of me. What was I supposed to do?"

"You were supposed to do what I told you to do. Stay home."

"I called you, but you didn't pick up or return the call. Visiting hours were only until four o'clock. We had to leave when we did."

"If you'd waited for me to call you back, I would have arranged a police escort. Police don't need visiting hours to talk to witnesses."

"Oh," was all Holly could say.

"Listen to me. You stay where you are. I'm sending a car to get you."

"Is that really necessary?"

"Ms. Donnelly, stay where you are until a Pineland Park police car comes to get you. Do you understand me?"

"Yes, sir." Holly rolled her eyes and made a face at Ivy.

"Ms. Donnelly, if you leave the house again to talk to a material witness in this case, I will arrest you for interfering in a police investigation. Do you understand me?"

"Yes." Holly sighed.

"And this time I won't release you until the investigation is over."

"Fine. And you're welcome for the information, Detective." Holly disconnected before he could reply.

Ivy smiled. "I think he's in love with you Holly."

"Ivy..."

"I know, I know. Shut up."

54 SPEED DIAL

"You think that was funny, huh?" Manelli snapped looking over at Rivera.

"No, sir," Rivera said, turning her head to look out the passenger side window.

"Call headquarters. Have them send a squad car over to Hackensack Hospital. Give them that lunatic's phone number and have them call her to tell her they're on their way. Then call Dina Hagel and tell her I want to see her."

When Rivera finished, she glanced over at Manelli, grinning.

"What's so amusing, Rivera?"

"It's just some of the female patrolmen were talking about Ms. Donnelly, that's all."

"Why?"

"They weren't sure why you arrested her, seeing as how you released her the next morning without questioning her. But now I understand."

"What do you understand?"

"Why you arrested her. The same reason you threatened to arrest her just now. She sounds like a handful."

Manelli didn't say anything and kept his eyes on the road. They passed exit 140 and would be back in Pineland Park in less than an hour.

"The girls said the Donnelly woman was kind of cute for her age," Rivera said.

"I didn't notice."

"She's about your age, isn't she, sir?" Rivera pushed.

"If you want to go back to writing parking tickets, Rivera, just continue this line of questioning."

Manelli's phone rang. Rivera hit the speaker phone button.

"Detective Manelli, this is Officer Jensen. The Stiles family just got back home."

"Good. Keep the patrol car there, Jensen. Officer Rivera and I are on the Parkway and should be back in Pineland Park in about forty minutes. We'll go directly there."

"Yes, sir."

In thirty minutes, Manelli pulled up in front of the Stiles residence. He and Rivera got out of the car and went up the walk to the red-brick Georgian home. Manelli rang the bell.

"Yes?" A rather tall woman in her early forties answered the door. Her beads perfectly matched the pink jacket and short set she wore. "Can I help you?" she asked through the screen, making no move to open the door.

"Ma'am, I'm Detective Manelli. This is Officer Rivera. We're with the Pineland Park Police Department." Both displayed their badges for her inspection.

"Police?" she said carefully comparing the photos on the badges to the faces in front of her.

"We have some questions to ask you regarding the murder of Mrs. Edna Hagel. May we come in?"

"Edna was murdered! That can't be! When? How?"

"May we come in?" Manelli repeated.

"Of course. Of course, come in." Renee Stiles opened the door wide. "Let's go into the living room."

She closed the door and followed Manelli and Rivera into the living room. "Sit down. This is just awful. Was Edna murdered in her home next door?"

"Yes, she was."

"That explains the police car across the street. I noticed it when the limousine dropped us off. This is just unbelievable. What happened?"

"Someone switched Mrs. Hagel's medication which brought on a heart attack."

"Are you sure she didn't just make a mistake herself?"

"She was also stabbed with a gardening tool to make it look like the gardener killed her," Manelli said.

Mrs. Stiles' eyes widened. "What! Who would do such a thing?"

"That's what we're trying to find out. Where have you been for the last few days, Mrs. Stiles?"

"Me? I was on a cruise with my daughter. We just got back a little while ago."

"How long ago did you book the cruise?"

"We didn't book it. It was a gift."

"A gift from whom?"

"My brother, Richie. He won a trip for two and had to work, so he came over and said Rita and I--Rita's my daughter--should use it. He said no reason it should go to waste."

"When did you learn about the trip?"

"Just the day before we left."

"Why did your brother wait to the last minute to give the trip to you?"

"Wait a minute. Why are you asking me that?"

"Please just answer the question, Mrs. Stiles? Manelli said.

"Richie said he was hoping he could get someone to cover for him at work, but at the last minute they backed out."

"Where does your brother work?"

"Evergreen Landscaping."

Manelli paused, remembering the logo on the matchbook cover scan. "Is his last name Stiles?"

"No. Stiles is my married name. My maiden name was Mazer."

"Does your brother have a key to this house?"

"Yes. This house belonged to our mother and father. When I divorced, Rita and I moved in with them. Richie lived here then, but he got his own apartment before Mom and Dad died. But why all these questions about Richie? You can't think he'd have anything to do with this."

"We think your brother may have been in your house while you were away and may have seen something that could help us find the murderer," Manelli replied.

"I guess that's possible. Richie comes and goes when he pleases. I actually told him to drop by and check on the place while we were away. To even stay here if he wanted."

"Where does your brother live?"

"Clifton."

"The exact address, please," asked Officer Rivera.

"2200 Van Houten Avenue. But he's not there."

"Where is he?"

"When we got back we found a message Richie left saying he was leaving for his cabin in the Catskills to go fishing."

"When?"

"The message was dated yesterday."

"How can we reach him?" Manelli asked.

"You can't. The cabin's in the woods. No electricity. No phone."

"But he has a cell phone, doesn't he?"

"There's no coverage where the cabin is. Richie has to hike down the mountain to use his cellphone."

"Can you give us the exact location of the cabin?" Rivera asked.

"There's no real address, but somewhere we have directions. Rita?" Mrs. Stiles called, turning toward the kitchen.

A teenage girl with purple hair and three rings pierced through her right nostril came in the room.

"Rita, these people are detectives from the police department."

Rita's eyes opened wide and the color drained from her face. Manelli had seen that look before. He wondered what she'd been up to. Probably smoking pot.

"Do you remember where we put the directions to Uncle Richie's cabin in the Catskills?"

Rita finally exhaled and said, "I--uh --I dunno. Why?"

"Because Mrs. Hagel's been murdered and the detectives think Uncle Richie may have witnessed something. They need to reach him."

Rita looked relieved and the color began to return to her cheeks. Mrs. Stile's continued. "Remember I asked Uncle Richie to give us something to let us know where he goes when he's fishing or hunting?" Mrs. Stiles turned to the detectives. "I realized one day that if something happened, and we needed to get in touch with him, we had no idea how to reach him or even how to tell someone where he was, so I asked him to write something down for me."

"Yeah, right," Rita said. "Wait a minute." She left the room and the familiar sounds of a junk drawer being rifled through came from the kitchen. Rita returned with a piece of paper and handed it to her mother.

"Yes, this is it. It's even got a map. See," she said, handing the paper to Manelli.

"Can we borrow this?" Manelli asked. "Officer Rivera will scan it and return it to you."

"Certainly," Mrs. Stiles replied. "Detective, should we be scared? Do you think there's a crazy killer running loose in the neighborhood?"

"I wouldn't leave any windows or doors unlocked if I were you."

"This is just awful. I can't believe it. And Mrs. Hagel was such a lovely person and a good neighbor."

"One more question, Mrs. Stiles. Did your brother ever do work for Mrs. Hagel?"

"No. Richie tried to get her to hire Evergreen, but Edna preferred to work with day workers. I'll never understand it. Dina told Richie her grandmother liked the day workers because they did exactly what she asked them to. Edna was a bit of a bleeding heart, I think."

"Dina Hagel knew your brother?"

"Yes. They went to Pineland Park High School together. They even went to the prom together. But Mr. Hagel put an end to that. He didn't think Richie was good enough for Dina." Mrs. Stiles raised her eyebrows and wiggled her head from side to side.

Manelli stood up and got a business card out of his pocket. "Thanks for your help, Mrs. Stiles," he said, handing her the card. "If you hear from your brother, please have him call me."

"I will," she said as she followed him and Officer Rivera to the door.

On the stoop outside, they heard the door locks turn. Manelli looked at his watch. 8:15 PM. He looked at the map and handed it to Rivera. "Have a squad car sent to Mazer's apartment. If he's there, tell them to bring him in for questioning. Then find out how long it'll take to get to the last spot you can drive to on that map," Manelli said as they got in the car.

Rivera placed the call, then loaded the information into her GPS and said, "Three hours and twenty minutes to the parking area on the map."

"You got hiking boots?"

"Yes."

"I'll pick you up at 9:00 AM tomorrow," he said.

"Cool. What about Dina Hagel?"

"She'll probably lawyer up and call us on Monday anyway. In the meantime, I think Richie Mazer mugged Ivy Donnelly and very well may be the one who plunged that garden knife into Mrs. Hagel's chest. He probably ran the Nowicki woman off the road, too."

"Because the matchbook Holly Donnelly found was from Evergreen Landscaping and Mazer works for Evergreen, right?"

"You caught that, huh? Very good, Rivera," Manelli said as he headed to her apartment building. He dropped her off and drove home. After pulling into the parking spot in front of his apartment, he got out his phone and called Holly's cell number. It went straight to voice mail. *Figures*. He tapped in the house phone.

"Hello," Ivy said.

"Hello, Ms. Donnelly. I see you got home safe and sound."

"Yes, we did. The two policemen you sent were just dolls. We drove in the police car with Officer Watson and Officer Jefferson drove Holly's car home. I'd never been in a police car before."

Manelli smiled. "Glad you enjoyed it. Is your sister there?"

"Holly? Uh--she went to bed."

"Could you wake her? I really need to talk to her."

"Uh,sure. Hold on."

Manelli could picture the scene--Ivy handing Holly the phone, Holly shaking her head, refusing to take it.

"Hello," Holly finally answered.

"Just wanted to make sure you got home, Ms. Donnelly."

"Yes, your policemen delivered us home safely."

"I'm really glad to hear that. Now, I think our call got cut off in the car before, because I know you wouldn't hang up on me, and I just want to make sure, we're clear about what staying home means."

"We're clear."

"Good. I've got your cell number now, so why don't you keep your cellphone on you at all times. In fact, I'm going to put you on speed dial number 1, and I think you should do the same with my number. I'll feel a lot better knowing you're just one touch away."

When Holly didn't say anything, he smiled. "You still there?"

"Yes."

"So you'll put me on your Speed Dial?"

"Whatever you say, Detective."

"Hmm. I like the sound of that."

"Good night." For the second time today, Holly disconnected before he could say any more.

This time Manelli laughed out loud as he put the phone back in his pocket.

55 HOUSEBOUND

"UGH! I can't stand this. I feel like a prisoner." Holly dropped onto the patio chaise, pulling off her gardening gloves.

Ivy handed her a glass of ice water and sat down on the loveseat. "It's better than being in a hospital bed."

"I know you're right, but what kills me is we don't even know what's going on. I mean, what are the police doing today? What are they doing with the information we gave them? Have they arrested Dina Hagel?"

Ivy sighed. "I'd like to know that, too, but no sense making yourself crazy."

"On the bright side, we got a lot of weeding done today." Holly smiled. "I'm always amazed at how much we accomplish together."

"It is better working as a team."

Holly's smile turned into a frown. "I just realized that your flight back to South Carolina is just three days from now."

"I know. I looked at my ticket on the dresser this morning." Ivy took a long draught from the water glass.

"We didn't get to do anything we planned. I'm so sorry." Holly shook her head.

"Don't be. We can always tour historic homes and go see plays. We actually got to do something amazing this week. We helped Juan and Leonelle."

"I guess we did, didn't we? Listen, I know I promised not to bring it up, but I really do want you to move up here with me."

"I know you do, but…" Ivy looked down at her lap then back up at Holly. "I don't want to."

"Why not?" Holly asked, her facial expression registering disbelief.

"I love you, Holly, but after taking care of Dave and all those years of being the primary caregiver for Mom and Dad, I need a little time to be on my own. It's funny, but after all that's happened since I got here, I actually feel--I don't know--a little braver, a little more confident that I can take care of myself. Besides, I think you need to deal with some issues on your own, too."

"Like what?"

"Like why you've never moved on after your break-up with Brian."

"I've moved on."

"In ten years, you've never had another relationship. That's not moving on."

"I can't help it if I haven't met anyone."

"You've met Nick Manelli."

"You can't be serious."

"How can you not see that he's interested in you?"

"What do you want for lunch?" Holly asked, standing up.

"Changing the subject doesn't change things, Holly."

"Hey, I know. Let's go down to the Boathouse Café."

"Manelli told us not to leave home."

"We can see home from the Café. C'mon. Let's shower and change. I'm up for a veggie wrap and a double scoop of ice cream."

"That does sound, pretty good. I guess you're right. We can see the café from the house and vice versa. Just make sure you take your cell phone. Did you put Manelli on speed dial, like he asked?"

"IVY! Were you listening to our conversation?"

"Yes, I was, which is why I know this man is crazy about you."

"We're not going to discuss this." Holly picked up her glass and went in the house.

****

"What a gorgeous day!" Ivy said as she licked the outside of her mocha ice cream cone.

"Yeah, it doesn't get much better than this. You sure I can't talk you into staying at least through the fourth of July?"

"No. I have just enough time to go home and get in some groceries and prepare for your visit. You drive down with Lucky like we planned. You know you love the pool and the Greenville Fireworks. There are some new restaurants downtown I'm dying to try, too."

"Yeah, I guess we must keep up the tradition. After these past two weeks, some time poolside does sound appealing."

The sisters finished their ice cream cones, watching the geese paddle around the pond.

"I have to use the rest room. I'll be right back," Ivy said.

"Okay. I'll wait for you here."

Holly sat watching as some mallards glided by. At least she and Ivy got this one perfect day at home. She started making a mental checklist of things she needed to do before leaving on her drive to South Carolina in another week. Stop the paper and the mail. Pack.

About five minutes went by and Ivy hadn't returned. *Must have been a line.* Holly looked at her watch. 2:15 PM. When a few more minutes passed, she got up, threw her water bottle in the recycle bin, and went in the back door and through the Boathouse, out the front and around the side. She tapped on the Ladies' Room door, and heard a flush. She stepped back and waited for Ivy to finish. When the door opened, a young girl emerged.

Where's Ivy? Holly walked along the outside of the boathouse to the back deck. Ivy wasn't there. She ran up the steps and into the café. No Ivy. Trying to keep the panic she felt out of her voice, she asked at the counter if they'd seen her sister. When the girls working the counter said no, Holly started to tremble. She ran back out the front door and scanned the park. No sign of Ivy. D*ear Lord! Please don't let this be happening.*

This time Holly didn't hesitate. She pulled her cellphone out of her pocket and Manelli's number was the last call made to her. She hit 'Return Call' and wanted to scream when the phone went to voice mail.

"Detective, this is Holly Donnelly. I really screwed up..."

56 MISSED MESSAGES

"So why do you think Mazer told his sister he was up here, when he wasn't?" Rivera asked as she and Manelli descended the mountain trail.

"Good question," Manelli replied.

"It doesn't bother you that we came all the way up here for nothing?"

"Don't you need to take your physical test next month? Consider it practice."

"Seriously? I just don't get people. Why would anyone do this for pleasure?"

"You never went camping?" Manelli asked as they reached the parking spot.

"No. How about you? You don't impress me as the camping type." Rivera drank from her water bottle.

"I'm not. My last camping experience was courtesy of Uncle Sam."

"In the army? Where?"

"Viet Nam."

"You're a Viet Nam vet? You never talk about it."

"Nothin' to talk about," he said, as he unlocked the car and threw his jacket on the back seat.

The clock on the dashboard read 4:30. "Check for messages," Manelli said as he started the car and got on the road. Rivera plugged his phone into the speaker jack and called in.

"Detective, this is Holly Donnelly. I really screwed up. Ivy and I walked down to the Boathouse Café for lunch. She went to use the ladies room and when I went to look for her she was gone. Just disappeared. Please call me. I don't know what to do. I'm walking back to the house right now. I know I was wrong, but please, please call me. I'm terrified."

"What time was that?" Manelli asked, looking in the rearview mirror and stepping on the gas.

"2:30."

"Great! Hit the "return call" for me. You call headquarters on your phone. Find out if she called there, and if not have them send a squad car over to her house right now before she does something stupid."

Rivera hit "return call" and it went to voice mail. "This is Manelli, Holly. Don't do anything until I get there. Call me back as soon as you get this."

When Rivera completed the call to the station, Manelli said, "Call her home phone."

Again, it went to voice mail. "Holly. This is Manelli. I know you're there. Pick up." When she didn't answer, he continued. "Listen to me. If you get a call from a kidnapper, do not attempt to respond to it yourself. You have to trust me. A police car is on its way over to you. Let us deal with this. I'll be there as soon as I can." Manelli shook his head, keeping his eyes on the road.

"Anything else you want me to do, sir?" Rivera asked.

"Pray." Manelli said as they got on the Thruway, and he moved into the fast lane.

58 THE MATCHBOOK PLAN

Holly sprinted up the block to the house. She unlocked the door and ran inside going straight to the answering machine. No messages. *Manelli call me.*

Lucky stood looking up at Holly. "Lucky, what have I done? Why didn't we just stay home? Please, dear God, don't let anything happen to Ivy."

She stared at the phone willing it to ring. Nothing. She walked into the living room, sat down on the couch, stood up, paced. *He'll call. He'll call.*

She screamed when the phone actually rang. "Hello."

"Holly Donnelly?" It wasn't Manelli.

"Yes."

"You have something I want, and now I have something you want."

"Let me talk to my sister."

After a brief lull, Ivy's voice came on the line, "Holly, I'm okay…"

Before Holly could say a word, the male voice returned. "That enough for you? I've got her and she's alive as long as you cooperate."

"What do you want from me?"

"You know what I want."

"No, please, I don't. Please just tell me."

"The matchbook."

"The matchbook? But don't..." Holly caught herself. "We gave it to the police."

"Don't lie to me."

Holly heard Ivy cry out in pain.

"Hear that? She'll get much worse if you don't stop lying and get me the matchbook."

"Okay, okay. I'll give you the matchbook. Just don't hurt my sister."

"You meet me in Mrs. Hagel's backyard at midnight. Don't bring the police. If you do, I'll kill your sister. Whether they get me or not, I'll make sure she's dead."

"No, I won't contact the police. I'll be in Mrs. Hagel's yard at midnight."

He hung up.

What am I going to do? If he doesn't have the matchbook, where is it?

"If he wants a matchbook, he's going to get a matchbook," Holly said out loud, heading downstairs to her office. She turned on her computer and found the scan of the matchbook cover. On the supply shelf, she located some glossy photo paper and put it in the printer. She flipped on the printer switch, sat down at the computer and sent the scan to print.

Removing the printout from the print tray, she examined it. Too big. She resized and reprinted it. This time, when she examined it, she was satisfied. She found a piece of cardboard in the file bin, opened the desk drawer and got out the X-acto blade. Carefully, she cut along the outline of the image. She ran upstairs and found a pack of matches in a glass dish on the fireplace mantel. Returning downstairs she used the stapler remover to detach the matches from the pack. Next she carefully folded the scanned image along the same folds as the match pack cover. Finally, she stapled the matches into the scanned cover. *This could work. It better work. Ivy's life depends on it.*

Holly went back up to the kitchen, got out a sandwich bag and placed her fake matchbook inside. *Now, how am I going to make this exchange without getting both of us killed?*

Holly sat down, closed her eyes, and re-constructed Mrs. Hagel's backyard in her mind. She mentally retraced her steps the day Lucky chased the groundhog. She went back over every step from the patio to the bush in the corner, and back again to the path blocked by the rosebush, then to the shed. *I can do this, but I need help.*

She jumped up, ran down stairs and rummaged through her inbox. *Thank, heaven!* She picked up a piece of paper with a phone number on it, reached for her cellphone.

"Peppy? This is Holly Donnelly. Do you remember me?"

"Holly Donnelly. How could I forget you? You callin' with that GED info?

"No, I need your help."

"What can I do for you?"

"Where are you?"

"Hangin' with my posse on Market Street."

"Give me the address and I'll come and get you."

In ten minutes Holly spotted Peppy on the sidewalk in front of a bodega on Market Street. She tapped the horn. Peppy waved and crossed the street. Holly hit the unlock button, and Peppy got in.

"Cadillac? Nice wheels, Mami," Peppy said, smiling in admiration as she pressed the button to move the seat back. She looked over at Holly, and the smile left her face. "You look awful. What's wrong?"

"My sister's been kidnapped and the kidnapper wants something from me that I don't have. He said not to call the police or he'd kill her. He wants me to meet him in Mrs. Hagel's yard at midnight tonight. I'm afraid this man will kill us both, but I have a plan for how to get my sister away from him. The only thing is I need you to help me."

Peppy raised one eyebrow. "You helped my cousin, Juan. I don't see how I could say no. What's your plan?"

"Let's go back to my house first, and I'll explain everything there." Holly pulled away from the curb.

"Do you know who has your sister?" Peppy asked as Holly turned onto Pineland Avenue.

"I think it's the man who made it look like Juan stabbed Mrs. Hagel with the garden knife."

"Hijo de puta! Let's get this scum."

Holly finished describing the phone call she'd gotten when they reached her driveway.

"Hey, what's this?" Peppy said, reaching down and picking up a plastic bag that had fallen out of the car when she opened the door.

Holly's eyes widened. "I don't believe it!" she said grabbing the bag, staring at the matchbook cover inside. "You may have just saved my sister's life. Peppy, this is what the man wants in exchange for my sister." For the first time since she picked up Peppy, Holly smiled. "C'mon."

Inside the laundry room, Lucky greeted them.

"You got a dog! Nice puppy," Peppy said, kneeling to pet Lucky.

"Let's go upstairs," Holly said. In the kitchen, she showed Peppy the fake matchbook she had created.

"So what's this one?" Peppy asked as she continued to pet Lucky who'd followed them to the kitchen.

"I made it from a scan of the matchbook Ivy made before she left to go to the police station. What do you think? Could it pass for the real one?"

"Looks the same to me."

"Great! Maybe we can actually get my sister back and still keep the real one."

"Why does this guy want this matchbook so bad?"

"I don't know, but it's got to be some seriously incriminating evidence for him to resort to kidnapping to get it back," Holly explained. "I can't believe this was in the car all the time."

"Yeah, it must have popped out from underneath when I moved the seat back."

"That's right. The night I was in jail with you, my sister got mugged. She was taking that down to the police station, when she got knocked out in the driveway. When she came to, the matchbook was gone so we thought the mugger got it. But it must have fallen out of her bag and slipped under the seat when he grabbed the bag. Now I remember! She bought a stupid bag when we were in the Catskills. She wanted to buy me one…" Holly started crying. "I said no because it didn't zip on top and I knew stuff would fall out." Holly wiped her eyes with her sleeve.

The phone rang. Holly didn't move. "Aren't you going to pick it up?" Peppy asked.

"No. Let's just listen."

"Holly. This is Manelli. I know you're there. Pick up. Listen to me. If you get a call from a kidnapper, do not attempt to respond to it yourself. You have to trust me. A police car is on its way over to you. Let us deal with this. I'll be there as soon as I can."

Peppy looked at her. "You want to wait for him?"

Holly grabbed her keys. "No. I called him before I got the kidnapper's call. That's why he's calling me back. I can't wait. I can't take any chances with my sister's life. The kidnapper said he'd kill her if I called the police. We have to get out of here before that police car gets here." Holly ran to the living room and through the window saw a police car turning the corner.

"C'mon. They're here already. Follow me." Holly grabbed the two plastic bags with the real matchbook and the fake. "Sorry, Lucky. You have to stay."

Peppy followed Holly out the back door. They heard the front doorbell ring as Holly closed the door.

"We have to climb the fence. We can get to the park through the other side of my neighbor's yard," Holly whispered. She struggled as she tried to climb the plastic coated chain link fence that separated the two yards. Peppy gave her a push and she was over. Peppy got one leg up and the other followed in one fluid motion. Together they crossed the yard and made it safely into the park.

58 THE THRUWAY

Manelli was cruising at 80 miles an hour. They passed the Saugerties exit and were making much better time than they had on the way up.

"Call headquarters again," Manelli said. "I want a car to go over to the Hagel's and bring Dina Hagel in for questioning tonight."

Rivera called in and relayed Manelli's order.

"Put him on speaker," Manelli said.

Rivera hit the speakerphone.

"Who's this?"

"O'Rourke, Detective."

"O'Rourke, you tell whoever goes there not to come back without her. If she's not home, find out where she is and go get her. You hear?"

"Yes, sir."

Rivera disconnected the call. A moment later the phone rang. She hit the speaker phone button again.

"Manelli here."

"Detective, it's Jensen, sir. We're at the Donnelly house. There's no one here. What do you want us to do? Stay here?"

"No. No point. Go back to headquarters.

"Yes, sir."

Rivera disconnected. "You don't think Donnelly's hiding in the house?"

"No. She probably got a call from the kidnapper who told her he'd kill Ivy if she called the police. She'd already called me, and so she knew she had to get out of there. When she got my message saying I was sending a squad car over, she bolted."

"Why would she do that?"

"Because she's going to do what she apparently always does--try to handle it herself. She's not going to risk her sister's life. Whatever he wants, she's going to try to give it to him in exchange for her sister."

"What do you think he wants?" Rivera asked.

"That's a good question. I don't know."

"Where do you think she went?"

"I don't know that either." Manelli sighed.

"I could try to have her cell phone located."

"Go ahead, but I'll bet you'll find it's sitting on her kitchen table."

"This woman's really somethin', isn't she?" Rivera asked looking over at Manelli.

"Yep, she's really somethin'." Manelli replied stepping even harder on the gas pedal.

.

59 TIA SELENA

"So what's the plan?" Peppy asked.

"Give me a minute. I need for my heart to stop pounding in my ears," Holly replied as they crossed Pineland Avenue to the baseball field.

Peppy laughed. "Lemme guess. This is the first time in your whole life you ever ran away from cops."

Holly laughed. "Yes, Peppy. At my age you'd think I wouldn't have any 'first times' left, wouldn't you?"

"Yeah, this could be the start of a whole new life for you," Peppy teased.

"I don't think so." Holly shook her head.

"Listen, we can't hang in the park until midnight. Manelli will probably have cruisers out looking for you," Peppy observed looking around. "I got an idea. My Tia Selena lives down on Main. You up for a walk? What am I sayin'? Of course, you are. Let's go. You can tell me the plan on the way."

In fifteen minutes, they were in front of one of four apartment buildings angled perpendicular to Main Avenue. Peppy knocked on the door of Unit 20. "*Tia Selena. Es tu sobrina favorita*," she called out.

The door opened and Tia Selena, a small woman with gray hair pulled back in a bun, opened her arms widely to greet Peppy. "*Bienvenido, Chica, ven aqui*." Holly was unable to understand all of the words in the rapid fire exchange that followed between the aunt and her "favorite" niece, but there was no doubt Tia Selena was delighted to see Peppy.

After a moment, Peppy turned and introduced Holly. "*Tia, es mi amiga,* Holly Donnelly."

"*Tu amiga*?" Tia Selena asked, raising one eyebrow, looking Holly up and down. Whatever she was thinking, she extended her hand and said, "*Mucho gusto.*"

Holly replied, "*Mucho gusto en concerse.*"

"*Adelante, por favor,*" Tia Selena said, opening the door wide and gesturing Peppy and Holly inside.

After locking the door, she pointed to a chair and said to Holly, "*Tenga un asiento, Señora.*"

"*Gracias,*" Holly said as she sat down on a red colored couch covered in plastic. The room was small and cramped with furniture. A vase filled with silk flowers was centered on a dark wood coffee table. An ashtray shaped like a sombrero also sat on the table with the word "Acapulco" painted across the side. The TV was on mute, a telenovela on the screen. The smell of spicy food cooking filled the apartment. Holly smiled, feeling a bit uncomfortable under Tia Selena's gaze. She knew the woman was suspicious of her, wondering what this older woman was doing with her young niece.

"*Ven conmigo, Peppy,*" she said turning and heading through the door to another room that had to be the kitchen, the source of the spicy aromas.

Peppy looked at Holly. "I'll be right back. Don't worry," she said, appearing to have picked up on Holly's concern.

"Listen, Peppy. I hate to ask you to lie to your aunt, but I don't think it would be good to tell her the truth."

"Don't worry," Peppy repeated. "When I tell her you're the woman who helped Juan, she'll be fine. I'll just make something up about why you need my help today. I got this." Peppy smiled and jaunted out of the room.

Holly could hear voices, but couldn't make out the words. She turned her attention to the television program. Even without sound, she was able to make out who was out to get whom and who was in love with whom. After about ten minutes,

Peppy and Tia Selena came back into the living room. Tia Selena sat beside Holly. She took Holly's hand in hers and said, "*Señora*, thank you for help *mi sobrino*, Juan. *Mi casa es tu casa. Vamos a comer*. Come. Eat."

Tia Selena led Holly into the kitchen where the table was set for three, and a platter of enchiladas was steaming in the middle of the table. Continuing to hold Holly's hand, Tia Selena gestured for Holly to take a seat. With her other hand, she reached out to Peppy. "*Gracias a Dios por esta comida*." She released both their hands sat and said, "*Por favor, come*."

"*Muchas gracias*," Holly said, feeling just a bit overwhelmed by this woman's hospitality. She had so much less than Holly, yet she offered the best she had to her, a total stranger. Holly closed her eyes a moment and offered up her own prayer. *Please keep my sister safe*.

After dinner, Tia Selena chased both Holly and Peppy out of the kitchen as she cleaned up. Peppy sat down and said, "So let's go over this plan again."

"Okay, Holly said. This is what we're going to do."

60 POLICE HEADQUARTERS

Manelli pulled into his parking space at Pineland Park Police Headquarters. He and Officer Rivera got out of the car and went inside.

"Is Dina Hagel here?" Manelli asked O'Rourke at the front desk.

"Yes, sir. They found her at her fiancé's in Montclair Heights."

"Excellent," Manelli said, walking over to his office. He dropped his keys and gun on the desk, grabbed his notepad, and headed directly to the interview room where Dina and her lawyer, Herbert Ralston, were waiting.

Ralston wore a three piece Navy Blue suit, white shirt and red bow tie. His round tortoise shell glasses gave him the appearance of an owl. He glared at Manelli as he took his seat.

"Detective, may I begin by saying that sending a squad car to pick up my client on Sunday evening was entirely unwarranted."

"Duly noted, Mr. Ralston," Manelli said, flipping through his notebook.

Ralston crossed his arms and grimaced. Manelli had dealt with Ralston in the past and knew that nothing irked him more than "civil servants", his pejorative epithet for policemen, who just refused to acknowledge how important he was.

"Look, Detective," Ralston began. Manelli just stretched back in his chair, tilted his head and made direct eye contact with Ralston, a move that caused Ralston to sputter. "You--you have no--there is no basis for this treatment of my client or for this interview."

"Mr. Ralston, the last time I spoke with Ms. Hagel, she said she wanted to help the police in any way she could in the investigation of her grandmother's murder. Am I right, Ms. Hagel?"

Until now, Dina had simply sat quietly, examining her manicure. She looked up at Manelli, and said, "That's right, Detective."

"So this is how you can help. By answering a few questions, like why did you make an appointment with Novardo Development the day your grandmother's body was discovered?"

Ralston put a cautionary hand on Dina's arm. "No, Herb. I can answer this. Detective, I never made an appointment with Novardo Development. Not ever, let alone the day of my grandmother's murder. What was it? Two, maybe three or four days ago--I don't remember--a woman from Novardo called me to follow up on an appointment she said I called about. I told her the same thing I'm telling you. I never made any appointment to meet with anyone at Novardo."

"Ms. Hagel, why did you lie to us about your brother's whereabouts the day of your grandmother's murder?"

This time Dina turned to Ralston. Ralston said, "How dare you accuse my client of lying?"

Manelli flipped through his pad. "It says right here she said Phillip was at the office. She even said he was home for dinner. But Phillip said he was at an all-day barbecue and didn't return home until around midnight."

Ralston and Dina exchanged whispers. Manelli smiled, knowing he had her on this one.

"As far as Dina knew, Phillip was at work, Detective. She may have been mistaken about his being there for dinner."

Manelli closed his pad and asked, "So did you see Phillip at all the day of your grandmother's murder?"

For the first time, Dina looked uncertain. Again she and Ralston had a whispered exchange. When they finished, she looked at Manelli and said, "I saw Phillip at breakfast, Detective."

"Excuse me, please," Manelli said. "I just need to check on something."

Ralston began to object. "Just a minute..."

"I'll be right back, Mr. Ralston."

Manelli walked out of the interview room and strolled over to Rivera's desk.

"Got anything for me?" he asked.

"Nothing good. You were right. Donnelly's phone was pinpointed to her home address. Also, a report was in my inbox from forensics. They couldn't see anything on the scan of the matchbook cover. Jensen reported no one's been in or out of Mazer's apartment. And none of the patrolman has seen hide nor hair of Holly Donnelly. How's it going in there?"

"Dina Hagel denies making the appointment with Novardo. She seems pretty confident no one can prove otherwise. I got her on the lie about her brother's whereabouts the day of the murder. I walked out just to make them stew a little."

Manelli walked over to the vending machine and bought three bottles of water. He opened one and took a long swallow. Slowly he walked back to the interview room. When he re-entered the room, Ralston once again began to complain.

"Detective, this is outrageous. You have no right to keep us sitting here like this."

"My apologies. I'm so sorry." Manelli feigned concern as he placed a bottle of water in front of each of them. "I got a call I just had to take while I was out there. I have just a few more questions for Ms. Hagel."

"When was the last time you talked to Richie Mazer?" Manelli asked.

Again, Ralston placed a cautionary hand on Dina's arm, but this time Dina brushed it off. "Richie Mazer? I haven't spoken to Richie Mazer in at least two years. I remember he wanted to do landscaping for my grandmother, and he caught me when I was leaving her house one day. His sister lives next door. I told him to forget it. Grandma only hired Mexicans to help her."

"Really?" Manelli replied. "And if we check cellphone records, we won't find any calls between you and Mr. Mazer."

"No, absolutely not. I have no reason whatsoever to call Richie Mazer. What is this all about?"

Manelli stared at Dina Hagel. She appeared genuinely baffled by the question about Mazer.

"Teresa Nowicki is the Novardo secretary who called you. The day after she called you, she was run off the side of the road and almost killed. The night before, a woman was mugged in her driveway at 7 Park Place. We have reason to believe Richie Mazer was responsible. We also have reason to believe Mazer was the one who plunged the garden knife into your grandmother's chest after she was already dead in order to frame the gardener."

At this Ralston smiled, stretched his neck and straightened his bow tie. "You may have reason to believe, but you don't have proof, do you, Manelli? And so this has been a fishing expedition intended to link my client to Mazer. We're done here," he said, standing up.

Manelli knew he'd gotten as far as he could. He stood up. "Thanks for your cooperation, Ms. Hagel," he said, smiling at her.

She said nothing, waiting for Ralston to open the door for her. They exited the room and didn't look back.

Manelli sat for a moment, stood up and kicked the metal filing cabinet in the corner, leaving a dent. He was running out of time.

61 A THORNY SITUATION

"Ms. Donnelly," Peppy said, tapping Holly's shoulder. "Ms. Donnelly, it's time to go."

Holly blinked, looked around, remembering where she was. She sat forward and shook her head, blinking her eyes, surprised she'd fallen asleep so soundly, amazed she'd fallen asleep at all.

"We need to go," Peppy said, staring at her. "You sure about this?"

Holly stood up. "I'm sure." She went into the bathroom and splashed water on her face. She stared in the mirror and whispered, "All you Gods and Goddesses in the Galaxy, please give me what I need to do this."

She came out of the bathroom revived and determined. Tia Selena was asleep on the chair. She and Peppy tiptoed out, closing the door gently behind them. They walked the fifteen minute walk to the park in silence. Entering the park through the main entrance, they followed the path past the now closed Boathouse Café along the duck pond directly across from the Hagel house. As they neared the part of the road that emptied back onto the street, they stopped in the shadows and faced each other.

"Okay, you know what to do. I will owe you forever for this. Just remember--no matter what--you get my sister and run. Leave the rest to me."

"That's the part of the plan I don't like."

"Believe me. I know what I'm doing. It will work," Holly said. She wasn't at all sure it would. The only thing she was sure of was that she had to rescue Ivy.

"Okay," Peppy answered, squeezing Holly's hands, then turning and moving quickly down the road. Dressed all in black, Peppy disappeared into the shadows on the east side of Mrs. Hagel's house. Holly looked at her watch. At exactly ten minutes after she and Peppy parted, she swallowed hard and licked her lips. As she started to move, she felt the ocean roar in her ears. No, this couldn't be happening. She bent forward placing her hands on her knees and took a deep breath. She could not pass out. She breathed deeply and slowly, and her head began to clear, but her limbs felt weak. *Snap out of it, Holly!*

She stood up straight and tossed her head back, rolling her shoulders and shaking her arms, then her legs one at a time. *Okay, let's go.* Stepping out of the shadows, she walked down the road, across the street and up Mrs. Hagel's driveway. Her heart began fluttering as she rounded the corner on the west side of the house and started up the path to the back patio. A bead of perspiration slid from her forehead into her eye. She stopped and ran the back of her right hand across her forehead. *Get a grip. Ivy's all that matters.*

Again she began to walk slowly forward. The path got darker the farther she got from the street light. When she reached the back corner of the house, she stopped and peered around. Slowly her eyes adjusted to the darkness. She wondered where he was, where Ivy was. She had to get past the shed to where the gravel path began if her plan had any chance of working.

She bit her lip and stepped past the house, scurrying in a diagonal line across the patio to the shed.

"Where do you think you're going?" a voice in the dark called out.

Holly felt the adrenaline course through her limbs and her entire body began to tremble. She stopped and turned to face the house trying to pinpoint exactly where the voice came from. She couldn't see anything, not a silhouette or a shadow.

"You said the backyard." Holly's voice cracked.

"That's far enough. Have you got it?"

"Yes," Holly answered, slowly inching backward.

"Show me," the kidnapper commanded.

Holly reached into her jeans pocket and pulled out the plastic bag containing the matchbook. A flashlight beam appeared, darting around, finally landing on her. Her hand shook as she held up the plastic bag.

"All right. Come over here and give it to me."

"Where's my sister?" Holly moved back just a bit. She had to get to the shed.

"You'll get your sister. Now come give me the bag."

"Uh-uh. You don't get anything until I see my sister."

Holly heard the back door, and the flashlight beam left her and landed on Ivy seated on a chair, gagged and bound. Holly was relieved when she saw Ivy nod her head. She just prayed Peppy saw her from wherever she was hiding, too. Then the door slammed shut. As the flashlight beam left Ivy, Holly turned and moved as quickly as she could over to the steps beside the shed.

"Hey, where are you? Do you want me to kill her right now?" the kidnapper threatened as he scanned the yard with the flashlight. "Stop with the games and give me the damn bag," he said when he finally located her.

"Untie my sister, and let her go first." Holly's voice now trembled.

"Enough of this, bitch. You don't call the shots here. Give me the bag."

"You want it? Come and get it," Holly said, turning and running up the two steps and down the path straight to the back of the yard. She heard the kidnapper's heavy footsteps crossing the patio. She knew she couldn't outrun him, but that didn't matter. She just needed to give Peppy enough time to get Ivy.

Knowing she was nearing the part of the path that was overgrown with weeds, Holly slowed down. Her pursuer was now just a few feet behind. Looking back over her shoulder she saw the flashlight beam on her. She stepped slowly onto the weeds that she and Lucky had tamped down just a few days before and stopped completely. She heard the kidnapper's heavy breath, he was so near.

"You dumb old bitch. Didn't you know there was no way out of here?" he laughed, so close she could smell him. *Now.* Holly dove over the weeds to where there was a small clearing in the path. Her pursuer lunged at her, but tripped in the weeds. Holly rolled over, got up and headed across the yard. In the near complete darkness of the back end of the yard, she was not sure where to turn. She had to just trust her memory.

As she stumbled over some branches, barely managing to stay upright, she again heard the kidnapper moving toward her. Looking back she was relieved to no longer see the light beam. He must have lost the flashlight when he fell. Without the light, he couldn't see any better than she could. If she could move quietly, she might make it over to the cleared bit of path on the other side of the yard, and if she could do that, she might actually get away from him.

Suddenly, Holly heard the crunch of branches and heavy breathing very nearby. She held her breath. She didn't exhale until she heard the kidnapper move in the opposite direction from where she stood. She turned slowly and started to move forward. When she put her foot down, a loud snap broke the silence.

Holly grunted. She could hear her pursuer running directly towards her. She screamed as he lunged managing to lock his arms around her legs, tackling her to the ground. He, too, fell and as she tried to roll away, he grasped her right ankle.

"Give me that bag," he growled.

Holly struggled to get her leg free, but couldn't break his grip. She grabbed on to some shrubbery in front of her and tried to pull herself forward. Holding on to her ankle, the kidnapper struggled to get up. As he did, Holly used every bit of strength she had to turn over and kick out with her free left foot. She hit him squarely, she didn't know where, but it was enough to cause him to loosen his grip. She rolled and scrambled to her feet. It was too dark to see where she was, and the skirmish left her disoriented. She decided she just had to move forward. As she did, she felt a distinct change underfoot. She was under the pine tree.

"Where are you, bitch?"

Good. He's facing the back. He doesn't know where I am.

Holly moved slowly one step at a time, but now she knew exactly where she was going.

"When I get you, I'm going to kill you and your sister."

Perspiration rolled down Holly's neck and back. Suddenly she caught a whiff of moonflower and smiled. Inching her way through the weedy area as quietly as she could, she positioned herself exactly where she wanted to be.

"All right I had enough of you," snarled her pursuer.

This time Holly replied. "Over here." He covered the distance between them in just a few seconds, and lunged at her again. A hideous howl pierced the quiet as his body stopped midair, caught in the branches of the Gertrude Jekyll rose bush. Holly turned and raced through the weeds, skirting the rosebush, her whole body shaking. As soon as she reached the footpath she ran as fast as she could. Crossing the patio, she rounded the corner of the house, running smack into someone coming up the path. Holly screamed.

"Holly! Holly! It's me. Nick."

"Nick?" Holly said, confused.

"Nick Manelli."

It took a moment for what she was hearing to make sense to her.

"Are you all right?" he asked, his hands holding her by her upper arms, his head lowered looking into her eyes in the dim glow cast by the street light in front of the house.

She nodded, unable to catch her breath, now a ball of quivering nerve endings.

"Where's Mazer?" he asked her.

"Mazer? You mean the kidnapper? He's tangled in the rose bush."

Manelli laughed out loud and pulled her tightly to his chest, wrapping his arms around her. She didn't resist.

Two patrolmen came up behind them shining powerful flashlights. "Looks like we didn't need the sharpshooters after all," he said. "Check out the rose bush."

Holly suddenly jerked back. "Ivy?"

"Ivy's fine. She's with the EMTs out front, which is where you're going." He turned her around, his arm around her waist, guiding her down the path to the driveway."

"Really, I'm okay. I don't need EMTs."

"Holly, for once, don't argue with me. Just get checked out, please."

Holly let him lead her to the emergency vehicle parked in front. She broke loose from his hold when she saw Ivy sitting on the back of the truck, wrapped in a blanket.

"Holly!" was all Ivy could say as Holly threw her arms around her and hugged her close. When she finally let go, one of the EMTs came over, took her pulse and asked her a few questions. Just as the EMT was finishing with her, Peppy appeared looking quite pleased with herself.

Holly jumped up and grabbed Peppy, hugging her tightly. "How can I ever thank you?"

"Okay, okay. Loosen up a little. You're chokin' me, Mami." Peppy turned and said something in Spanish that Holly couldn't make out. The EMTs burst into laughter.

"What did you say?" Holly asked.

"That I'd come up with a way for you to thank me. That's all."

Holly laughed. "It worked just like we planned."

"Hey, like you planned. And why didn't you tell me your sister was your twin? Dios mio, I nearly flipped when I opened that door and saw her. I thought somehow the guy got you and she was the one running away."

"Oops. I didn't even think about that."

"Doesn't matter. I knew Manelli wasn't going to let anything happen to you."

"How did he know we were here?" Holly asked.

"Sorry, Mami, but I called him. I didn't like your plan."

"I don't believe it," Holly laughed, shaking her head. Suddenly the smile left her face as she turned to Manelli. "You mean you were here all the time?"

"Yep," Manelli answered. "With two sharpshooters with night vision goggles targeted on Mazer from Louie Brunetti's backyard."

"So, I was safe the whole time?"

"Until you started running," Manelli answered. He bent down, moved in close to her ear and whispered, "I think there's a message there for you."

"Detective Manelli," a patrolman called coming down the driveway followed by two other patrolmen on either side of Richie Mazer, who was now in handcuffs, bloody scratches appearing through the rips in his clothes.

Manelli straightened up as the officer approached. "Sir, his skin is ripped up pretty bad. We had a helluva time getting him untangled from that bush. Do we need to take him to the hospital?"

Manelli turned to the EMT in charge. "Do these ladies need to go to the hospital?"

"Are you kidding?" the EMT answered. "They're in better shape than your perp." At that everyone laughed.

Manelli turned to the policeman holding Mazer and said, "Just a minute and the EMTs can take a look at him."

Walking back over to where Holly and Ivy were sitting on the back of the EMT truck, Manelli said, "A police car will take you home and stay parked outside your house tonight. Officer Rivera will come by and take your statements in the morning." The two sisters just nodded, their arms around one another. As Manelli walked back to talk to a patrolman coming down the driveway, Holly turned to Peppy.

"Do you want to go home with us tonight?" Holly asked.

"No, Mami. I want a police escort home," she laughed. "I'll be the first person on my block brought home by police instead of being carted away."

Holly left Ivy's side, and hugged Peppy again. "You call me tomorrow."

"You got it." She turned and headed over to the waiting patrol car, but then stopped, pivoted abruptly and ran back to Holly who was about to get into another patrol car with Ivy.

"I almost forgot." Peppy pulled out from her pocket the plastic bag with the real matchbook in it and handed it to Holly.

"Me, too," Holly laughed. "After all this, how could we forget the evidence?"

Peppy waved, running back to the police car that would take her home.

"Detective Manelli," Holly shouted. He walked over and she handed him the bag.

"Where did you find that?" Ivy asked in disbelief.

"Peppy found it. All this time it was under the car seat. When she moved the seat back, it popped out. It must have fallen out of that bag you bought up at Reddington Manor."

"Wait until we tell, Kate! Even she had a role in catching this guy," Ivy giggled getting into the car.

Holly turned to Manelli. "I don't know who this Mazer guy is or what he has to do with anything, but I hope this matchbook helps."

"It may be the only solid piece of evidence we have, so, yeah, I think it will help," he smiled. "Go home. I'll talk to you tomorrow." She got in the car and he closed the door, tapping the roof signaling the officer inside to leave.

Holly leaned her head on the back seat of the patrol car as they pulled away. Her eyes now felt leaden and she couldn't wait to get into bed, and fall asleep remembering how good it felt to be in Nick Manelli's arms.

63 RICHIE MAZER

Manelli walked into the interview room with a folder, his notepad and the plastic bag with the matchbook.

“Richie, we’ve got you on kidnapping and assault charges. Our team searching your apartment right now found some jewelry I suspect belonged to Edna Hagel, so we’ll probably be adding robbery to the charges. You want to tell me about your role in Edna Hagel’s murder?”

“I want my lawyer,” Richie said.

“You know, cooperating with us could make the difference between being charged as an accessory to murder, or being charged with first degree murder.”

“I didn’t murder anyone. I want my lawyer.”

“Okay. Whose your lawyer, Richie?”

“Herbert Ralston.”

Manelli raised his eyebrows. “Really, Richie? You can afford Herb Ralston?”

“Just get me Ralston.”

“I think it’s pretty interesting that you have the same lawyer as Dina Hagel.”

“Dina?”

“Yeah, Richie. If it’s between you and Dina, who do you think Ralston’s going to defend?”

Richie looked confused. "You’re just tryin’ to trick me.”

Manelli stood up. "It really would go easier on you, if you'd talk to me, Richie, but if you want to talk to Ralston instead, we'll get him for you. It's just that once we get a print off this matchbook, and we track the cell number written inside to Dina, I think you'll be looking for a new lawyer."

"I'm not sayin' another word until I see my lawyer."

"Suit yourself." Manelli got up and left the interview room. He paused out in the hallway. The guileless Mazer seemed genuinely surprised at the mention of Dina's name. If it wasn't Dina's number in the matchbook, whose was it?

63 STATEMENTS

Holly awoke with a start. She lifted her head and looked at the clock. 9:30 AM. She never slept this late. Then she remembered all that happened the night before. *It's over.* She sank back into her pillow and stretched her arms and legs, feeling a few achy spots as she did. *Is that coffee I smell? And bacon!* She jumped out of bed, grabbed her robe and went down to the kitchen. Officer Rivera and Ivy were eating fried eggs and bacon.

"Good morning, sister dear!" Ivy greeted. "Have a seat and I will make you breakfast. You are hungry, aren't you?"

"Famished," Holly said, sitting down. "Good morning, Officer Rivera."

"Good Morning, Ms. Donnelly. You can call me Yolanda," Rivera replied.

"Then you better call me Holly," Holly said, accepting the mug of coffee Ivy handed her. "I can't believe it's finally over."

"Not exactly," Rivera said. "We don't know who the killer is for sure. I phoned Detective Manelli earlier. We don't have a confession, so the killer is still at large."

"Really?" Holly said. "I thought it was Dina Hagel."

"Detective Manelli says Mazer won't talk and he's waiting for his lawyer, but from the little Mazer did say, Manelli's not so sure it's Dina. They've got a warrant to search Hagel Printing and Paper records to determine who was assigned the cellphone number that was written inside the matchbook. Once we get that, it should be a slam dunk."

Ivy handed Holly a plate with two-fried eggs and a mountain of bacon. “Ivy! Did I manage to escape a crazed kidnapper last night, only to have you kill me with a cholesterol spike?”

“Splurge a little. I’m sure it won’t really kill you,” Ivy said, sitting back down at the table. “I gave my statement to Yolanda, and you’ll need to do that, too. Look at this adorable little computer she’s got. I have to get one.”

“Oh, no,” Holly groaned. “Then I have to, too, because you’ll be calling me every day with questions. How do I do this? I didn’t do anything and the screen just went blank. What do I do? I can’t find my email.”

“I’m not that bad, am I?”

“Yes, she is,” Holly said to Rivera

“I wish I had a sister,” Yolanda said, appearing to enjoy the sisterly banter.

“Yeah,” Holly said. “It’s good to have a sister.”

“Especially when you’ve been kidnapped,” Ivy added.

Holly finished breakfast and Yolanda took her statement, typing everything into her Notebook.

“Let me see that thing,” Holly said. “It really is cute. Hey, does Dina Hagel have a Facebook page? I’d like to see it. Maybe we could find something that could help prove she’s guilty.”

Holly looked up from the screen and Yolanda was just smiling at her.

“What?” Holly asked. “You probably already did that, huh?”

“No, actually, I didn’t, but I was just thinking about what Detective Manelli said about you.”

Holly just looked at her, but Ivy, who was rinsing dishes, stopped, picked up a towel to dry her hands, sat down directly across from Yolanda and asked, “What did Manelli say about Holly?”

“Just that she was really something,” Yolanda answered.

"That's it?" Ivy said, sounding disappointed.

Yolanda smiled, started to say something and stopped.

"C'mon, Yolanda. Dish," Ivy demanded. "It's just us girls."

"Ivy, stop it," Holly warned.

"No, I won't. Yolanda?" Ivy persisted.

"Look, I probably shouldn't be saying anything, but..." Again she hesitated.

"Go on," Ivy encouraged.

"I kind of felt that the Detective was sweet on one of you." Both Ivy and Yolanda looked over at Holly.

"Aha!" Ivy said. "I've been saying all along that he liked Holly. Why do *you* think that?"

"Because when there are female witnesses in a case, he usually turns them over for me to handle, and after our first visit, Manelli always came here himself. Of course, we haven't had any women quite like you two before."

"You see, Holly."

"Shut up, Ivy."

Ignoring her, Ivy continued probing. "So what's Manelli's story, Yolanda? Does he have a girlfriend?"

"No. The women at work are always trying to fix him up with their friends."

"A guy that good-looking doesn't date? Is he..." Ivy paused.

"No, no," Yolanda stopped her. "His wife died of cancer two years ago, and he just seems to have thrown himself into the job since then."

"How awful!" Ivy said.

Holly, who had logged onto Facebook on Yolanda's computer, stopped and looked up.

Looking at Holly, Ivy said, "So Yolanda, would you characterize Nick Manelli as a womanizer or a tease?"

"Are you kidding? No way." She frowned and shook her head.

"I rest my case," Ivy said, raising her eyebrows at Holly.

Holly said nothing and went back to Facebook.

"Oh, boy!" she exclaimed.

"What?" Yolanda asked.

"There's a copy of Dina's wedding invitation on her Facebook page. It says: "Steven and Delia Elaine Hagel request the honor of your presence blah blah blah.... D. Hagel is Elaine Hagel!"

Yolanda grabbed her phone. "It's Rivera. I need to speak with Detective Manelli immediately."

64 THE BEGINNNING

At 2:00 PM Officer Yolanda Rivera escorted Holly and Ivy Donnelly into Detective Manelli's office. He stood up, smiling and said, "Ladies, have a seat." As Holly and Ivy sat down in the two chairs in front of his desk, Rivera turned to leave. "You, too, Rivera." She smiled and pulled up a third chair that was against the wall.

"Delia Elaine Hagel is in custody, charged with the murder of Edna Hagel. She tried to pin the whole thing on Mazer, but Mazer, of course, told us everything once he knew she wasn't going to protect him as she promised when she first came up with the scheme."

"So what was the scheme?" Rivera asked.

"Elaine Hagel seduced Richie Mazer and enlisted him to help her murder Edna Hagel."

"Mrs. Robinson!" Yolanda exclaimed.

"If Mrs. Robinson was a murderer," Manelli replied. "The plan was for her to switch Edna Hagel's medications, causing her to have a heart attack. Mazer would go into the house with a key she gave him after Leonelle Gomez left for the day. He was to plunge the garden tool into Mrs. Hagel's chest, making it look like Juan Alvarez did it."

"Why did she kill Edna?" Holly asked. "Steven was the only son and would inherit everything. Besides, Edna wasn't well and probably didn't have a lot longer to live."

"Time was running out on the Novardo Development deal. Elaine knew that Novardo Development was starting to pursue other properties for their project. If they found another site, the Hagels would be left out of the deal."

"But the Hagels are so rich already," Ivy said. "I don't understand why she'd risk murder."

"The Hagels stood to make between ten and fifteen million dollars if they sold to Novardo. That kind of money would move them into a whole other class. That didn't matter though because she planned to divorce Steven Hagel. Even if she got only half of everything, the money from the Novardo deal would ensure she could live the life she wanted without him."

"Was she really going to leave her husband for Richie Mazer? I mean, Mazer didn't do all this just for sex, did he?" Rivera asked.

"No and no. She, of course, just used Mazer. She was planning to dump him as soon as everything settled down. He didn't know that though. She also assured him that she would pay for Herbert Ralston to defend him in case anything did go wrong."

"So Mazer is the guy who mugged Ivy and stabbed Edna Hagel post mortem?" Holly asked.

"Yep. He also ran Teresa Nowicki off the road," Manelli answered.

"Why did he do that? How did he know I spoke with Teresa?" Holly asked.

"He didn't know you spoke with Teresa. Neither did Elaine, but I have to say she's got some powerful survival instincts. She had Mazer run Teresa off the road because she was starting to get worried. Her scheme wasn't working quite like she planned it. Juan Alvarez had been released and we were still questioning the family after we had Leonelle Gomez in custody. She'd been talking to the partners at Novardo Development privately. She had their direct numbers and never dealt with anyone and never left messages with a secretary. She knew if anyone found out she was keeping the deal alive, she would become suspect number one. When Dina just happened to mention Teresa's call to her, Elaine panicked. Rightly, she figured someone was looking beyond Leonelle Gomez and she wanted to stop them. She figured eliminating Teresa Nowicki would end that line of inquiry."

"Unbelievable," Holly said. "But I'm still confused about Richie Mazer. Can I see his picture? I never even got a good look at him."

Manelli handed her Mazer's mugshot.

"I don't believe it!" Holly said, showing the picture to Ivy.

"That's the guy from the garden center parking lot," Ivy exclaimed.

"Now I know why that logo seemed familiar to me," Holly said.

"What happened in the garden center parking lot?" Manelli asked.

Holly looked up. "Oh, nothing."

"Really?" Manelli said.

"Yeah, really. Nothing that matters now. You were about to tell us how Mazer got involved in this."

Manelli just smiled and continued. "Mazer went to high school with Dina. They were an item, but the Hagels didn't approve. They didn't think he was good enough for Dina, so after graduation, Elaine and Dina went to Europe; then Dina went to college, and that ended things between them."

"Then why in the world did he help Elaine and put himself at risk for her? How did Elaine even re-connect with Mazer? It just seems all so unbelievable," Holly said.

"Mazer's sister lived next door to Edna Hagel. Apparently, Elaine Hagel ran into him one day when she was scheming and got the idea to use him to help her pull it off. Mazer says she just seduced him at first, telling him she was always so sorry about how Steven had treated him, that she always liked him as a match for Dina, but Steven said he wasn't good enough for her. Mazer admits that he slept with Elaine at first just as payback for Steven breaking them up."

"So, has Elaine Hagel confessed?" Rivera asked.

"No. Ralston wouldn't let her plead guilty, but the evidence we have now is pretty damning. The number on the matchbook was a cellphone assigned to her by Hagel Printing and Paper. Her phone record doesn't show calls to Mazer, but it shows a series of calls to a burner phone that Mazer admitted he used to keep in touch with her. Also, Richie paid $5,000 cash for the cruise that got his sister and her daughter out of their house. That matches a $5,000 withdrawal from the Hagels' joint account made by Elaine Hagel, the same day Richie booked the cruise."

"The matchbook made a difference, after all," Ivy marveled.

"So, it's really over? Leonelle is free?" Holly smiled. "No more Jonathan Grabnick?"

"Leonelle Gomez is being released from Pineland County Prison as we speak," Manelli confirmed. "And, by the way, Grabnick is Herbert Ralston's brother-in-law. Ralston threw Grabnick some small jobs, so Grabnick, the lowly public defender, probably fed information about the case to Ralston, a prosperous law firm partner, just to keep on his good side."

"Small world," Holly said.

"Never mind that. It's so good to hear that Leonelle is free," Ivy exclaimed, grabbing and squeezing Holly's hand. Holly just nodded, a satisfied grin on her face.

"Rivera, good work. Now, go home. You deserve the day off," Manelli said.

"Thank you, sir," she said, standing up to go. Holly and Ivy both got up, and in turn hugged Officer Rivera.

"Thank you, Yolanda," Holly said.

"It was so nice to meet you," Ivy said. "We'll call you next time I'm visiting Holly, and we can all go out for lunch."

"I'd love that," Yolanda said. "You have a safe flight home. It was a pleasure working with both of you."

After Yolanda walked out the door, Holly and Ivy turned back to face Manelli, who was also standing. Ivy reached across his desk to shake his hand.

"Thank you, Detective. I hope you can forgive us for making your job so difficult. I'm just happy that I can fly home tomorrow knowing that Leonelle is back with her family. It really has been a pleasure knowing you."

"Likewise," he said. "You have a safe trip home. Hopefully you won't run into any more muggers or kidnappers. Here. Take another card, just in case," he joked, releasing her hand and taking a card from the card holder on his desk to give her.

"Don't take this the wrong way, Detective, but I hope I don't have to call you again," Ivy laughed as she took the card and put it in her handbag.

"Could you give me a minute with your sister?" he asked.

"Take more than a minute," Ivy replied smiling, turning to leave. "Take as long as you like, Detective. I'll wait in the car, Holly."

"Have a seat, Holly Donnelly," Manelli said, sitting back down behind his desk. "So, have you baked any more honey oat bread?" he asked.

Holly smiled and answered, "It's on my to-do list."

"I'd like to see that to-do list. 'Weed the garden. Bake bread. Catch a killer'," he teased.

"I know you don't believe me, but I never wanted to do any of the things I did. You must be happy you won't have to see us anymore."

"I'm certainly glad the murder is solved. But actually, I was wondering if you'd like to go to dinner with me tomorrow night."

"Dinner?" Holly said. "Uh--yeah. Yes, I'd like that."

"Good. Maybe you can tell me then about what happened at the garden center."

"Really, it wasn't' anything," Holly grimaced, scratching the back of her neck.

Manelli smiled. "What kind of food do you like?"

"Food? Italian is my favorite." As soon as she said it, she felt the blood rushing to her cheeks.

Manelli smiled that 100-watt smile of his and said, "No need to blush. Italian is my favorite, too. Seven o'clock good?"

"Seven's good. Listen, I better go," Holly said standing up, dropping her bag on the floor. As she bent to retrieve it, Manelli came around to the front of the desk. She stood up, reached the door, turned back and asked, "Did you want me to meet you some place?"

"No, Holly. It's a date. You get that, right? I'll pick you up. I know where you live."

She reached for the doorknob and started to open the door. With the flat of his left palm, Manelli closed it. Holly looked up at him, uncertain what to do.

"There's something I didn't get to do the other night." Manelli leaned forward and brushed his lips against hers. Not much of a kiss Holly thought, when, suddenly, he put his right arm around her waist, pulling her against his chest, firmly placing his mouth on hers, his tongue parting her teeth with the same slow certainty he did everything. Holly felt her body dissolving into liquid. When he stopped she was afraid to move, fearful she might just melt into a gooey mess on the floor.

"So, I'll pick you up at seven tomorrow night," he said.

"Right," she replied.

He stepped back from the door, releasing his hold on her. She fumbled reaching for the door knob, struggling to regain control of her limbs. Mortified, she finally grasped the knob, opened the door and walked into the outer office without looking back.

"Holly."

She stopped, turning around to face him.

"I'd really love some of that honey oat bread."

"Really?" she replied, hearing herself actually giggle.

"Really. I bet it's great for breakfast." He winked, a teasing grin on his face.

She just smiled, turned and said, "Good-bye, Detective."

"That's Nicky to you," he called after her.

Holly laughed out loud, and gave a wave over her shoulder. She continued down the hallway smiling. She'd stop for yeast on the way home.

ABOUT THE AUTHOR

An avid reader, Sally Handley has been a mystery lover since she read her first Nancy Drew book as a young girl. An English major, she graduated from Douglass College at Rutgers University and became a public school teacher. Transitioning into business, she worked as a professional services marketer for 30 years, and returned to teaching as an adjunct professor of English before retiring in 2015.

Now a resident of Mauldin, SC, Sally devotes her time to writing cozy mysteries and gardening. President of Sisters in Crime Upstate SC Chapter and a member of SinC Guppies, Sally also writes a blog entitled "On Writing, Reading and Retirement" at www.sallyhandley.com.

Made in the USA
Coppell, TX
16 May 2023

16890848R00173